MAKING A MEDIUM

A LOST SOULS LANE MYSTERY

ERIN HUSS

Copyright © 2019 by Erin Huss

Written by Erin Huss

Cover design by Sue Traynor

Author photo by Ashley Stock

All rights reserved. Without limiting the rights under copyright reserved above, no part of this publication may be reproduced, stored in or introduced into a retrieval system, or transmitted, in any form, or by any means (electronic, mechanical, photocopying, recording, or otherwise) without the prior written permission of both the copyright owner and the above publisher of this book.

This is a work of fiction. Names, characters, places, brands, media, and incidents are either the product of the author's imagination or are used fictitiously. The author acknowledges the trademarked status and trademark owners of various products referenced in this work of fiction, which have been used without permission. The publication/use of these trademarks is not authorized, associated with, or sponsored by the trademark owners.

 Created with Vellum

PRAISE FOR ERIN HUSS' BOOKS

"Hilarious and fun!" -**The Huffington Post** (*French Vanilla & Felonies*)

"Laugh-out-loud funny, and written in such a descriptive way that you could picture everything that was happening." -**Readers' Favorite** (*French Vanilla & Felonies*)

"This enchanting novel has hit a home run!" **Night Owl Suspense** (*Rocky Road & Revenge*)

"Simply hilarious!" -**Chick Lit Chickadees** (*For Rent*)

"Uproariously funny. Erin Huss is certainly one to watch!" - **InD'Tale Magazine** (*For Rent*)

"Five stars!"- **Cozy Mystery Book Reviews** (*Rocky Road & Revenge*)

"Fun! I highly recommend." -**KRL Reviews** (*Double Fudge & Danger*)

Silver Medal Winner in the International Readers' Favorite Awards. (*French Vanilla & Felonies*)

FREE BOOK

Sign up for Erin's newsletter to be the first to know about new releases, special bargains, and giveaways, and as a bonus receive a FREE ebook of the #1 Kindle bestseller, *Can't Pay My Rent!*
erinhuss.com

ACKNOWLEDGEMENTS

Thank you to my editor, Wendi Baker, so fun to work with you again; Sue Traynor for taking my horrible mock-up and making it ten times better; Paula Bothwell for the editing (you're amazing); Morgan Searcy for the series name; Jed Huss for being the wonderful supportive husband that you are; Debby Holt, Ann Rohrer, Miriam Packard, Ruth Bigler, Jessica L. Randall, and Nina Johns, for beta reading. A huge thank you to my favorite authors, Melissa Baldwin and Kathryn R. Biel for holding my hand through this process.

Dedicated to my son, Noah.
doing hype dance

CHAPTER ONE

"Take a seat."

I do as told. The chair is straight-backed with no arms. Not constructed for comfort or style, this chair is practical and to the point. Much like the man sitting behind the desk. I cross my ankles, pick off the few strands of cat hair stuck to my skirt, and rub my hands together.

"Are you cold?" Brian Windsor asks.

"No." I pull my scarf tighter.

He checks the thermostat. "It's seventy-five degrees."

"I'm perfectly fine, thank you," I say with a smile, even though it feels like we're sitting in an igloo. "Here is my application." I slide the papers across the desk and concentrate hard to keep my teeth from chattering.

Brian skims the first page. "Zoe *Lane*. Any relation to Mary and John Lane?"

"They're my parents."

"I didn't know the Lanes had children."

"It's just me."

Brian's brow is wrinkled. I'm sure he's wondering how in a town of fewer than 800 people, he and I have never crossed paths. He's not much older than I am, and my parents are real estate agents. Their faces are on everything from grocery carts to park benches. Everyone either knows John and Mary Lane or they know of them. Heck, this is Fernn Valley. Everyone either knows or knows *of* everyone.

Except me.

I don't get out much. I would blend in with the wall if I could. And nearly do. The floral wallpaper in the lobby looks awfully close to the pattern on my blouse.

"Why do you want to work at *The Fernn Valley Gazette?*" Brian leans back and adjusts his glasses.

"*The Gazette* is a respectable publication," I say, trying not to sound too eager. "I read it every week. My favorite column is 'Squirrel of the Month.' I enjoy the crossword puzzle and reading about the town events. The article you wrote about our Fourth of July parade was compelling journalism."

Brian blinks a few times then flips to the second page of my application. "You forgot to fill in your work experience." He clicks a pen and stares at me. I think he's waiting for me to rattle off my previous employers. There's only one problem.

"I've never had a job, per se."

He flips to the first page of my application to verify that, yes, I am in fact twenty-three years old.

"I write the MLS descriptions for my parents' listings," I quickly add and hike up my sock, which has managed to slip below my kneecap. "I just don't get paid to do it. But I'm a quick learner."

Brian puts my application down and rocks in his chair with his fingers steepled. His desk is pristine, and the room smells freshly Lysolled. His brown hair is parted on the side with wisps around his forehead. His glasses are dark-rimmed, and he smiles without showing his teeth—all this, of course, I know from his black-and-white editorial picture printed in the paper every week. What I didn't know before now was that behind those glasses are gray eyes with specks of brown in them. I didn't know he had freckles across his nose. I didn't know he was tall, at least a foot taller than I am.

I didn't know he was even more gorgeous in person.

"Unfortunately," Brian starts to say, and my stomach plunges. "We're looking for someone with more experience."

"But the ad said it was an entry-level position." I pull the paper from my briefcase. "See, right here. *Entry-level position*," I read aloud. "I'm happy to do office tasks like faxing papers, answering phones, or making a fresh pot of hot chocolate in the morning. Whatever you need."

Brian appears a bit shell-shocked, and I'm not exactly sure why. I make an excellent pot of hot chocolate. "We're looking to bring someone on who has fresh ideas. To shake things up around here."

"I have fresh ideas," I say louder than I mean to. "For example, what if you did squirrel of the *week* instead of the month? Papers would fly off the shelf!"

"I don't think it's a good fit." Brian stands and extends a professional hand. "I wish you luck."

Guess that's my cue to leave. "'Thank you for taking the time to meet with me." I slip my hand into his, and he flinches.

"Your hand is ice cold."

"It's a glandular issue," I say with instant regret.

"Uh ... I'm sorry to hear about that." Brian avoids eye contact. "Let me get the door for you."

I pick up my briefcase and wait until his back is turned before I smack myself on the forehead. *Wow.* Brian is right. My hands are cold. Like touching fresh snow. Even my fingertips are numb. I've had bouts of cold flashes before, but nothing like this. If I weren't currently standing and breathing, I'd swear I was dead. I check my pulse just to be sure. Blood is pumping. Heart is pounding. Good.

Brian clears his throat to grab my attention.

Oh, right. Didn't get the job. Need to leave. Got it.

I exit into the main working space. Desks are pushed together in groups of two. It looks very much like a busy newsroom—minus the busy. Two employees are playing solitaire on their computers, and the woman in the corner is filing her nails. Everyone is dressed casually and appears pleasant, except for the man standing beside the copier, the one wearing a fitted tan suit, dark tie, shiny black shoes, and a vintage homburg hat. He's staring at me with such intensity that a sharp chill runs down my back and through my legs. I rush out to the lobby and push on the door several times until I realize it must be pulled open.

Outside, I take a seat on a bench and check the time. The interview took ten minutes. I have an hour before my ride will be here, which gives me enough time to walk down to Butter Bakery and buy two glazed donuts and a scone. I hate to eat my feelings, but I can't help the disappointment.

Jobs are nearly impossible to come by in Fernn Valley. When I read the help wanted ad in last week's paper, I sincerely thought this was the perfect opportunity for me to enter the workforce, gain independence, and maybe even move out —one day.

My parents and I have been reading *The Gazette* together since I was a child. What a thrill it would have been to work for a newspaper. What a thrill it would have been to receive a paycheck. What a thrill it would have been to work alongside Brian Windsor, editor-in-chief.

I'm not exactly sure where it went wrong. I was professional and polite. My handwriting on the application was pristine, and I have on my best outfit.

Brian wants fresh ideas?

Pfft.
I have plenty of fresh ideas ... I just can't think of what they are at this moment, but I know they're in there. If only I'd been given the chance.

I slip off my pumps, place them in my briefcase, and pull out my walking shoes. There's a smudge near the sole, and I scrub it off with a wet wipe. The shoes mold around my feet, just as the infomercial promised they would. I stand at the crosswalk, look both ways, and step onto the street. My body has finally warmed, and I unwrap the scarf from around my neck. My favorite scarf—a chic, pink chiffon fabric my mother bought me for Christmas—

A blaring horn grabs my attention. I look up just in time to see the car racing toward me. Next thing I know, I'm staring up at the blue sky, and dots dance around my periphery until my vision tunnels and the world goes black.

"You're not dead."

"It sure feels like it." I sit up slowly. A whoosh of nausea hits me, and I fall back down. I'm in Dr. Karman's office, lying on an exam table, and I have no recollection of how I got here.

"I promise you're very much alive." Dr. Karman swings his stethoscope around his neck and flashes a light into my eyes. "You do have a mild concussion."

"Mild?" This doesn't feel *mild*. This feels like a high school percussion band has taken up residence in my cranium. "But earlier today, I was freezing and my hands were—"

"Zoe, dear," Dr. Karman cuts me off. "Like I've told you many times, it's perfectly normal to get cold now and then. You're a healthy young woman with no glandular issues."

"Except for a concussion."

"Except for a *mild* knock on the head." He turns around and washes his hands in the sink.

I've never been a fan of Dr. Karman. He's got more hair in his nose than he does on his head, and he smells like corn. So does his office. The room has white walls with red trim and a picture of a clown framed above the exam table. The same creepy clown that's been staring at me since I was seven.

"It was Old Man LeRoy." Dr. Karman pulls two paper towels from the dispenser and dries his hands. "I've been telling him for years it's time to stop driving, but he won't listen. This should give him a wake-up call. He's badly shaken up."

That makes two of us. "Where is he?"

"We had an ambulance take him to the hospital in Trucker to be sure he's okay."

Old Man LeRoy is shaken up and taken to the hospital. I get hit by a car, lose consciousness, and am sitting in the pediatric wing of the town doctor's office.

This feels *off*.

"You need to watch where you're going, dear," the doctor says with a stern shake of his finger. "Old Man LeRoy said you appeared out of nowhere."

"Well, Old Man LeRoy is also like a hundred years old." I rub my head. "Shouldn't I get an X-ray or a CT scan?"

Dr. Karman steps on the pedal of the trashcan, the lid flips up, and he tosses his dirty towels in. "All you need is Motrin. I'll be right back." He leaves and closes the door behind him.

I sit up, more successfully this time. My skirt is covered in dirt, presumably from Old Man LeRoy's clunker of a car. I'm not sure he's ever washed that thing.

"What the hell is wrong with you?" intones a deep male voice.

I yelp and nearly fall off the table. It's Homburg-Hat Guy

MAKING A MEDIUM

from *The Gazette*, and he's standing right in front of me. "Wh-wha-what at are you doing in—"

"Are you trying to get yourself killed?"

"No. I-I was in the crosswalk and—"

"Everyone can hear LeRoy's Buick clanking from a mile away."

"But ... but ... I was in the crosswalk." I don't know who this man is or why he's here, but I shouldn't have to defend myself to anyone. Pedestrians have the right of way!

"This is just great," Homburg-Hat Guy paces the room, mumbling to himself. "What a waste of my time."

"Excuse me?"

"You're a dud!" He waves his arm around. "You're wasting my time, and you dress like an old woman."

"I do not." I grasp my pearls. "No one asked you to come here."

"You will do your job." He narrows his eyes. "Do you understand me?"

"I didn't get the job!"

There's a knock on the door, and the doctor returns. Thank goodness. He can kick this rude man out of here.

"I have eight hundred milligrams of Motrin for you. It should take the edge off." He drops the pills into my palm and hands me a small cup of water.

"Thank you." I sit up a little taller and take my meds. "Now, can you please ask this man to—"

Oh, no.

I can smell the Aqua Net coming.

"Where is my daughter?" Mom comes barreling into the room. "There you are, my baby girl." She hugs me so tight my back pops. "I heard you threw yourself in front of a car. Did the interview go that badly?"

7

"I didn't *throw* myself. I was in the crosswalk and Old Man LeRoy hit me."

"Oh, you sweet dear." Mom smooths a strand of hair off my forehead. "Everyone can hear Old Man LeRoy's car from a mile away. You need to be more vigilant."

"Told you," says Homburg-Hat Guy. He's now in the corner under the ABC poster, picking at his back teeth.

"She has a mild concussion," Dr. Karman explains to my mom. "I gave her Motrin, and she can have another dose in eight hours." He hands her a pill bottle. "I suspect she'll feel fine by tomorrow."

"Good thing your mommy came to help you," Homburg-Hat Guy says. "How old are you again?"

"You know what?" I leap off the table, and the world goes a bit tipsy.

"Hold on." Mom snakes her arm around my waist. "Goodness, Zoe. You're so cold. Let's get you home."

"Good idea." I drape my arm around her shoulders, and she helps me outside. The sun hurts my eyes, and I use my hand as a visor. Dad is at the helm of our minivan and gets out to slide open the door.

"That's your car?" Homburg Guy folds over in a laughing fit like he's never seen a real estate agent's vehicle before. On the sliding doors are pictures of my parents in matching denim, with my dad sporting a Tom Selleck mustache and my mom sporting a perm. He's giving her a piggyback ride, and they both are giving the camera a thumbs-up. *We're in your lane* is printed in blocky neon-green lettering along the bottom. It's the same picture and slogan they've had since they got their license. *It's memorable*, my mom had said. Can't argue with that.

"It's the tacky mobile," Homburg Guy says, still laughing.

"Leave me alone!"

"I don't think you should be walking on your own," Mom says.

"Not you."

Dad helps me into the back of the van, and I slump down into the captain's chair and close my eyes. My head beats in time with my heart, and all I want to do is sleep.

Dad starts the car and eases away from the curb. "Do you want to stop and get ice cream?"

Homburg Guy is in the seat beside me. "Ice cream? Do they spoon feed it to you, too?"

"Wh-wh-how did you get ..." *Gah!* I can't formulate a sentence. Must be the concussion. I rub my temples and try again. "What are you doing here?"

Mom turns around in her seat. "We were at an open house when we got the call from Dr. Karman and rushed over."

"Couldn't you have come by yourselves?"

Dad looks at me in the rearview mirror. "I'm not sure what you're talking about, pumpkin."

"Pumpkin?" Homburg Guy shakes his head.

"Leave me alone!"

Mom and Dad share a glance then stare straight ahead. "I know you're in pain, sweetie, but there's no need to be so rude," Mom says.

"Me being rude? Wha-how-my. *Gah!* Never mind." I cross my arms and close my eyes.

When I open them, we're home and Homburg Guy is gone. Hallelujah! Mom and Dad must have dropped him off somewhere. It's a good thing I didn't get the job. I'd hate to have to deal with him five days a week. He has a lot of nerve showing up at the doctor's office and making fun of my clothes and calling me a dud.

I'm not a dud.

I'm a respectable, educated, and self-reliant woman!

My parents help me inside, and Mom makes a bed for me on the couch. Dad pulls a blanket up to my chin. "Are you comfortable?"

I nod yes. I'm quite comfortable. There's no place like home.

Jabba, my cat, jumps up onto the couch and nestles close, purring so loudly it sounds as if he's about to explode. I've never heard Jabba purr before. I didn't think he knew how. He showed up on our doorstep ten years ago, and he has never allowed us to pet, cuddle, get near, or look him directly in the eyes. He mostly lies around and eats.

Also, he looks like Jabba the Hutt.

Hence the name.

Mom puts a cool washcloth over my eyes, and it feels wonderful.

"I'll stay with her, and you go finish with the Attwood listing," Mom says to Dad.

"No, I'll stay, and you go."

"Neither of you needs to stay." I peek up from under my washcloth. "I'm fine. Stop fussing. Go work."

"Are you sure?" Mom asks.

"Dr. Karman said it's a mild concussion," I say. "Nothing to worry about. You can't afford to lose the Attwood listing. Please go, and if I need anything, I'll call you."

They hesitate but with a little more coaxing agree to leave and promise to be back shortly. I replace the washcloth and cuddle up with the blanket. Jabba curls up on my chest and even allows me to pet his head a few times before he bites my hand.

What a day.

I didn't get the job, got hit by a car, and was harassed by a man in a hat.

What's his problem anyway? He sees me once and is able to ... oh, I get it.

I chuckle to myself.

It's obvious.

He's in love with me.

Homburg Guy is the town's bad boy, and I'm the shy girl. He's no good for me and he knows it. But he can't help himself and it kills him. When he witnessed the accident, it scared him and he took it out on me. He's angry now, but then one day, while we're passing by each other at the market or when we're caught alone in an elevator, he'll pin me up against the wall, rip open his shirt to expose his chiseled abs, and kiss me. Then he'll stalk off and pretend it never happened. We'll do the back and forth thing for a week or two until I either get knocked-up or we wake up one morning hung-over and married.

I read a lot of hot romance novels, so I know how this kind of thing goes.

Homburg Guy is handsome, I'll give him that. Light hair, blue eyes, square jaw, very All-American Boy.

I'm short with dark blonde hair and big brown eyes. Mom's hairdresser said I should add in highlights, but I don't have a source of income, so dark blonde it is.

Jabba interrupts my thoughts by digging his claws into my chest and hissing.

Ouch!

I throw the washcloth off my face and jolt upright, sending Jabba to the floor.

"Good, you're up," says a familiar voice.

I turn my head. Homburg Guy is in my living room!

Okay, so maybe it's not a hot romance novel but more so a psychological thriller and this guy is my stalker. Or this is some freaky version of *Fifty Shades of Grey*. Either way, I don't do bondage.

I scream again.

Jabba hisses.

We do this for a while.

"Stop that. Do you want your neighbors to hear?" Homburg Guy says.

"Yes!" I run to the kitchen and pull out a butcher knife. "Stay away!"

Homburg Guy looks at me as if I'm being ridiculous. Like his breaking into my house is completely normal. As if I'm the one acting crazy in this scenario.

"Back away!" I hold the knife up. "Back off!"

"Put that thing away and get to work," Homburg Guy says.

"I already told you, I didn't get the job!"

"Not at the newspaper, you nitwit. If you want to write about this crap town, I don't care."

"Watch your language."

He squints his eyes. "Crap."

"Stop it."

"Crap. Crap. Crap. Crap. Dammit!" He runs his hands down his face.

Jabba strolls into the kitchen and rises to his back legs, as if to appear taller, and bares his teeth.

"That is the ugliest cat I've ever seen," Hamburg Guy says, staring down at Jabba. "I can't believe I'm stuck with some crazy cat lady."

"I am not a crazy cat lady!" My hands are shaking so badly the knife slips from my grip and falls to the ground. "Leave my house at once," I demand.

"No."

"Leave my house right now!"

"No!"

I grab the cookie jar and hurl it at him with all my might. It goes right through him and crashes against the wall.

Through him!

The cookie jar went *through* his body and is now shattered into tiny pieces on the ground.

I fall into the fetal position. This is the concussion. I'm hallucinating. That's it. Once the swelling in my brain goes down, I'll be fine. Perfectly fine. Fine. Fine. Fine.

"Are you done with your nervous breakdown?" he asks.

"No," I say, rocking with my head between my knees. "You're not real. Leave me alone."

"I can't leave you alone. We have work to do. Now get up and do your job."

"I saw you at *The Gazette,* and now my injured brain has manifested an intense hallucination."

Homburg Guy grunts. "If I were a hallucination, could I do this?" He looks around the room and shakes his head. "I've got nothing, actually ... Look"—he lowers to one knee—"you need to put on your big girl panties and act like an adult, because we've got stuff to do and not a lot of time to do it. Suck it up."

My hallucination is mean.

I reach my arm up and feel around on the counter until my hand lands on the cordless phone. My fingers shake as I dial.

"Are you calling Mommy and Daddy?"

I put the phone to my ear. "Mom, I need you to take me to the hospital."

Homburg Guy slaps his hands over his eyes. "We don't have time."

"Right now!"

CHAPTER TWO

The ER doctor pulls open the curtain. Mom and Dad each have one of my hands, and I hold my breath while I wait for the news. A brain bleed. Tumor. Stroke. Aneurysm!
"You're anemic," the doctor says.
I blow out a breath. "That's it?"
"Considering you've been hit by a car, I think you're in great shape." The doctor doesn't look old enough to have MD behind his name. I need a second opinion.
One hour later:
"CT scan looks normal. Urine sample is fine. The only thing I found is low iron. I'm recommending you start on an iron supplement and follow up with your regular physician," says the second opinion. His name is Dr. Girt, and he's not much older than the previous MD, but I've been told they're busy and a third opinion is not an option.
"Hold on." I yank my hands free from Mom's and Dad's grasps. "No one else can see that man at the nurses' station? The one with the hat on?"
Everyone switches their attention to Homburg Guy, who is reclining in a chair with his feet propped up on the desk,

ankles crossed, hands behind his head, looking like he owns the place.

"Who?" Dad asks.

"The man with the shiny black shoes. Right there. He's checking out the nurse with the curly hair. Do you see him?"

Mom's smile goes tense, and she tugs on her blazer, which is black with shoulder pads and gold buttons. "Can we speak to you privately?" she asks the doctor. The three of them take five steps, pull the curtain, and begin talking like there's a brick wall between us, not a thin piece of fabric.

I tune them out and drop my head into my hands. This is not happening. This is *not* happening.

"Does your mom always dress like a member of that ... what was that group called?" Homburg Guy is sitting at the foot of my bed. "Bratty Pack? Brat ... something *brat* from the eighties. They were in all those high school movies."

"What in the world are you ... wait! No, no, no, no. I'm not talking to you. You're not real."

The curtain slides open. "Did you call me?" Mom asks.

"No," I smile what I hope is a reassuring I-am-not-crazy smile. "I'm fine."

Mom's brow furrows, and she yanks the curtain closed.

"Look," I say at a whisper. "Please, please go away."

"No." Homburg guy cocks a thumb. "They're talking about admitting you to the psycho ward, woman. You're no good to me if you're drugged up."

Psych ward? My parents would never do such a thing. I mean, *yes*, I am being harassed by a figment of my imagination. Still, I don't want to be drugged up or locked up. I close my eyes and take a deep breath. "You are not real. You don't exist. I am fine." I repeat this to myself until I believe it.

"I'm still here," Homburg Guy whispers in my ear.

Darn it!

The curtain flings open, and the trio returns with fake smiles plastered on their faces, like they all just received heavy Botox injections.

"Good news!" I say before they whip out the straight jacket. "I'm feeling much better. I was so concerned about possible internal damage caused by the accident that ... um ... I talked myself into a panic attack. That's why I threw the cookie jar. I'm all better now."

Dad places a hand on my shoulder. "So you're not seeing anyone?"

"Not at all," I manage to say. "Only you three." And the Homburg Guy hovering behind the doctor.

"You weigh a hundred and five pounds?" He's reading over the doctor's shoulder. "I would have guessed you had another thirty on you. That outfit isn't doing you any favors."

"Totally fine," I say through gritted teeth. "How about that ice cream, Dad?"

"Honey," Mom smooths out the blanket draped over my legs. "I would feel more comfortable if you talked to—"

"Dear," Dad cuts her off. "She said she's better."

"But, *dear*"—Mom juts her jaw—"it won't hurt for her to talk to *someone*."

"You heard her, *dear*. She had a panic attack. She's fine."

"People don't typically see men in hats when they're having a panic attack, *dear*."

"Do they always talk about you like you're not here?" Homburg Guy asks.

"Pretty much." I lay back against the scratchy hospital sheet and wait for them to finish.

"What was that, pumpkin?" Dad asks.

"Um ... errr ... um." My parents are politely arguing over me. I'm getting fashion advice from a hallucination. And my doctor looks like he recently hit puberty. It takes every ounce of self-control I have not to completely freak out, but I'd rather not spend my days in a padded cell. "I'm *pretty much* fine. Can we please leave?"

Mom lets out a sigh. "I don't think—"

"Ice cream it is." Dad turns to the doctor. "Can we get the discharge papers?"

We're home by sundown. My hallucination is still here but quiet. When we stopped for ice cream, he chose to sulk in the car, and I was afforded a few moments by myself. Well, not technically by myself. I was sandwiched between my parents who silently watched me eat my single scoop of vanilla ice cream as if I might spontaneously combust at any moment.

It was exhausting.

Almost as exhausting as having to pretend a man isn't following me around.

"I'm going to sleep," I announce as soon as I exit the car and then proceed straight to my room and close the door. Jabba is sprawled out on my bed, fast asleep. I nudge him out of the way and bury my head in my pillow. I already know what Homburg Guy is thinking. Probably because he's a figment of my imagination. "Don't say it."

"What am I about to say?"

"You're going to make fun of my daybed or the fact I have a porcelain doll collection. But I'll have you know that they're vintage and worth a lot of money."

"I wasn't going to say anything about your room," he says, his tone softer than before.

I sit up. "You weren't?"

"Of course not," he scoffs. "This doll collection is impressive, and I like the drapes. The white lace goes well with the wallpaper ... oh, hell. I can't do nice. Your room looks like it belongs to one of those people you see on TV who eats deodorant. Now that your helicopter parents are gone, it's time to get to work."

I'm too tired to fight. "What is it exactly that you want me to do?"

"Find out how I died."

I put a pillow over my head and fall back on my bed, careful not to disturb Jabba. "This is not happening."

My body goes cold, like I just dove into an ice bath. I throw the pillow off my head. Homburg Guy is sitting on my legs. "What are you doing?"

"I'm not leaving until you help me."

I attempt to move but my legs are frozen still. I suck in a breath, about to scream, when I remember the look my parents exchanged in the hospital. I can't give them more reason to believe I'm crazy. Even if I clearly am.

"Fine," I say, giving up. If I help my hallucination, then perhaps he'll disappear. Or so I hope. "All you want is to know how you died?"

"Yes." He stands, and I can move my legs again.

"If you're dead, then why don't you ask God, or an angel, or someone in heaven how you ended up dead?"

Homburg Guy shakes his head. "It doesn't work like that. All I need you to do is get on the computer and find out how I died. Then I'll go."

"You promise?"

"Trust me, woman. I don't want to be here anymore than you want me to be."

I can't believe I'm even considering this. I can't believe I'm talking to a hallucination. I can't believe the only thing wrong with me is a lack of iron. I need a third opinion.

In the meantime ...

"There's one problem," I say. "The laptop is in the living room."

"And?"

"*And* my parents are out there. It's their work computer. They're not going to just let me use it. I'll have to wait until they go to bed."

"We don't have time!" He paces the room and strokes his chin until he comes to a halt. "I've got it. Tell them you need to fill out the papers online for your new job and grab the computer like a big girl."

"B-but I don't have a new job."

"It's called a lie. Like what you did earlier in the hospital when you said you weren't seeing me anymore. They don't know if you got the job or not. They never asked. You never told them."

My hallucination makes a good point. I don't want to lie to my parents. But I don't want to keep arguing with imaginary people either.

If this doesn't stop soon, I will happily commit myself.

Mom and Dad are sitting on opposite ends of the couch watching a documentary on penguins. I wet my lips and smooth back my hair. I suddenly realize I'm still in the same ripped socks and dirty skirt ensemble. This won't work.

I quickly retreat back to my room.

"Did you get it?" Homburg Guy grabs ahold of the bed railing and stares at me anxiously.

"Get out. I need to change."

"What? Why?"

"Because they'll be less suspicious if I'm dressed and ready for bed." I open my closet and pull out my nightgown.

Homburg Guy moans and walks through the wall. My room feels eerily empty.

I get dressed, brush my teeth, wash my face, and comb my

hair. My hands are shaky, and I can't believe I'm even doing this. Looking up a man who doesn't exist on the internet is only going to prove that I have, in fact, lost my marbles.

All dressed for bed, I peek my head out of the bathroom door to see if Homburg Guy has returned.

Coast is clear.

I tiptoe to my bedroom.

"Get the damn computer and get on with it." He's at the end of the hallway, arms crossed, foot tapping. "I want to get out of here!"

"Fine," I grunt and go to the living room. Mom has fallen asleep. Her head is back, mouth open, drool slithering down her chin. This is good. Dad avoids conflict like the stomach flu, while Mom grabs conflict by the balls and forces it to comply.

"Dad," I whisper so as not to wake Mom. "I forgot about the paperwork for my new job that I need to fill out online. It's due tonight. Can I use your computer for a bit?" I unplug the laptop from the wall and wrap up the cord.

"I didn't know you got the job, sweetie. Congratulations." He yawns and runs a hand through his dark hair. "When do you start?"

"Um ... tomorrow."

Dad rubs his eyes. "Don't stay up too late."

"I won't. Good night." I kiss the top of Dad's head and scoot out of the room before he realizes what he's done. In the past, they've only allowed me to touch their computer for homework purposes or to update MLS listings. *We have sensitive client information on there,* Mom had said. Can't argue with that.

I'm back on my bed with the laptop open. I click on the internet icon and go to Google. "What's your first and last name, date of birth, and date of death?" I ask.

Homburg Guy is pacing the room. "Willie MacIntosh,

spelled with a capital *I*. Born September fourth, nineteen twenty-six. Died sometime in the last day or so."

"My fingers freeze over the keyboard. "You're kidding me, right? You want to know how you died? You were ..." I click on the calculator icon on the desktop and type in the dates. "You were ninety-three years old," I loudly whisper in shock. "Why do you look so young?"

"I'm no expert, but it appears that you are restored to your prime after you die. The fifties were good years for me."

"You're ninety-three."

"Age is only a number," he says defensively. "Before I died, I was in great shape. I played golf on Tuesdays and Thursdays. Cross-country skied in the winter. Took my boat out every weekend. I was the picture of health."

"You were *ninety-three years old*," I repeat, because I don't think he's getting it.

"Just tell me how I died so I can go," he snaps. His nostrils flare when he's mad.

"Okay, okay." Not that any of this matters anyway. He's not real. I'm only humoring my hallucination.

I type in his information, and much to my horror, Google pulls up several articles. Most of which I can't open because of the parental controls my mom must have installed. I click on the only website I'm allowed to access, the local news station. Front and center is a picture of a wrinkled old man with large, droopy ears, bushy brows, and a frown. A little lower in the article is a picture of the same sharply dressed All-American Willie that's standing in front of me.

Ahh!

I shove the computer off my lap and scramble to my feet.

"What are you doing, woman?"

"You ... you ... you ..." My back is pressed against the wall, and I'm frantically pointing at the computer. "You ... you were real." How can Willie be a figment of my imagination if my imagination has never met him before? I don't watch the news. I don't read the obituaries. I don't socialize. There's no way I could have known Willie. The only time I ever saw him was at *The Gazette* before I was hit in the head.

Before!

Jabba hisses.

Ah! My cat can see Willie!

"Stop hyperventilating and get to work," Willie says, nostrils flaring. "Tell me how I died."

"B-but. You're dead ... that means"—I inch toward the only logical conclusion—"you're a ghost."

"Tell me how I died!"

"Okay. Okay." *Okay.* I pick up the laptop, still reeling from the realization that I'm not crazy, I just see dead people. Which doesn't make me feel any better about the situation. "Um ... so, according to the article, you died ... *today*. This morning, actually. It says you were influential in the space program?" I look to him for clarification.

"I created part of the filter system. Patented the design. Made millions. Keep going."

So I'm seeing rich dead people. Great. I wet my lips, feeling parched, and keep reading. "It says your wife confirmed that you passed away at home." I look up at Willie. "If you have a wife why don't you go bother her instead?"

"Don't you think I've tried? No matter what I do, or how hard I concentrate, I can't leave you. It's like I'm stuck. You move, I move. You run out in front of a car. I run out in front of a car."

"For the last time, I was *in* the crosswalk," I say, feeling a bit annoyed.

"Who cares? Now, how'd I die?"

"Why do you need me to tell you how you died?"

"I don't know!" He throws his hat on the floor. "Don't you understand? I'm still trying to figure out how death works. But I have this pressing *need* to find out how I died, and I lack the ability to find out. Now, tell me so I can get out of here! I hate Fernn Valley."

"You can say please."

"*Please.*"

"Okay." I read through the rest of the article and ... crud. "It doesn't say how you died. Just that you grew up in the Fernn Valley, died at home, and you were ninety-three."

"That's terrible journalism."

"Willie, maybe you were in great shape for being *ninety-three years* old. But all your internal organs were almost a century. You understand this, right? You died because you were old."

Willie takes a moment to digest. "No," he decides. "There was nothing natural about the way I died. I can feel it. Someone killed me. I know it. You need to keep searching."

Murder seems like a stretch, but I humor him. Only one problem. "I can't click on any of the other articles because of the parental controls. They're blocked."

Willie gapes at me. Then he does his pacing, rubbing chin bit until he comes up with an idea. "'Tomorrow morning, we'll go to the library, use the computer there, figure out how I died, then I'll disappear, and you can go back to your dull, sheltered, ugly life."

As appealing as that sounds, we have two problems. "I don't have a car, and there's no way my parents will take me to the library without accompanying me. The library is sort of our thing. We check out books together."

"You're killing me!" Willie explodes. "When I was your age, do you know what I was doing?" He doesn't wait for a response. "I was living in Mexico. No parents. No one was buying me ice cream, or driving me around, or changing my diaper."

"Wait." I do the math in my head. "When you were my age wasn't World War Two going on?"

"Yeah, so?"

"Didn't you get drafted?"

"It's not important. What's important is that we find out how I died and who killed me so I can get out of here." He rubs his temples. "Go to sleep, and tomorrow morning your parents can drop you at *The Gazette*. Then we'll sneak over to the library." He stalks toward the door.

"Where are you going?"

"I'll wait in the hallway. Your cat gives me the creeps."

CHAPTER THREE

Communicating with the dead is exhausting, and I sleep through my alarm.
"Zoe!"
I stretch my arms, roll over, and fall back asleep.
"Zoe!"
I blink to focus. Mom is leaning over me. Her hair is extra permy, and she has blue eyeshadow covering her entire lid.
"What do you want?" I throw the pillow back over my head. The room is too bright and my head hurts.
"Dad said you start work this morning."
"No, I don't," I moan, and my body goes cold. I peek out from under my pillow. Willie is hovering over me frantically pointing at my mother.
Huh?
Mom's eyes slide to the laptop at the foot of my bed.
Willie pulls at his hair. "Get up and get ready for work, woman! We need to go to the library."
"But—" I start to say, then think better of it. Talking to Willie in front of my parents is not a good idea. "Oh. No." I

bring my hands to my cheeks. "I. Am. Late. For. Work. I. Need. To. Get. Up. I. Need. To. Get. Dressed. Oh. No."

Willie slaps his forehead.

I jump out of bed and accidentally step on Jabba's tail, sending him ducking for cover under my desk.

Mom follows me to the bathroom. "Are you sure you're feeling okay?"

"I'm good." I close the door but can feel her presence on the other side. She's concerned. She thinks she should talk to a man ... a man named Phil ... then there's an S. Something with an S ... I see an S. I can see an S burning in a pit of fire. "Ahhhh!"

"What's wrong?" Mom tries to open the door, but it's locked. "Zoe Matilda Lane, open this door right now."

My breath hitches in my throat, and I wring my hands. I'm overcome with emotions: fear, anger, anxiety, menopause!

"What are you doing?" Willie hisses.

"I can read my mom's thoughts," I whisper in horror. "I can *feel* her."

He shrugs like this is no big deal. Like hearing thoughts and feeling others' feelings is totally normal. "You need to calm that woman down so we can go," he says. "Also, you need to find her a new hairstylist. Did your people stop evolving in nineteen ninety? I'm almost a hundred, and I have a better style than her."

My head is spinning. "How do I stop feeling her feelings?" I ask, still at a whisper.

"How the hell would I know? I only talked to people with a pulse when I was alive."

Well, he's of no help.

I grip the edge of the counter and close my eyes. When I do this, I can more easily separate my feelings from hers.

Gah! This is weird.

Mom rattles the knob. Panic rises inside of me. "I am

breaking down the door if you don't open up right now." And she means it. She's trying to remember where Dad keeps his sledgehammer when it dawns on her that she can use a bobby pin to pick the lock.

Crud.

I suck in a deep breath, blow it out slowly, and open the door. Mom is frantically trying to yank a bobby pin free from her head.

"Tell her you saw a spider," Willie says.

"There was a spider," I say.

"You're sorry to scare her," Willie says.

"I am sorry I scared you," I say, trying to sound less robotic.

We stand there, mother and daughter, staring at each other. Mom wants to believe me, but her gut tells her I'm lying. She ultimately convinces herself she's being overly sensitive. "You have ten minutes before we need to go. I've left a muffin and an iron pill on the counter," she says and goes to her room.

Willie is in my ear. "You need to keep it together, woman."

"Leave me alone." I feel like I'm about to have a stroke, but I manage to brush my teeth and pull my hair into a ponytail. In my room Willie is waiting for me. I open my closet and pull out a blue pantsuit and pink blouse.

"Do you own anything not ugly?" He walks through my clothes. "Guess not."

"It's a sensible pantsuit. Why are you so concerned about how people dress?"

"Not people, just you. You're way too young to dress so old."

"I do not dress ... you know what? If you want my help, you're going to have to be a lot nicer," I angry whisper. "Got it?"

"Fine. Wear the ugly clothes. I don't care." Willie walks through the wall.

This ghost is seriously testing my patience!

I get dressed in my *non*-ugly pantsuit and stand in front of the mirror while I button my blouse. If only I were starting a real job, with real people, and real money today. My mood falls at the thought. Twenty-four hours ago, I stood in front of this mirror while getting ready for my interview. Mom was sitting on my bed, trying to convince me that I didn't need the job at *The Gazette*. That I could continue helping them manage listings. "You're a talented writer," she had said. "We could even put you on the payroll."

I'm not sure how they could pay me. It's not like real estate in Fernn Valley is exactly booming. They barely make enough to cover their expenses as it is.

Had I known I'd be hit by a car and harassed by a ghost, I may have taken her up on the offer, though.

Mom, Dad, Willie, and I drive to *The Gazette* in silence. The only feelings I have are my own—which is quite nice. Mom is reading through a contract, and Dad's holding tight to the steering wheel like he's afraid it might fall off. I shift my focus to the window and watch the trees go by as we take the dirt road into town. Fernn Valley is a quaint community with brick buildings and brightly colored awnings, wide streets, and medians filled with grass so green it almost hurts your eyes. Nearly every house and business has an American flag proudly hung outside. In the center of town is Earl Park, named after Fernn Valley's founder, Earl Fernn. It reminds me of the setting from a sweet romance story: large willow trees, beveled walkways, a beautifully constructed gazebo, and a pond with a family of ducks that fly in every spring.

Across the street from the park is *The Gazette*. A two-story brick-faced building with a red awning and an American flag waving in the wind. Dad pulls up to the curb, and I grab my briefcase and slide open the door. Dad cuts the engine and starts to get out.

"What are you doing?" I ask in a panic.

"I want to take a picture of you on your first day of work in front of the building," he says while holding up his camera.

"Um ... er ... no. Please don't."

Mom turns around in her seat. "It's for your scrapbook, honey."

Oh, geez. I can't deny my parents the pleasure of documenting their only child's first day of work, but I also can't deny my parents the blissful unawareness of the fact that their only child is conversing with the dead.

Also, I'm twenty-three not seven.

It takes a bit of convincing, but Dad finally agrees to take the picture from the inside of the car.

"Pumpkin, you feeling okay?" Dad asks from behind the camera.

"Yes," I say in a rush.

Dad frowns. "You look tense. If you're not feeling up to it, you can call in sick. I'm sure they'll understand."

"Why would I not feel up to it?"

Dad lowers the camera. "Because you were hit by a car yesterday."

Oh, right. That. I completely forgot. Now that I think about it, my back does hurt, and my neck, and my arms, and my legs, and my feet. But there's no time to dwell on my limbs—I have a ghost to get rid of.

Per Dad's request, I say, "Cheese." Willie leans over and smiles for the picture. This is by far the most bizarre experience of my life.

"Before you go"—Dad reaches into his pocket—"this is for you." He places a silver pen into my hand with *Lane* engraved on the side. "My dad gave this to me on my first day of work. I've been saving it for you."

Great. Now I feel guilty.

"Thank you, Dad. I'll take great care of it." I tuck it into my inner jacket pocket, step outside, pull the van door closed, and walk slowly toward *The Gazette*, pausing a second to wait for my parents to drive off so I can make a swift U-turn and head to the library. Except they aren't moving. I stop at the door and wave. They wave back. Willie waves. I wave some more, and I realize they aren't leaving until I am inside the building. Great.

I pull on the door a few times until I remember you must push. Once I'm safely inside, Dad starts the car. I watch with my palms and forehead pressed against the glass of the door, waiting for them to disappear out of my sight.

"Ms. Lane?" a voice comes from behind.

I spin around and accidentally smack Brian Windsor in the stomach with my briefcase. "Oh, my gosh. I'm so sorry. It was an accident. Are you okay?" I ask.

"I'm o-okay." He plays it off, but I can tell he's in pain by the lack of color in his cheeks and the way he's hunched over mumbling profanity under his breath.

"You just nut-punched your fake boss." Willie shakes his head. "I feel for the guy. A briefcase to the balls hurts." He shudders at the thought.

"I didn't nut-punch anyone," I say.

"Yes, you did," Brian huffs out.

"Oh." Oops.

Brian drops onto the couch positioned below a black and white picture of Fernn Valley and puts his head between his knees.

"Oh, no." I stutter around, not really sure what to do. "Should I get a heat pack?"

Willie takes a seat beside Brian and puts a protective arm

around him. "Are you crazy, woman? You don't put heat on throbbing testicles."

"How would I know how to treat injured testicles?" I ask.

Brian grimaces up at me, and I want to die. I cannot believe I just said *testicles* in front of Brian. I want to crawl under the couch and never return. Of all the people in the world, why did my briefcase have to crash into *him*.

Brian may be sheet white, but I have a feeling I'm tomato red.

"I'll be fine." He manages to roll upright. Willie is at his side, his face full of concern.

"Are you sure?" I ask. "I'm so sorry. You scared me, and I-I ... I'm sorry."

"Don't worry. I'm fine." He pauses to catch his breath. "What are you doing here?"

"Um." Good question. One I don't have an answer to. I look to Willie for help.

"Say you came to inquire about advertising for your parents."

Oh, that's good. "I came to talk about advertising for ... um ... my parents' real estate business. They ... um ... need a bigger ad."

Brian adjusts his glasses, keeping one hand on his stomach. "Bigger than the full-page ad they already run?"

Oh, crap!

I mean ... *crud*. Stupid Willie is rubbing off on me.

Crap or crud. Either way, I completely forgot about my parents' weekly advertisement in *The Gazette,* and now Brian is staring at me expectantly with those gray eyes, and I don't know what else to do.

So I do what I do best.

Disappear.

I pull open the door and take off down the sidewalk.

"Ms. Lane, wait!" Brian calls after me, but I don't dare look back. I keep my briefcase swinging at my side, feet moving so fast Mrs. Clark from the beauty salon steps outside and asks if I'm training for a speed-walking competition.

"No!" I say and keep going until I'm able to turn down the alleyway between the dry cleaner and pharmacy. There's a pile of crates, and I take a seat and wait for my breath to return.

Willie makes a *W* with his arms. "What was that about?"

"Nothing." I open my briefcase and take out my walking shoes, still struggling to catch my breath. If I die right now at least I'd know how *I* went.

Cause of death: extreme mortification.

"First you nut-punch the guy. Then you take off," Willie says. "Did you not learn how to socialize in school?"

I slip on my sneakers and place my pumps into my briefcase. "I was homeschooled."

Willie rolls his eyes. "There's a shocker."

"That's it." I stand up. "Stop treating me like I'm an idiot with no feelings!"

Mr. and Mrs. Batch peek around the corner. Mrs. Batch is chewing on a donut, and Mr. Batch has a pipe hanging out of his mouth.

"Now you've gone and done it." Willie shakes his head. "Might as well drive yourself to the loony bin. Oh wait, you don't have a car."

"Shut up," I hiss.

Mr. Batch steps forward, squinting at me. Mr. Batch is the mayor, and Mrs. Batch owns the antique shop. They play Santa and Mrs. Claus in the Christmas parade every year.

I fidget with my fingers until I'm struck with a brilliant idea. I grab my cell phone from my briefcase and hold it to my ear. "Shut up ... That's right ... Wait, can you hold on a second?" I cover the receiver and look at Mr. and Mrs. Batch. "I'm sorry to be so loud." I smile sheepishly.

Mr. Batch pulls the pipe from his mouth, a slight expression of concern on his face. "You're the Lane kid, right?" His voice is rough, like there's a baseball size of phlegm stuck in his throat.

I nod, my hand still covering my phone.

"Huh." He returns his pipe to the corner of his mouth. "Okay, then. Be sure to keep it down. This is a nice quiet town, and we intend to keep it that way."

"I will. Thank you, Mr. Batch." I smile until he turns around and walks back to wherever he came from.

I just about pass out.

"The phone idea is genius," Willie says. "But why don't you have one of those smart phones?"

I sandwich my non-smart cell between my shoulder and ear and finish tying my shoes. "My parents bought me this one. iPhones are expensive."

"And a waste of money, if you ask me. Everyone has their face glued to a screen these days, and they need to know what every person is doing. Back when I was younger, if you wanted to know what someone was doing, you walked to their house or you called them. No one was twittering."

"That's great," I say, not quite paying attention to what he's saying. I'm still trying to recover from my run-in with Mr. Batch. I grab my briefcase and go down the alleyway, in the opposite direction.

"This isn't the way to the library," Willie says.

"No. We're taking the long route," I say into the phone. "We'll go around the back road and cut through the parking lot of Gladys's Diner."

"You don't seem like the type that gets out much. You sure you know where you're going?"

He's right. I don't get out much. But I've been to the library many times. Fernn Valley is small, and I've got a keen sense of direction—it's like my sixth sense.

Or ... er ... my seventh, I guess.

"You don't have many friends, do you?" Willie asks.

"I'm not very social." My blood pressure has dropped from stroke level to mild heart attack, and I'm able to relax a bit. The back road is empty, but I keep the cell to my ear in case anyone happens to come strolling by.

"Why don't you socialize?" Willie asks.

"I'm shy."

"You don't strike me as shy. I'd say you're more socially awkward."

"Thanks."

"Why is that?"

"I don't know. Because I grew up an only child." I cut through Gladys's Diner's parking lot. "We moved here when I was seven, and I never made any real friends, I guess."

"Why?"

"Why are you suddenly so interested in me?"

"Because you're strange. Where did you live before you moved here?"

"I don't remember."

"That doesn't make sense. You were seven?"

I shrug. "I don't have any memories prior to seven. I was young. It's not that uncommon."

"I'm ninety-three years old, and I still remember my first day of kindergarten."

"Congratulations." We stop at the curb, and I triple check to be sure no cars are racing down the road.

Coast is clear.

The library is a single-story, small clapboard building with a yellow awning and a revolving door. Inside smells of damp wood. The carpet is maroon, and the walls are painted with a mural of Fernn Valley. A sign asking all patrons to please silence their cells phones is mounted to the wall by the drinking fountain, and I slide mine into the outer pocket of my briefcase.

We step into the main library area, and behind the desk is Rosa, the librarian, on her cell phone. Here's what I know about Rosa: her mother has early stages of dementia, and Rosa spends a great deal of her time on the phone fighting with the insurance company, or fighting with the nursing home, or fighting with her family. I don't know if she's ever been married, but I do know she's single now and has three sons, five grandchildren, and another one on the way. I've never asked how old she is, but I'm assuming she's in her late sixties, early seventies. Rosa is the closest thing I have to a friend.

"You have to put the cream on first." Rosa pounds the counter and berates the caller in Spanish. A dark bun of messy hair is secured by a pencil on the top of her head. Red-rimmed glasses hang by a chain around her neck and colorful beaded earrings adorn each ear.

"Guess she didn't get the no-cell memo," Willie says.

"You can't do that!" Rosa yells. "Hello?" She looks at her phone then replaces it to her ear. "Hello?" With a grunt, she slides the phone across the desk and falls into her chair.

I clear my throat.

She looks up and claps her hand over her mouth. "I'm sorry, Zoe, sweetie. I didn't know anyone was here. It's my mother. The nursing home charges an arm and a leg, yet they can't ... you know what? Never mind." She slips on her readers and scoots her chair closer. "The fifth book in the Sizzling Hot Fireman series came in yesterday, and I saved it for you."

Willie gives me a look. "*Sizzling* fireman?"

My cheeks go red. "Actually, I'm here about something else. Do I have to pay to use the internet?"

"Of course not, silly thing. But I do need to sign you in. Follow me." Rosa takes off down an aisle of non-fiction books, and I run my hand along the colorful spines. Books of every shape, color, and width.

Rosa stops at a table with a boxy computer atop. "Copies and printing are a quarter. Internet is free." She wiggles the mouse and types in a ten-digit passcode. "Here you go, my dear."

"Great. Thank you. And, can you save the book for me?" I'm dying to find out who the fire captain ends up with.

"Of course I will," Rosa says with a wave of her hand. "No else checks them out, anyway."

"Thank you, and, um, if maybe you could not mention to my mom I was here, that would be helpful."

Rosa touches my shoulder. "I never saw you." She winks and hurries back to her desk. I can hear her on the phone again, yelling in Spanish. Which is lucky for us, because I can talk to Willie freely without worry of Rosa overhearing.

I take a seat, place my briefcase at my feet, and get to work.

"Why do you carry a briefcase?" Willie is on the ground staring at it.

"Because I'm supposed to be going to work." I roll my eyes. Honestly. Has he completely forgotten about our ruse?

"It's twenty nineteen. Do people still use briefcases?"

"Yes."

"It's ugly."

"Well, it's a good thing it's not yours. Why don't just go and ... *ugh* ... never mind." It doesn't matter what Willie thinks about my wardrobe or accessories or that he can remember kindergarten; he'll be gone soon. I type in his full name and birthday into Google and wait for the slow internet to show me the results. I read through each article. They all say the same thing: Willie MacIntosh, millionaire inventor, originally from Fernn Valley, retired in Trucker, died at ninety-three years old.

With each passing article, Willie grows more quiet. At one point, I think he's gone and push away from the table only to find him lying atop a bookshelf with his hands clasped over his chest, staring at the ceiling.

I return to the computer and keep reading until, finally, I find a helpful blurb in *The California Post*. "Got it. Got it. Got it," I almost sing.

Willie appears at my side. I highlight the sentence using the mouse. "It says you died of natural causes. No one killed you. You died because you were old. Congratulations." I spin around in my chair—happy this is all over.

Except Willie is still here.

"What's wrong?" I ask.

"That's not how I died."

"How do you know?"

"Because I just *know*. Someone else was responsible." He grunts. "I didn't want to do this, but it looks like we have no choice."

I'm scared to ask.

"You need to talk to Betty," he says.

I'm scared to ask.

"She's my wife," he says, sensing my hesitation.

"Where does she live?"

"In Trucker. Let's go." He starts toward the exit.

"Um, one small problem," I say from my chair. "Trucker is a forty-minute drive, and I don't have enough money for the bus."

I wait for Willie to stop kicking at the wall.

"All right," he finally says with a long exhale. "I've got an idea. Let's go."

I'm scared to ask.

CHAPTER FOUR

"Why are we at Old Man LeRoy's house?" I ask.
"You'll see."
I have a sinking suspicion I'm not going to like this.
Here's what I know about Old Man LeRoy: he lives in a double-wide on the outskirts of town. His yard consists of dead grass, broken lawn chairs, sun-faded plastic flamingos, and his dirty brown Buick that has a hula girl on the dashboard. Per *The Gazette,* he's the one who ran over the mailbox on Second Street last year. He's single, not sure if he's ever been married, and two months ago, he listed a golf cart in the classified ads, which didn't sell, obviously, because it's parked and rusting out front.
Oh, and he can't drive.
I follow Willie down a dirt driveway. The front hood of Old Man LeRoy's car is still smudged from where my body slid across. If I weren't so busy trying to convince a ninety-three-year-old dead man that he died of old age, I might be more upset about the accident.
"Now what?" I ask. "I'm not getting a ride from him."
Willie looks at me as if I'm being ridiculous. "I'd never let

LeRoy drive me around. Dead or alive. We're going to use his car."

"What? No, no, no, no." I retreat toward the main road.

Willie appears in front of me. "That old man takes a three-hour nap every day. We'll borrow the car now and return it before he wakes up."

"I draw the line at grand theft auto."

"It's not theft if we return it. Look at it like this, he owes you one."

"No."

"He's a good friend of mine. We've known each other since grammar school. He'll understand."

"No."

"He'll never know."

"No!" I step around him. This entire situation is bananas, and I'm done.

"If we don't find out today how I died, then I'll be stuck here with you forever!" Willie hollers after me.

I spin around and study the old man trapped in a thirty-something's body. In his tailored suit and black shoes that, despite the dusty road, are still shiny. He looks ready for a photo shoot. "You're bluffing," I say.

"Am I?" He pulls the sleeve of his jacket up and reveals a watch. "Time is running out. This is our last option. Either get in the car or you get me for the rest of your life."

Willie has me and he knows it. I can tell by the smug look on his face. Even if he is bluffing, and I suspect he is, I can't risk being stuck with him. The thought gives me indigestion. I drop my head into my hands and massage my temples. I wouldn't mind taking a three-hour nap as well.

"Fine," I say with a relenting sigh. "Where are the keys?"

"Good girl." Willie claps his hands and runs into the trailer, disappears, and returns a moment later with a triumphant smile.

I'm not sure I'll ever get used to watching someone who looks so real walk through walls.

"Good news," Willie says. "The door is unlocked, and the keys are right inside on a hook. LeRoy is sawing logs, so we have at least two hours."

"And you're sure he won't wake up?"

"I've known LeRoy my whole life. He's my best friend. The man is as predictable as stale bread."

I don't understand the analogy, but I go with it. I'd rather risk jail time than spend another day with Willie.

As promised, LeRoy's door is unlocked. I step into his entryway, if you can call it that. I'm basically in his living room, and there's LeRoy, fewer than five feet away, lying back in a recliner, snoozing away. Old Man LeRoy looks like a shar-pei dog—wrinkles upon wrinkles upon wrinkles. It's no wonder he hit me. He probably couldn't see.

The keys are on a hook by the door, and I snatch them up and exit as quietly as I entered.

"Hot damn, she did it." Willie throws his arms up in the air as if I just scored a touchdown. "Let's beat feet."

I don't know what that means exactly, but it dawns on me that there are two very real problems with Willie's plan.

First, "Everyone knows Old Man LeRoy's car. Someone will definitely see me driving it through town."

"I live by the lake. We can take the back road to get there. No one will notice."

Easy for him to say, he's invisible.

The second problem, "I've never driven a car before. I don't know how."

I wait for Willie to stop cursing and kicking the ground.

It takes a while.

... Still waiting ...

Finally he runs his hands down his face and says, "Do you have a watch?"

"Yes."

"Set the timer for one and a half hours."

I do as told.

"Good. Now get in, and I'll teach you how to adult."

This seems like a very bad idea.

But I do it anyway and slide into the driver's seat. "What in the world is that awful smell?" I check the backseat to make sure there's no dead body back there. No body. Just moldy sandwiches and grease-stained bags from fast food restaurants. I spot a Wendy's wrapper crinkled on the floor. The Wendy's in Fernn Valley closed down three years ago. Gross.

"LeRoy is a slob," Willie says as he settles into the passenger seat. "And has been since Gail died in eighty-nine."

I pinch my nose. "Was Gail his wife?"

"No. German shepherd." Willie tips his hat back and leans closer. "First you want to put that key into the—"

"I know how to start a car," I cut him off. "I'm not a complete imbecile. I *do* watch movies." I shove the key into the ... round key thing and turn it. Nothing happens.

"You have to press the brake," Willie says.

Oh, right. I put my foot on the brake and try again. The car turns on, and I feel a moment of pride, until I remember that I'm stealing an old man's car to run an errand for a ghost.

After a bit more instruction, we are on our way to Trucker. My hands hurt from clutching the steering wheel. The *clank, clank, clank* coming from under the hood is almost deafening, and there's an alarming burnt rubber smell coming from the air vents. I'm scared to push too hard on the gas pedal, convinced the car will explode along the curvy frontage road we're currently traveling on.

Willie bounces his right leg and keeps checking his watch, even though I'm fairly certain it doesn't actually tell time anymore. "I drive faster than you, and I'm almost a hundred years old, woman."

"Stop calling me woman."

"Why? You *are* a woman. When I was your age, a woman was called a woman and that was that. People are too easily offended these days."

"When you were my age, Nazis occupied Germany and smoking was considered good for your health. I would appreciate it if you called me Zoe." I turn on the blinker.

"The off-ramp isn't for another two miles, wo—" He adjusts his hat and takes a deep breath. "Person! Why are you using the blinker?"

"Because I don't know how to drive!" I turn off the blinker and return my hands to the steering wheel. Maneuvering this land ark is more difficult than I anticipated, and my nerves aren't making anything any easier. All it will take is for one police officer to pull me over and I'm done—off to jail, or solitary confinement, or both.

"How are you twenty-three years old and don't know how to drive?" Willie asks.

"We can only afford the one car, and my parents drive me where I want to go."

"Speaking of crazy." He turns to face me and rests his elbow on the back of the seat. "Did they forget to cut the umbilical cord at birth?"

"They're protective, that's all."

"They made you weird."

"You don't even know me or my parents."

"They're suffocating. Don't you want to experience life? Get in the car and just drive. Backpack through Europe. Wake up in a beachside cabana in Tahiti. Fresh macarons in Paris ..." his voice trails off, and he shifts in his seat. "I miss living already."

In my periphery, I see him staring out the window with a distant look in his eyes. Perhaps this is why Willie came to me. It's my job to help him accept his death and peacefully transition to the next life.

Except I have no idea how to do that. I'm not a psychologist. Nor am I particularly good with people—dead or alive, apparently. I wonder if there's a book at the library about how to help the deceased deal with death? I should look into that.

In the meantime ... "Willie, why do you think you came to me?"

"I don't know. One minute I'm alive, eating oatmeal and the next I'm watching you struggle through an interview for a job you're not qualified for."

"It was an *entry-level* position," I say, not that it matters, but still.

"You dotted your *I*'s on the application with swirls."

"I was making it personal."

"And you're sweet on that editor."

"I am not," I say as convincingly as I can. "Anyway, this is not about me. This is about you. How can I help you deal with your death?"

"Find out who killed me."

I withhold a grunt and keep going. "Tell me more about yourself, Willie. How long have you lived in Trucker?"

"Forty years."

"Where did you live before then?"

Willie blows out a breath. "I was born in Fernn Valley. Moved to Houston after the war. Moved to Trucker when I retired," he says in monotone.

"Do you have kids?"

"Had a vasectomy in fifty-five. Best decision I ever made—turn right!" He reaches for the steering wheel, but I've already turned the wheel so hard only two tires stay on the ground. The car swerves to the right ... to the left ... to the right. Willie has one hand on his hat and the other on the dashboard screaming at me to, "Pump the brakes!"

I do as I'm told, and we spin around in two complete circles before coming to a stop. Willie floats through the door and does a walk around the car while I work through a panic attack.

"Good news. No damage." Willie is back. "At least you're facing the right way. Two streets down, make a left, and I'll give you the gate code."

My hands are white knuckled on the steering wheel, and I'm scared to blink.

Willie snaps his fingers in front of my face, except they don't make the *snap* noise, which only makes the situation ten times worse. "Zoe?"

I turn my head slowly.

He gives me an encouraging smile. "Drive forward." He points. "That way."

I nod and press the gas ever so lightly with my foot, and we inch forward. Eventually, we roll up to a tall iron gate with Lakeshore Estates engraved in the center in lovely script. Willie dictates the gate code, and I type it into the keypad. The gates part, and we're granted entrance. LeRoy's clunky old car couldn't be more out of place. Even the road looks expensive. There are no sidewalks or street lamps. Only houses that look more like hotels. We drive past mansion after mansion. Each one bigger than the next.

"There it is." Willie points to a colonial-style home at the end of the street, and I stop the car.

"Willie," is all I can say. The house is gorgeous. The most beautiful home I've ever seen. Which is saying a lot. With real estate agent parents, I've seen a lot of gorgeous homes. Well, pictures of gorgeous homes. Willie's mansion has a stone facade with more windows than I can count. Each window is adorned with dark blue shutters. The door is red and the landscaping pristine. Despite its vastness, the house is warm, approachable, and friendly. The kind of house you see on a Christmas card or on a picture hung in the doctor's office.

"Park around the corner out of sight," says Willie. "You're not pulling this thing into my driveway nor are you parking it in front of my house. That's the rule when LeRoy visits me, too."

"What a nice friend you are." I park around the corner at the curb. Well, more like *on* the curb, and the front right wheel might be *on* the grass. But, hey, this is my first attempt at driving. I open the door and ... "Whoa! Why is the car moving?"

"You have to pull the parking brake!"

"Oh, right." I jump back in and yank the parking brake. The car stops, and I exit again. This time the car stays where I put it.

"What am I supposed to say?" I ask Willie as we climb up the long circular driveway. "Hi, my name is Zoe. Your dead husband thinks he was killed."

"Tell her you're a reporter doing an article on me and ask if you can interview her."

Willie is much better at crafting lies than I am. "Should I grab my briefcase then?"

"Why in the world would you do that?"

"To look more professional."

"So help me, if I had the use of my hands, I'd burn that monstrosity."

"It's a good thing you don't because that briefcase was almost thirty dollars." We step up to the door, and I ring the bell. A melody of chimes announces our arrival, and a dog barks in the distance. "You're not a very nice person, do you know that?" I add.

"Yeah, yeah."

The door opens, and I come face-to-boob with a life-size Barbie in a black bikini. This can't possibly be ... "Mrs. MacIntosh?"

She gives me the once-over. "That's me."

I thought Betty MacIntosh would be, gee, I don't know, *old*. I pictured her with white hair and arthritic hands. The real Betty can't be more than thirty. If that. She has a raspy voice and eyes so blue they're almost see-through. The dog at her feet is a little terrier mix with scruffy gray hair, a brilliant red collar, and an impossibly long tongue.

Willie walks past Betty and disappears.

Gee, thanks. Guess I'll do this alone.

I clear my throat to buy time. Betty's beauty, and house, and cute dog intimidate me. And it's really hard not to stare at her cleavage. Not because cleavage is my thing. But because it's at eye level and quite impressive—as far as cleavage goes. I guess. "Um ..." I tuck a strand a hair behind my ear, feeling self-conscious. I should have worn my navy pantsuit today. "My name is um ... Zoe and I'm a reporter for um ... the ... um ... the *paper*?" That's the best name I can come up with. "Can I ask you a few questions about Willie MacIntosh?"

Betty surveys me from head to toe with a skeptical tilt of her head. "You said your name is Zoe? With a *Z*?"

"Um ... *yes*." I have a feeling that I'm about to get a door slammed in face.

Betty props one hand on her hip. "What's your last name?"

I'm hesitant to give her my real name, but something tells me I should. And that something is Willie who has returned and is yelling in my ear to, "Hurry the hell up! Tell her your name and get on with it!"

"Lane," I say. "Zoe Lane."

Betty claps a hand over her mouth. "Lane? With an *L*?"

"Um ... yeah."

Her eyes gloss over and, before I know it, her arms are wrapped around me. She smells like vanilla. Unsure of what else to do, I keep my arms plastered to my side.

Betty releases me and fans her face. "Come in. Come in." She opens the door wider. "Come. Come. I'm so happy you're here."

That was easy.

Too easy.

I step inside and realize I'm still wearing my sneakers. They're almost unrecognizable, dirty from Old Man LeRoy's driveway and unworthy of the marble floor I'm standing on. "Would you like me to remove my shoes?" I ask, but Betty is already gone. She's on the couch in the living room with her feet tucked under her little butt. The dog is curled up at her side, tongue still dangling from its mouth.

I decide to slip off my shoes and place them by the umbrella holder in the entryway. I'm cold, and I shove my hands into my pockets to keep them warm. My socks are slippery, and I nearly tumble down the single step into the living room—if you can call it that. It looks more like an Ethan Allen showroom with large bay windows overlooking a small garden and the calm lake.

"Go ahead and have a seat." Betty gestures to one of two chairs. I pick the one closest to her and sink three feet into the cushion.

Oh, my. I want to take a nap in this chair.

"I'm sorry about the temperature." She sweeps her golden locks into a bun at the top her head, and, of course, it looks perfect. Like she spent thirty minutes pinning every hair into place. "The thermostat is stuck at eighty-five."

Willie appears in the other chair with one foot propped on the ottoman. "That's because I put a lock on the heater."

I roll my eyes, but Betty doesn't notice.

"The temp is fine." I bite at my lip, not sure where to begin. I've never interviewed anyone before, and coming right out and asking how Willie died feels insensitive. So I start with the obvious. "I'm very sorry for your loss, Mrs. MacIntosh."

She looks up and frowns. "You can call me Betty, and thank you. You know what? You're the first person to say that to me. Everyone assumes I was with Willie because he was rich. I'm totally heartbroken. I mean, look at me." She opens her arms, and I'm not sure what exactly I'm supposed to be looking at. "I'm obviously in a state of mourning here."

Still confused.

"She's wearing black," Willie clarifies.

Oh, right. Black bikini. State of mourning. Got it.

"How long were you two married?" I ask.

"Almost two weeks. I know it may sound silly, but I thought we had at least another year together. Willie was in great shape for his age."

"Told you." Willie smirks.

"I mean, he couldn't ... *you know* ... but I was fine with that."

Ew.

Willie shrugs. "I'm ninety-three years old. Been there, done that. Don't need to do it anymore."

Oh, geez.

"How did you two ... um ... meet?" I ask.

"Why does it matter?" Willie scoffs. "Ask how I died and get on with it."

"I'm conducting an interview," I say through a smile. "I need to ask more than one question."

"You can ask whatever you want. I'm an open book," Betty says. "I worked as a waitress at the country club where Willie and his friends played golf on Tuesdays and Thursdays. One day, Willie asked me if I'd like to marry him, and I said yes."

"Just like that?" I ask in shock. "You just *married* him?"

"No, silly. Not just like *that*." She snaps her fingers. "We dated for two months before we went down to the courthouse to make it final." The memory curves a weak smile on her face. "He said he didn't want to spend the time he had left in this big house alone and that I could stop waitressing and spend my time doing what I'm passionate about."

"Which is?" I ask, half expecting her to say something like shopping, or working out, or hot yoga. Not that I enjoy stereotyping anyone. But a beautiful young blonde marrying an old rich man is the premise for the entire Hot Bazillionaire series—which is my least favorite of all the romance books I've read.

Betty grabs a magazine off the side table and uses it as a fan. "I'm passionate about humanitarian work."

Oh.

"She spends her free time volunteering at the Trucker Teen Center, working with kids who are struggling at home," Willie says proudly. "Bet you pegged her for a blonde bimbo, huh?"

"*Pffft* ... no."

"What was that?" Betty asks.

"Um ... I said ... that's great."

"I'm finishing my master's in social work," Betty says. "Do you know how many children are currently in the foster care system?"

"Uh ... no."

"Over sixty thousand children in California alone," Betty and Willie say in unison.

So Willie MacIntosh *does* have a softer side. Who knew?

"It's awful, Zoe. I know I'm just one person, but I think I can help," Betty says. "So when Willie said I could quit my job and concentrate solely on my charities and education, I said yes."

"It was a bet," says Willie. "The guys didn't believe I could still get any girl I wanted, so I proved them wrong."

"Excuse me?" I ask.

"I said that I took him up on the offer," Betty repeats. "Shouldn't you be writing this down?"

Probably. "I, um ... am recording it."

"Really?" Betty asks. "Where is the recorder?"

I blow out a breath. That's a good question. I pat around my pockets and pull out the pen Dad gave me. "This is a recording device." I give it a click.

Betty looks skeptical but doesn't question me on it.

"Can you tell me more about how Willie died?" I feel intrusive asking, but I only have so much time before Old Man LeRoy wakes, and Willie looks as if he's about to have a coronary if I don't ask soon.

Assuming ghosts can have coronaries.

Betty lowers her head and picks at a scab on her leg. "It's still weird to think he's gone. I'd been away shopping all morning. When I came home I dropped my bags in my room then came downstairs ..." She points directly at Willie and his eyes go wide.

Oh, my ...

"Holy hell. Can you see me?" he asks.

"He was on that chair, sitting in a weird position," she says, still pointing. "I thought he was asleep, but when I tried to wake him, he just ... fell over." She blinks, tears pooling in her eyes. Willie jumps out of the chair and moves to the other side of the room. "He wasn't breathing. I tried to do CPR, but it didn't work. By the time the paramedics got here, he was already ... *dead.*"

I can feel her shock and sorrow. But there's another emotion there ... one I can't quite place. I'm still figuring out this whole feeling other peoples' feelings thing. "Do you know how he died?" I ask.

"The medical examiner said it was likely natural causes." The tears spill down her cheeks, and she buries her head into her hands. I move to the couch. Too afraid to touch her, I keep my hands on my lap. I know they're cold, and she doesn't have much clothing on. *This* must be why I'm here. Both Betty and Willie need closure, and it's my duty to provide that for them.

Willie tilts his hat back. "It's one-two-three-four."

I mouth, *"What is?"*

"The code to the thermostat. It's one-two-three-four. I never told her because I didn't want her changing the temp. She thought keeping the house at eighty-five wasn't good for my arthritis. But I don't care. I'm old, and if I want it to be eighty-five, then I'll keep it at eighty-five. But I suppose she doesn't have to live in tropical conditions if she doesn't want to."

"Betty," I say. "I can help you with your thermostat."

She looks up at me with mascara-stained cheeks. "You can?"

"Yes." I take her by the hand, and she flinches. "And please know that Willie cared for you more than he ever thought he could. You made him a better man. The way you put others before yourself. The way you looked after him. Like how you'd go to Butter Bakery in Fernn Valley and buy him those bran muffins he likes every Saturday morning. Or how you'd make him his overnight oats in the evening before you went to bed. Or when you insisted on attending all his doctors' appointments and took notes. He noticed everything, and even though he never said it, he cared for you. You made these last few months remarkable ..." I shake my head, as if waking from a daydream. Willie is standing silently with his hat in his hands, starring at the floor, and I realized those were Willie's thoughts. He did care for Betty. He is more than a grumpy old man (mostly). Maybe dating Betty started off as a bet, but that's not how their relationship ended, which makes me feel a whole lot better about the situation.

When I look at Betty, her mouth is wide open. "She was right!"

"Huh?"

Betty squeezes my hands. "Aleena said you'd come with a message from Willie, and she was right."

I'm confused.

"Aleena is her psychic," Willie says with an eye roll. "She spends an hour a day on the phone with her. Costs five dollars per minute. Waste of time and money."

Huh. Two days ago I would have agreed that psychics are a scam. Now, I'm not so sure. I wonder if I can charge five dollars a minute for my services.

Hmmm ...

"Concentrate, person," Willie says.

Right. Back to Betty.

"Aleena said Willie would send me a sign today. She specially said it would be a person with the name *L*," Betty says as a single sticky tear rolls down her cheek. "I've always believed certain people had the ability to communicate with spirits. You're Willie's messenger, right? Is he here?"

Wow.

I want Aleena's number.

"Um ..." I yank my hands free. "No. I um ..."

Willie gets in my face. "Ask about an autopsy."

I stifle a grunt.

"Tell her," he demands. "I want an autopsy!"

Betty is staring at me with an unreadable expression. I clear my throat, forcing the words out. "Have you ... um ... thought of ordering an autopsy for Willie?"

"Oh ... I didn't think it was necessary." She shifts her focus to the ground, and I catch the slightest hint of remorse from her.

"Where is my body now?" Willie is still in my face.

Gah! He's making it hard to concentrate.

"Betty, what are your plans for Willie's funeral and remains?" I ask her.

"He's at Trucker Funeral Home. Willie said he wanted to be cremated and his ashes to be scattered in the lake."

"Stop her!" Willie explodes, and I almost fall off the couch. "I cannot be cremated before they do an autopsy. I was killed. I know it! Tell her!" He presses his mouth to my ear. "Tell her! Tell her! Tell her! Tell her! Tell her!"

"Betty," I say and shoo Willie away like he's a fly, "can I bother you for a cup of water?"

"Of course." She jumps up and retreats to the kitchen.

I wait until she's out of earshot. "Willie, listen to me," I whisper. "You were seven years away from a century. The doctor said it looked like you died of natural causes. She found you sitting in a chair, not in a puddle of blood with a gunshot wound to the head. This does not sound like foul play. This sounds like you had a long wonderful life, and now you can peacefully go to wherever it is you're going."

Willie narrows his eyes. "I want an autopsy."

I wish it were possible to strangle a ghost.

Betty returns. "Here you go." She places a coaster on the coffee table and puts down a glass filled to the brim with water.

"I was just thinking." Betty takes a seat in the chair Willie died in, and the little dog curls up at her feet. "You now, I read somewhere that when you die you go back to your prime age. Willie was so handsome when he was in his thirties, and I'm wondering if when I die the two of us will be able to meet up and start over at the same age. Can you ask Willie?"

"Um ..." Oh, geez. I'm not ready to admit out loud that I see dead people.

Not yet, anyway.

Willie lowers to one knee in front of his wife. "Betty, please. You need to order an autopsy. Please."

Betty freezes and tilts her head back. I think she can hear

Willie, or sense his presence, but then she closes her eyes and sneezes.

"Excuse me." She sniffles. "Since you're here, let me ask you something. When I was a little girl, my very best friend Daisy was hit by a car. It was tragic. She was the best little dog, and sometimes I can feel her. Willie said I was crazy. But do you feel her here, too?"

My eyes shift to the dog at her feet. Oh, my word ...

So I see dead, rich old guys and dead dogs.

I take a sip of water, needing a moment to digest this new information. "Daisy?" I say, and the little dog walks over and scratches at my leg with her paw, but I don't feel a thing.

"This is getting weird," Willie says.

Weird isn't the word I'd use to describe the situation. It's more so ... *beautiful.* Daisy returns to her owner, nestles close to Betty's leg, and whimpers. She's here to comfort and protect Betty.

I can't help myself. "She's here," I say. "Daisy is here. She has a red collar and scruffy hair."

"And a long tongue?" Betty says through tears.

I nod. "Willie is here, too."

"He is?" Betty drops her head into her hands. "It was my fault!" she suddenly cries out. "I'm the one who killed him!"

Willie stumbles backwards.

Didn't see that one coming.

Betty is trembling. "He called me yesterday morning to say he was out of blood pressure medication. I didn't think it was an emergency. So I finished shopping before I went to the pharmacy. But they had to get ahold of the doctor before they would give it to me. It took forever. If he'd had the medication on time then he wouldn't have died. It was a heart attack. Even Aleena confirmed that's what it was. She said he died of a heart attack because of his blood pressure medication, and she's never been wrong! She's one of the reasons I agreed to Willie's proposal. She said together we would create great change in Trucker. But now he's gone, and it's my fault. No one believes me, but I really do care about him. I completely failed him."

Um ... that was a lot of information to take in. I glance at Willie, who is shaking his head. "Nope. That's not how it happened. Tell her to order an autopsy."

Ugh.

Willie waves his arms to get my attention. "Tell her about the autopsy!"

Fine!

I first take another sip of water. Then I hold the cup in my hands, staring at the driblets of condensations slithering down the side. Then I clear my throat. Then I take another sip of water. Then I continue to procrastinate.

Truth is, Willie likely died of a heart attack, especially if he didn't take his medicine. Even the physic said so. Once this is confirmed, the guilt will haunt Betty for the rest of her life. And, even if Willie will haunt me for the rest of mine, it's not fair to her. She needs peace. She needs closure.

So I say, "Willie doesn't blame you."

She looks up. "He doesn't?"

"No. He understands it was his time."

Willie's mouth drops open. "That's not what I said!"

"He doesn't hate me?" Betty asks.

I shake my head no. "He adores you."

There's no argument from Willie on this one.

"Tell him I adore him, too," she says, and she means it. I feel the genuine adoration she had for Willie. Heaven knows why. Perhaps he was more pleasant to be around when he had a pulse.

"He knows you do." I check my watch. We don't have much time. "Can I help you with the thermostat before I go?"

Willie throws his hat on the ground. "You're horrible at your job!"

I ignore him and follow Betty down a hallway and into a masculine bedroom. A four-post bed with a green comforter towers in the middle of the room. Off to the side is a sitting area with a faux fur rug and a worn leather recliner.

Willie looks around. "Tell her not to touch anything in my room."

I'm confused. "Did you not share a room?" I ask Betty.

"No," she says over her shoulder. "He told me to take the master upstairs."

This is a weird marriage.

Betty hands me what looks like a mini iPad. "The heat and air are both controlled from this, but he put a lock on it. I've tried every code I could think of, but none have worked."

"Funny that Willie didn't believe in smart phones, but his house is controlled by an iPad," I say.

"Not really," Willie says. "There's a big difference between being able to change your thermostat without having to get out of bed and taking a picture of your lunch so you can put it on one of those social media sites."

He makes a point.

I type in the security code. Once I'm granted access, I hand it over to Betty, and she lowers the temp. I can hear the air pushing through the vents. Betty opens her arms wide and lets out a sigh.

My breath puffs out in a cloud and my hands go numb. I look around. Only Willie, Betty, Daisy, and I are in the room, but I have an uneasy, irritable, almost haunted feeling.

"We need to talk about the autopsy!" Willie yells directly into my ear.

"*No*," I mouth and return the tablet to the side table next to a row of pill bottles. "Were these all for Willie?" I ask Betty.

"Yes. This one is for acid." She points to each pill bottle. "This one is for his thyroid. This one is to prevent blood clots. This one is his blood pressure medication. This one is for blood sugar. This one is for arthritis. This one is for chronic constipation."

"That's *a lot* of pills for someone who was in perfect health," I say, looking at Willie.

"I was killed," he says. "I think *I* would know, being as I'm the only one in the room who was there."

The doorbell chimes, and the little dog barks.

"I wonder who that is?" Betty says and scoots out of the room, leaving me alone with all of Willie's personal belongings —expensive looking belongings, I might add. A Rolex watch collection, golfing trophies, nice suits lined up in the closet from light gray to black, and a deer's head mounted to the wall.

I grimace. "Did you shoot that yourself?"

"Why does it matter?"

"Because I don't know how I feel about hunting."

"At least that buck knows how he died. What is wrong with you? Aren't you supposed to respect the wishes of the deceased?"

"Why did you wait until you were out of blood pressure medication before you asked Betty to fill it?"

"I didn't wait until I was out!"

I pick up the blood pressure bottle and give it a shake, nothing rattles around. "See, it's empty."

Willie blinks a few times. "It doesn't matter. No one is going to have a heart attack because they went three hours without their blood pressure medication."

He makes a point.

I think.

I don't know too much about blood pressure medication or heart attacks. I should look into that.

"Listen to me, person." Willie squares his shoulders. "I was killed. I'm sure of it. We need to figure out how I died. Once we figure that out, we'll know who it was that killed me. I know it."

"But Betty's physic said it was a heart attack because of your blood pressure medication," I remind him.

"That's a bunch of hogwash. I was killed."

"Fine. Let's check your security footage and see if someone snuck in."

"I don't have security footage. What's the point of cameras when I live in a safe, gated community? I already fork out a thousand bucks for the HOA every month."

For the record, if I had a mansion, I'd have cameras.

"How can you be so sure—" I start to say when Willie shushes me and turns his ear toward the door.

"What's wrong?" I whisper.

"Stay here." He disappears through the wall and reappears a moment later. "Beat feet, person. Your parents are here."

CHAPTER FIVE

I've lost the ability to swallow. "Wh-ha-wh-wh ... Why are my parents here?"

"I don't know, but we need to get out of here before they see you." Willie runs out of the room, and I follow. He starts down the hallway then comes to a sudden stop, and I run right through him.

That was weird.

"What are you doing?" I angry-whisper.

Willie is poised in a battle-ready stance.

"What is it?" I ask in a panic. "Oh, no. Are they here with the police? Am I going to be arrested?" I feel a bit light-headed. "Are they going to take me away now?"

"Calm down, person. No one is taking you anywhere," Willie says and furrows his brow. "It's Weasel!" He takes off in the opposite direction, and I stutter around, unsure of what to do, or what Willie means when he says weasel, but if my parents catch me here, I'm doomed. There's no way I can come up with a reasonable explanation as to why I "borrowed" a car, without a license, to visit a dead-man-who-I've-never-met's life-size-Barbie of a wife.

Nope.

I need get out of here.

Except ...

I hear a crisp masculine voice coming from the entryway. Not the voice of my father. Nor anyone I've met before. Could this be the *Phil* I saw in my mother's mind? Or the S?

I'm conflicted: run away or see who else is here?

My natural instinct says run! But my curiosity overrides that feeling.

I tiptoe down the hallway, keeping my back against the wall. I peek around the corner and find Betty cowering before a man whose face is tomato red. Willie takes a protective stance in front of his wife. If this man is Weasel, then I can see why Willie calls him such. The man resembles a weasel: at least fifty years old, with thinning, slicked-back red hair, dark beady eyes, and a small nose and mouth.

My parents are standing shoulder-to-shoulder by the door and couldn't look more uncomfortable.

"I had to read about his death in the newspaper!" Weasel says to Betty.

Betty starts backing up and Daisy growls. "I haven't had a chance to make phone calls."

"I bet," Weasel makes a big U-turn, and my parents shuffle out of the way in unison. Weasel pauses at the door and peers over his shoulder back at Betty. "He's been gone a day, and you've already moved on to your next victim?"

Betty's face contours into a questions mark. "What?"

Weasel walks toward her like a cat approaching its prey. Daisy bites at his ankles. She doesn't like Weasel and, frankly, neither do I. He has a dark presence and an unsettling spirit, similar to what I felt in Willie's room. "Then whose shoes are by the door? There is no way they belong to Willie. He's not that cheap. They belong to your next victim. Don't they?

MAKING A MEDIUM

Don't they!" A vein pops out of the side of his neck. "Don't they!"

Hold on ... Is he talking about *my* shoes? Because the Weekend Walkers not only cost over twenty dollars ($19.99 plus tax and shipping) but were rated last year's As Seen On TV's best product. Weasel has a lot of nerve.

Mom raises a hand. "Perhaps we can come back when it's more convenient."

"Those aren't man shoes," Betty says, cowering.

"Yes, they are!" Weasel ignores my mom. "Those are old man shoes if I've ever seen them. You're nothing but a gold digger."

"That's it!" Willie throws a punch that goes right through Weasel.

"You're mistaken," Betty says. "I promise."

Weasel raises his pointer finger up to Betty's nose. "I was going to be nice and give you a month, but I think a week should suffice. I expect your things out of here before Sunday. We're putting the house on the market."

"But ... but ... this is my house," Betty says with a whimper.

"Maybe it was when you were dating my uncle. But he's gone now, and this is my house. You're trespassing."

"That's not true!" Betty disappears into a room and reappears with a blue file folder. "Willie and I got married a couple of weeks ago, and he changed his will." She hands the paperwork to Weasel.

Mom and Dad share a look, and I catch a hint of disappointment flicker across their faces. Not that I blame them—the commission from Willie's house would be more than they've made their entire career combined.

"You talked him into marrying you?" Weasel spits the words out.

"No. It was all his idea. I promise. And I never asked him to change his will, either. He came home one day with the paperwork and told me."

Weasel's hands tremble as his eyes dart down the pages. "He left you ... *everything?*"

"Damn straight, I did." Willie pushes up the sleeves of his jacket. "And if you come near her again, I'll ... I'll ..." He looks down at his clenched fists. "Zoe! Come punch this fool for me."

Um, *no.*

Weasel looks like he's about to fall over. "This is garbage." He tosses the will into the air, and papers flutter down around them. "You're nothing but a scam artist!"

Betty lowers to her knees and gathers the papers into a pile.

That's it! I don't care what happens to me, but no one deserves to be talked to like that. I stand and puff my chest, ready for a fight, but the timer on my watch goes off. It takes me a moment to remember why I set it in the first place.

LeRoy!

"What is that?" Weasel asks. "What's the beeping?"

Willie appears in front of me. "Follow me."

"But what about Betty?" I whisper.

"We're married. The will is legal. She'll be fine. Come on."

I hesitate, wrestling between helping Betty and saving myself.

"Hurry up, person!" Willie hollers from the end of the hall. "You're of no help to me if you're in jail."

Good point.

I follow Willie down another hall. He makes a left, then a right, then another left, and points to a door. "Open."

I rattle the knob, but it's stuck, and the deadbolt won't turn. Willie disappears through the wall and pokes his head back through. "There's a key broken in the lock." He looks at me. "Why is there a key broken in the lock?"

"How would I know?" I check the time. Crap. LeRoy will be

awake in thirty-eight minutes, and it takes longer than that to get back. "This way." Willie goes through a different wall, I use the door, and we are in an empty room. "Open the window and go out."

I go headfirst into a rose bush. Ouch.

I crawl out, pick the thorns out of my palms, and run behind Willie to the side of the house. We peek around the corner. Mom and Dad hurry to catch up to Weasel who is storming towards a black 4-Runner. He jumps into the driver's seat and starts the car. Mom and Dad climb in and swing the doors shut. Weasel peels out of the driveway, leaving a cloud of burnt rubber behind him. He makes it halfway down the road before his brake lights come on.

Oh, no.

He backs up just as fast as he left and stops near the corner where I parked LeRoy's car.

Oh no, no, no, no.

Weasel holds up his phone and takes two pictures then screeches down the street.

That's not good. That's not good at all.

Willie and I hurry to the car, and I nearly trip over my own shoeless feet. The sprinklers are on, and I must have run one over because it's spewing water all over the trunk of LeRoy's car. It's way too clean. "I'm screwed!"

"We'll fix it when we get back." Willie takes his position in the passenger seat.

I slide in beside him and turn the key.

"Foot on the brake, person," Willie reminds me.

Right. Foot on brake. Turn ignition. Car on, and we're off.

"You need to go more than fifteen miles per hour if we're going to make it to LeRoy's before he wakes."

I ease on the gas, and the car lurches forward. My heart is slamming against my chest. "Who is that guy?" I ask.

"It's my nephew, Daniel. The only reason he ever bothered to come around was because he thought he'd get everything once I was gone." He laughs. "Showed him."

I pull out onto the main road and manage to go only five below the speed limit. "You should have told him about Betty so she wouldn't have to deal with him."

"I planned to," Willie says. "He and I were supposed to meet at the club for breakfast this Saturday. I was going to drop the news then. Obviously, that didn't happen."

"Obviously." I clutch the wheel and check my rearview mirror to be sure no cops or black 4-Runners are following me. Coast is clear. For now. "So what do we do?"

"We make sure Betty gets the autopsy."

I feel like beating my head against the steering wheel. "But if an autopsy shows a heart attack, Betty will never forgive herself."

"I didn't die of a heart attack. Someone killed me."

"Even if someone did, we won't find out who it was by the end of the day," I say.

"Then we'll figure it out tomorrow."

"But you told me that if you don't know how you died by today, you'd be stuck here forever."

"I was bluffing," he says. "Obviously."

We're back at LeRoy's. Willie disappears. I grab my briefcase and silently close the car door behind me. I'm in my socks, but I don't have time to care. LeRoy's car is too clean. I grab a handful of dirt and sprinkle it on the trunk.

"He's waking up." Willie is back. "Hurry."

I grab another handful of dirt and dump it on the trunk and spread it around. "Um ... um ..."

"That's good enough, person!" Willie takes off toward the trees. I still have LeRoy's keys in my hand. If he's waking up, I can't very well enter his house. Instead, I open the car door, throw the keys on the seat, and chase after Willie. The sticks and prickly plants hurt the bottoms of my feet, but adrenaline keeps me going. I run through the forest and wait until we're at the creek before I stop to catch my breath.

"That was a close one," Willie says.

"If we keep this up, *I* am going to have a heart attack." I put my head between my knees. "I can't do this anymore."

"You can and you will until we figure out who killed me."

"Mother Nature killed you!" I blurt out and a flock of birds fly out of a nearby bush.

"Wanna make a bet?" Willie asks smugly.

"No." I wipe the sweat from my brow. "And what's with you betting to date Betty? That's awful."

"She's sitting in a ten-million-dollar home with three hundred million dollars about to be deposited into her bank account. How is that awful?"

I blink. "Three hundred million dollars. You left your wife of less than a month *three hundred* million dollars?"

Willie takes a seat on a stump. "The question is, who wanted to off me?"

"Three hundred million dollars."

He rolls and unrolls the bottom of his tie. "When we get back to your house, we'll make a list of suspects. Off the top of my head, I've got three people who threatened to kill me recently. We need to ask Betty about the key. I remember going out to the garage yesterday morning. I would have locked the door behind me. But I wouldn't have used a key. There's a code I can type in ..."

"Three hundred million dollars."

Willie stands. "What time are your parents picking you up from *The Gazette*?"

I'm having a hard time wrapping my brain around the three hundred million dollars.

"Zoe?" Willie waves a hand in front of my face. "You there?"

Right. Parents. I check my watch. "They'll pick me up in front of *The Gazette* in an hour."

"It will take you that long to get there." He starts walking along the creek and waves for me to follow.

I open my briefcase, grab my pumps, and slip them on. Not exactly walking attire, but I have no choice.

Wait a second … "Did you say three people threatened to kill you recently?"

"I rub some people the wrong way."

"Really?" I mock surprise. "I'm shocked."

We make the rest of the journey to town in silence. Willie spends the time trying to figure out who killed him. I spend the time trying to not cry. My feet. Back. Entire being hurts, and all I want to do is sleep.

Also, three hundred million dollars!

It takes us an hour to get into town, just as Willie said. I fall onto the bench in front of *The Gazette*, feeling like I just ran a marathon.

Not that I've actually run a marathon before.

But I'm assuming one would feel like her cartilage had been replaced with Jell-O once she'd completed the 26.2 miles.

"The tacky mobile is here," Willie says.

The van rolls to a stop. My parents' giant faces are staring at me, and part of my mom's right hand is peeling off. I guess it is a *little* tacky.

I slide open the door and drop into the chair. I pull the seat belt over my chest, and in my periphery I see Brian Windsor exiting the building. He peers into the van, but we're already moving by the time he realizes it's me.

I fall back against the seat. That was a close one.

"How was your first day of work?" Dad asks.

"Fine."

"Did you do anything exciting?"

"Fine."

"I think she's tuckered out," Dad says to Mom, and they begin to chat while I doze in and out of consciousness until I hear Dad say, "MacIntosh," and my eyelids pop open.

I can't very well ask how they became involved with Daniel MacIntosh or why they were at Willie's house because it's obvious they had no idea I was there. Mom would have said something by now.

"He thinks we should be able to put the house on the market by the end of the month," Dad says.

"Did you say MacIntosh?" I ask, trying to sound nonchalant. "As in Willie MacIntosh?"

Mom spins around in her seat. "How do *you* know about Willie MacIntosh?"

I look to Willie for help, but he's not paying attention. Um. "We're ... we're doing an article on Willie MacIntosh at *The Gazette*."

Mom and Dad share a look. They're confused, and I'm not sure why. They had to have known I'd be privy to news when I took a job at the *news*paper.

"Well," Mom says, turning back around to face the front. "We were contacted by Mr. MacIntosh's nephew this morning. He wants to put the house on the market as soon as possible."

Willie turns his head so fast I fear it will fall off. "I still can't believe that I've been dead a day and he's already planning to sell my house! What the hell is wrong with him?"

"What the hell is Daniel doing calling you?" I repeat and slap my hand over my mouth. Oops.

"Zoe Matilda Lane, that is no way to talk to your mother," Dad scolds.

"Sorry." I take a breath. "Why is Daniel contacting you? I, um ... it's just you're here in Fernn, and Willie lived in Trucker. You've never sold a house in Trucker before."

A smile spreads across Dad's face. "We put an ad in *The Trucker Times* last week. Worth every cent."

Mom and Dad both beam with excitement and rightfully so; Trucker is twice the size of Fernn Valley, and houses cost five times as much. I have no idea why they haven't branched out sooner.

"I heard Willie left the house to his wife," I say.

Dad looks at me in the reflection of the rearview mirror but doesn't respond.

Mom does. "A ninety-three-year-old multimillionaire meets a broke twenty-nine-year-old waitress, and two months later he marries her, cuts his only blood relative out of his will, and leaves her his fortune. That doesn't sound fishy to you? Daniel is distraught over his uncle's death. His lawyer is positive they'll be able to prove Betty MacIntosh is a scam artist."

Willie's mouth drops open. "He already has a lawyer?"

"But Mom, that's not right," I say. "Willie wanted her to have everything."

"How do you know so much about this?" Mom asks.

"Um ... I heard at ... um ... I heard it at work."

Mom purses her lips. "Daniel is his nephew, and I think he knows more about his uncle than you do."

"That worm." Willie punches the back of the seat. "He's been waiting for me to die so he can take my money. He's going to drag this out in court until Betty gives up." He rubs his temples. "Why couldn't I have died *next* Monday morning?"

Seeing Willie in so much anguish hurts my heart. I don't blame my mom for thinking the way she does. From an outsider's perspective it does look fishy.

I try to think of how I can help in this situation. Talk to Daniel? Help Betty find an attorney? Convince my parents to drop Daniel as a client? Not that he wouldn't find another real estate agent. Not that he can even list the house without fighting the will in court. My mind is churning through all the possibilities, and I barely noticed that we've turned onto our street.

I do, however, take notice of the sheriff parked in our driveway.

CHAPTER SIX

Here's what I know about Sheriff Vance: he's been the sheriff for possibly ever, and he looks like a sheriff. Gray mustache, gray hair, and appears to be about six months pregnant with a donut.

Dad parks the van in front of our mailbox, which is a mini replica of our single-story ranch-style home. "What's Vance doing here?"

"Surely I don't know." Mom unbuckles her seat belt. "Zoe, dear, stay in the car."

The two exit the van simultaneously, as if they'd been practicing their timing. Mom pulls at the bottom of her jacket and plasters a huge smile across her face. "Sheriff Vance, to what do we owe the honor?"

The three huddle near the front door, and I can't hear what's going on, but I can hear Mom's fake laugh, so I know it's not good.

"If you're arrested, plead the Fifth Amendment, and I'll give you the number of a good lawyer," says Willie. "Jackson Anderson. He's terrible at golf, but I wouldn't want to face him in court."

My gut sinks. "I should have never let you talk me into

taking the car. I don't know why I listened to you." That's not true. I know why. Because I thought he'd leave, and yet, here he is, and I'm about to be arrested. What's my defense? A dead guy made me do it?

I'm screwed.

"I'll be right back." Willie disappears and reappears beside the trio. When my dad gets upset, which isn't very often, he becomes a hand talker. Right now his hands are flinging around like he's conducting an orchestra.

This isn't good.

Willie returns. "You're in luck. The sheriff is here to talk about the accident yesterday."

I melt into a puddle of relief. So help me, for as long as I live, I will never break the law again. I'm not cut out for the criminal life.

"What else did they say?" I ask.

"The sheriff asked to speak to you, but they said you're too emotional and not up to it. After we figure out who killed me, we'll deal with your parents, because they need to get a life."

"This is ridiculous." I slide open the van door and walk up to the group. "Here is my statement," I say to the sheriff. "I don't want to press charges, and I'm fine."

The sheriff takes a wide stance. "Zoe Lane, I don't think I've had the pleasure." He extends a professional hand and offers a flat smile.

I slip my hand into his, and he flinches, probably because my fingertips are numb and my palms feel as if they're made of ice. I've always run cold, but since Willie's arrival, my body temp seems to vary between *a light sweater will do* and *go get the toe tag*.

Apprehension flashes across the sheriff's face, and I yank my hand free. "Are you sure you don't want to press charges?" he asks.

"I'm positive. I don't believe Willie should be driving, though."

The sheriff scrunches his brow. "Willie?"

Did I say Willie? Oops. There are too many old men in my life. "I mean LeRoy. I don't think LeRoy should be driving."

"You won't get any argument from LeRoy," the sheriff says. "I talked to him this morning, and he assured me he's retiring the keys."

"He's lying," Mom interjects. "He was in Trucker earlier today at the MacIntosh home. On the road we saw tire marks and swerve lines. Then hidden outside the house was Old Man LeRoy's car parked next to a broken sprinkler head that you could tell he'd run over. We have pictures to prove it."

Oh, no.

"Is that so?" the sheriff says with a shake of his head. He produces a notebook, clicks a pen, and jots this down.

This is bad.

"You know what I think," Mom says, and I want to shove a sock in her mouth. "Poor Willie MacIntosh died a day ago, and his wife has already moved on to her next victim. We're working with Willie's nephew, Daniel MacIntosh, and he warned us about her. She stole Willie's fortune. It's quite scandalous."

Willie throws his hands into the air. "Aren't you going to say something?"

Yes.

What, though?

I blow out a breath. "I believe that Betty is truly heartbroken over Willie and ... perhaps ... um ... LeRoy was there to comfort her?"

"Heartbroken my bum, excuse the language," Mom says to the sheriff. "Abusing the elderly is a crime. She was in a bikini, entertaining an old man one day after her husband died."

"All the perm solution is going to her head," Willie says. "Do something!"

"That's not true!" I yell, and now everyone is staring at me. Even the neighbors across the street who are outside doing yard work pause to see what the commotion is about. "Betty is a good person. I think Daniel is a weasel who wants his uncle's money. He's the one who killed Willie." I want to take it back as soon as I say it. Accusing someone of murder is an awful idea.

What is wrong with me?

"Zoe Matilda Lane," Mom gasps. "Mr. MacIntosh died of natural causes."

The sheriff strokes his mustache. "What makes you think Daniel MacIntosh was involved in Willie's death?"

I have no words.

My mind is a complete and total blank. I got nada.

Willie is making a *W* with his arms.

Pull it together, Zoe, and think. "Here's the thing," I start. Unsure of what exactly the *thing* is. "Twenty-four hours after Willie's death and Daniel MacIntosh not only has a lawyer but real estate agents ready to sell the house. That doesn't sound suspicious to anyone else?"

"Yeah!" Willie adds.

"What I know of Willie MacIntosh is he was in great shape for his age," I say, building momentum. "He still skied and drove his boat. He doesn't sound like a man easily persuaded to do anything he doesn't want to do."

"Exactly!" Willie says.

"Obviously, Willie cared for Betty, and she cared for him. Daniel was obviously sure he was going to get the money when his uncle died. But when this young woman, who—I think we all can agree is super hot—enters the picture, it threatened his three-hundred-million-dollar inheritance. So he killed his uncle before he could marry Betty, but he was obviously too late.

Because they were obviously already married. Obviously." If I had a mic, I'd drop it.

"Three hundred?" Dad chokes out.

The sheriff isn't quite sure what to make of me. "I came to get a statement about Old Man LeRoy. But I'll pass this information over to the sheriff in Trucker County."

"Surely you don't need to do that." Mom takes a step in front of me. "My daughter suffered a concussion yesterday. She doesn't know what she's talking about."

"Yes, I do," I say over her shoulder. "Daniel killed his uncle."

Mom nudges me in the side with her elbow.

"I'll relay the information. You folks have a good night," the sheriff says and saunters back to his vehicle, stealing one last look over his shoulder. We lock eyes, and a chill runs down my spine.

Yikes.

In hindsight, I should have probably kept my mouth shut.

Mom waits for him to leave before she snaps. "Zoe Matilda Lane, Daniel MacIntosh is a client of ours, and you just accused him of murder. That's it! You're quitting your new job. It's not healthy."

Mom stalks inside, and I follow. "I am not quitting my job!"

Willie is at my side, encouraging me to go on. "Tell her you're an adult who needs to learn to stand on her own two feet."

"I'm an adult with two feet of my own!"

"Not what I said, but close enough," Willie says. "Tell her you no longer want to be coddled. You want to break free and make your own choices."

"I want to make my own choices!"

"And you want money so you can dress better."

"I want money so I can dress—hey, I like my clothes." I tug at the bottom of my blazer and ... wait. I pat down my pockets.

The pen! Did I leave it at Betty's? Did it fall out in LeRoy's car? Last I saw it was when I was at Betty's. It must still be there. Oh please, please, please let it still be there.

"Concentrate, person." Willie claps his hands. "Your mom's looking at you like you're a nut."

He's right.

Mom's lip is curled, like she's doing a halfhearted Elvis impersonation. Even worse, I can *feel* her worry. She's thinking about the S again ... A person ... A person with a name that starts with an S ... There's fire, screams, and tears associated with that S ... A three-story building with mirrored windows and a palm tree out front ... Red, blue, white, heat ...

I'm so overcome with emotions—anger, sorrow, confusion, bitterness—it takes a great deal of effort not to collapse on the living room floor.

I can't do this anymore.

At least not today.

"I'm tired," I say and go to my room. It's already dusk. I don't bother changing out of my clothes before I shove Jabba out of the way and slip into bed. My world is spiraling out of control. I don't know how to stop it, but all I want to do is sleep. I pull the covers to my nose, ignore Willie who is sitting on my dresser and my mom who is knocking on the door, and fall into a deep, dreamless slumber.

CHAPTER SEVEN

It's like Groundhog Day. I sleep through the alarm. Mom wakes me up. Shoves an iron pill into my mouth. I get dressed in a sensible pantsuit. Willie hates my outfit. Mom begs me to quit my imaginary job. I refuse. I'm dropped off at *The Gazette*. Willie and I go the library. Rosa is on the phone arguing with the nursing home. Willie and I are at the computers.

"Okay, so you created the will using an online legal service. But did you have it signed by two witnesses?" I ask Willie, who is perched on the window seat, tossing his hat up in the air and catching it by the rim. Completely casual, as if it were a typical Wednesday morning, while I'm over here trying to obtain a Google legal degree.

"Why do you suppose your mom is against you growing up?" he asks.

"I don't know. Now, *please* concentrate. Was your will signed by two witnesses?"

Willie tosses his hat up in the air, and it lands on his head. "Yes, it was witnessed and signed by my buddies."

"Good. This is good." I grab a pencil and my notepad.

"You're left-handed."

"So?"

"Didn't your parents teach you to write with your right?"

"*No*, because I was born left-handed." Honestly. Can ghosts have ADD? "Now, concentrate. What are their names?"

"LeRoy Fillerup and Jerold Conway."

I drop my pencil. "Old Man LeRoy? Why would you have someone so old witness your will?"

Willie looks at me. "What do you have against the elderly?"

"Nothing at all. But the person you choose to witness your will should be someone younger and in better health than you."

"Says who?"

"Says Legadoc dot com, Online Wills dot com ..." I'm reading off the computer. "Preparing for Death dot org. Need I go on?"

"Please don't." He appears in the chair beside me and stretches out his legs in front of himself. "LeRoy outlived me, so it doesn't matter."

"Let's hope not." I write the names down on my notepad. "According to the internet, Betty needs to file the paperwork with the probate court, and if anyone contests, as I suspect Daniel will, then you have two witnesses to confirm that you were of sound mind when you created it."

"One."

"Excuse me?"

"Only one witness. Jerold died."

I smack my forehead. "How did he die?"

"Liver failure. Was yellow as a banana. He went a few days before I did. Such a shame. He had a great swing."

"Why would you ask someone in liver failure to ... *gah*. Never mind. Not important. Did you tell anyone else about your decision to cut Daniel out of your will?"

He gives a halfhearted shrug. "It's no one else's business anyway."

I push away from the desk and roll my chair closer to him. "This is serious, Willie. I'm worried about Betty. You created the will online. It was witnessed by one person who is dead and another person who just plowed over a pedestrian. If I didn't know you, if I didn't know Betty, I'd be suspicious as well."

Willie brushes off my concern. "Betty and I are legally married. I only changed the will to make sure he got nothing. Weasel doesn't stand a chance in court. What *is* suspicious is how I died. I think your theory about Daniel might be right."

My stomach lurches. If I could go back in time, I'd travel to yesterday and take back what I said about Daniel. I don't even know the man, and murder is a serious accusation.

"I could never stand the kid," Willie says. "He's a self-righteous brat."

"Then why were you going to leave him all your money and property to begin with?"

"Because he's my brother's boy, and Tod was a good guy. Died in ninety-two." A flash of sadness crosses his face. "I promised to take care of the kid, but he's nothing but a weasel. Only time he ever comes around is when he needs money for a house, or for college for his kids, or when his wife needs an emergency hysterectomy, or when he's gambled his four-oh-one K away."

"Hold on. He has a family? Don't you want your great nieces and nephews to get part of your fortune?"

"*Pfft*. I don't know them. Weasel never introduced me." Willie stands and studies a picture of Dr. Seuss pinned to the wall. "Aside from popping up now and then to ask for money, the only other contact I had was the newsletter his wife sends out every Christmas." He snorts. " Why do people send newsletters anyway? Do they think I have nothing better to do than to read about their year?"

"Hey, I like reading newsletters."

"That's because you have no life."
"No, it's because I'm not a jerk."
"That too."

I blow out a breath and tap my pencil on the notepad. I feel even worse about accusing Daniel of murder knowing he has kids and a wife who writes newsletters. Just because he hired a lawyer and real estate agents right away doesn't mean he killed his uncle. Everyone deals with grief differently. Daniel may believe he's doing what his uncle would have wanted. Even if he's not. The hurt Willie feels when it comes to Daniel is palpable. And I suspect Willie left his money to Betty to teach Daniel a lesson.

"I know what you're thinking," Willie says, still studying the picture. "You're thinking I cut Daniel off because he didn't come around, and because he didn't bother including me in his life, and because he treated me like a bank, and you'd be right."

"Oh." At least this is all starting to make a little more sense. "The good news is that even if Daniel contests the will and wins, he won't get everything. According to my online legal knowledge, he'd get half, if that. Which is still one hundred and fifty million dollars. I'm pretty sure Betty can survive on that."

Willie is shaking his head before I even finish. "I don't want Daniel touching my money. I want Betty to keep the house, and I want her to keep the boat, and the house in Aspen, and my cars, and clubs, and everything. I want her to have everything, and I want him to have nothing."

I'm not sure how I can make this happen for Willie, but at least it won't require autopsies and accusations of murder.

"And I want you to find out who murdered me," he adds.

Ugh.

I can't believe I'm even entertaining this idea. "Let's pretend for a moment that you were killed. What was the very last thing you remember?"

Willie takes a moment to think. "I woke up. Went to the bathroom. Took a shower. I went outside. Came back in through the garage. I locked the door. Then I went to take my morning pills. Realized I was out of my blood pressure medication. Called Betty. She said she was out shopping. Then I went to the kitchen and got my oatmeal out of the fridge. Heated it up in the microwave and ... that's it."

"You don't remember sitting in the chair Betty said you died in?"

"No."

"And who are the three people who threatened to kill you recently?"

"My neighbor, Arnie. He said he'd kill me if I touched his geraniums again."

"So you touched them."

"They were on my side of the property line! Took a weed whacker to them. He was livid." Willie laughs at the memory. "He still has that tall fortress of bushes in the front. He did it on purpose, you know. So that I couldn't see his house and he couldn't see mine. But they're against HOA."

"Weed whacker to geraniums and HOA ..." I write this down on my notepad. "And the next person?"

"Ron MacDonald."

I drop my pencil. "You're joking, right? Ronald MacDonald?"

"He's a golfing buddy. We got in a heated argument last week about Betty. He had a thing for her." He smirks. "But she picked me."

"After you offered a life of luxury and three hundred million dollars," I remind him.

"What can I say, I'm a charmer."

I roll my eyes. "What exactly did he say to you?"

"He accused me of using my money to trap Betty into an

unhealthy relationship. I told him that I satisfied her in ways he couldn't."

"Which is a lie."

"Not a lie," he says, mocking offense. "I satisfied her in *other* ways. None of them happened to be what was implied. But that's neither here nor there. Ron got mad. Then he told me he'd kill me if Mother Nature weren't going to take care of it for him. Oh, he also told me to rot in hell."

"*Rot in hell* ..." I write this down. "And the third person?"

"LeRoy."

"The man you had witness your will threatened to kill you?"

"Meh. It was a petty argument over ..." He pauses to think. "I can't remember. The older he gets, the ornerier he gets. Whatever it was, he lost his temper and said some things." He waves off the concern. "But he wouldn't have killed me. Punch me in the face, sure. Spike my drink with Ex-Lax, probably. Not kill. Man doesn't have it in him. I've known LeRoy my entire life. We would have played golf today if I were still alive."

Ironically, he almost killed *me*. But whatever. I write this down on my notepad. "The key stuck in the lock. Does Betty come in through the garage?"

"No." Willie crosses the room. "She parks in the carport on the other side of the house and enters through the back door. That's why you need to tell the police about the key. It was probably Daniel. They need to take fingerprints and DNA samples. They do that nowadays."

The thought of talking to the police again gives me heartburn. Especially since I'm not entirely convinced Willie— despite the alarming amount of people who'd threatened to kill him—didn't die of a heart attack, and all this talk of murder will do nothing but ruffle a lot of feathers. What we should concentrate all our efforts on is protecting Betty from Daniel. If only I could get Willie on board. Perhaps if he saw Daniel as a person, as a dad, as a husband, then he'd be less angry and be able to focus on peacefully transitioning.

Which gives me an idea.

I wiggle the mouse to wake up the computer and Google Daniel MacIntosh. His Facebook profile pops up at the top of the search. Perfect. I can show Willie pictures of his great nieces and nephews! Brilliant idea. If I do say so myself.

Willie appears behind me and looks over my shoulder at the computer screen. "What are you doing?"

"Looking at Daniel's Facebook profile."

"Good idea. We can see what he was doing Monday morning."

Not exactly what I was going for, but, sure, why not? I click on the link, and I'm taken to the Facebook sign-in page. "Shoot."

"What's wrong?"

"I don't have a Facebook account, so I can't see his profile."

"Then get one."

I bite at my lip. My parents are adamantly against social media.

Actually, that's not true.

My parents have a business Facebook page. I've seen them use it before. They're adamantly against *me* having social media. I've never contested it because I didn't have a reason to. It's not like I have a ton of friends who will care about what I'm doing on the daily.

Willie drops his head. "You're an adult, Zoe. If you want a Facebook account, you can get a Facebook account. You don't need your parents' permission to live."

"But..."

"You don't need anyone's permission."

"But..."

"You are a capable and smart woman with way too much to offer the world to be hiding behind Mommy and Daddy."

"You know what?" I roll my shoulders. "You're right. If I want a Facebook account, then I can get a Facebook account." I feel a surge of empowerment, and I'm not exactly sure why. I'm hiding in a library getting a pep talk from a ghost.

"Attagirl."

"Yeah. I can do this." With my head held high, I click on *create an account* and ... "It's asking for an email account, and I don't have one. I don't know ..."

Suddenly, Willie is in my face. "Fire!"

I scream and jump back, fall out of the chair, scramble to my feet, whack my head on the table, and stumble into a book shelf.

Rosa runs toward us, her glasses swinging around her neck. "Are you okay back here?"

I rub my head and look around. No fire alarm. No smoke. Rosa doesn't appear to be in distress. I take a whiff. Smells like damp wood and books.

"Ta-da!" Willie says like he just produced a rabbit from his hat. "Now you have help. Get on with it."

I shoot him a look, and he responds with a full-face sardonic smile. If this man weren't already dead, I'd happily escort him to the nearest cliff.

Okay, maybe I wouldn't do that.

But, geez.

Now I know how his friends felt.

Rosa looks at me expectantly, and I smooth out the front of my blazer and clear my throat to buy time.

Willie saunters up to Rosa and tips his hat back. "She needs help creating an email and Facebook account."

Rosa cocks her head and narrows her eyes.

Can she hear him?

I look at Willie, and he shrugs. "Help her with her Facebook page," he says directly into her ear.

Rosa's eyes glaze over like she's in a trance. Holy crap! She can hear him!

Willie cups his mouth around Rosa's ear and says, "Testing, testing! One, two, three. Testing, testing."

Rosa rubs her hands along her biceps. "Oh, heavens. I just got the chills." She looks directly at Willie.

He takes a step back. "Can she see me?"

I'm scared to ask.

Rosa shakes it off and slips on her readers. "Do you need help with your Facebook account?"

"How'd ... how'd you know that?" I ask.

"Because you're on the Facebook login page?" She points to the computer.

Oh.

"Is it not allowing you to sign in?" She moves the mouse and checks the internet connection. "Sometimes the Wi-Fi can be wonky in this place. I swear it's haunted."

If only she knew.

"The signal is strong." Rosa cups her hands and blows into them, trying to get warm. "Is there anything else I can do for you?"

Rosa can feel Willie's presence. I'm sure of it. Perhaps she doesn't know that she does, or maybe she's playing it off so I don't know that she has medium abilities. Either way, it would be nice to have someone to talk to about ... all of this.

I narrow my eyes and concentrate, hoping to read her thoughts.

"Anything ... else?" Rosa runs her tongue across her teeth, appearing uncomfortable.

Willie sticks his face next to mine. "Are you into girls?"

"What? No! I like men."

Rosa sucks in her lips. "That's nice, dear."

Oh, heck. That's it!

I need Willie to go ... wherever he's going. Up or down? I'm not so sure anymore. I'm also not so sure how to make that happen.

"Um ... actually ... since you're here," I say, desperately trying to sound normal, "do you happen to have any books on ...?" Oh, geez. How do you ask if she has books about communicating with the dead without sounding insane? "I'm researching ... um ... do you have books on *conversingwithghosts?*" I spit the words out so fast I'm not sure she heard me right.

"We do," she says without hesitation and walks down an aisle.

Phew!

I follow. She stops and runs her fingers along the spines of the books, whispering to herself, until she finds what she's looking for. "Aha. Here you go."

The book is two inches thick with *Reaching the Other Side* in swirly letters on the front. When I open the cover, it cracks, and even though the copyright says 1995, it smells of fresh ink.

Rosa's cell phone rings from her pocket. "What now?" She checks who the caller is and groans. "Do you need anything else, dear?" she asks me.

"No, I'm good," I say, and she slams the phone to her ear and retreats back to her desk, yelling in Spanish.

I turn the book over.

Medium Tabitha Corner began communicating with the dead when she was three years old but didn't fully accept her gift until she was forty-two. Now, she's helped hundreds of people connect with their deceased loved ones using her remarkable gift. In this book, Tabitha helps those with the same gift cultivate their talent.

A picture of Tabitha Corner with purple hair, wearing a purple sweater, holding a black cat with a purple collar on, is under the blurb.

I flip to the table of contents, run my finger down the chapter headers, and stop at *Chapter Twenty-Two: How to Help Your Spirit Transition.*

Hallelujah!

I open to the corresponding page. Even though the book appears fairly unused, the first paragraph is underlined with a pencil. *There are many reasons why a Spirit will stay in his or her physical realm instead of transitioning to the other side. It's your job to be compassionate, set boundaries, and help the Spirit find the peace of mind required to cross into the light. Listen and remember he or she was once a person. Speak kindly and let the Spirit know you're here to assist him or her. Remember, most likely the Spirit is just as scared, if not more so, than you are. Especially if the Spirit has suffered a sudden and traumatic death.*

The last sentence jumps out at me.

A sudden and traumatic death.

I haven't been compassionate or patient. Nor have I considered how scary or frustrating this must be for Willie.

I take the book back to the table.

"What's that?" Willie asks.

"Nothing." I slip it into my briefcase and make a mental note to check it out before we leave, along with *Sizzling Fireman Volume Five.* "Willie, I'm here to assist you with compassion."

"Yeah, okay."

"But we must set boundaries," I say. "First, no more making fun of my clothes, my shoes, our car, my room, or any member of my family."

"Deal. Now, are we going to figure out who killed me?"

I heave a surrendering sigh. "I'm here to assist you to peacefully transition to the light."

Whatever that means.

CHAPTER EIGHT

"What happened to you?" Betty's voice cracks. Willie and I are on the greenbelt behind the library with her on speakerphone.

"I'm sorry for leaving," I say. "Are you okay?"

"No! It was awful, Zoe. Daniel accused me of coercing Willie into marrying me and changing his will to be sure I got everything. I'm not a gold digger, and I'm sick of people saying that. When Willie came home with the will, *I'm* the one who said I'd only feel comfortable with it if he told Daniel about our marriage."

"When did you and Willie have this conversation?"

Betty thinks. "It was ... last Thursday?"

I glance at Willie and cover the phone. "You changed your will Thursday? Why didn't you say that before?"

He shrugs as if this is of little consequence. When in reality, at least in my reality, the timing changes everything. Willie alters his will Thursday and is dead Monday. But if Daniel didn't know about the will, why would he kill his uncle so soon after the change? Could it be a coincidence? If anything, the situation looks bad for Betty. "Did you have a gut feeling you might die very soon?" I ask Willie.

"No. I was in—"

"Great shape," I finish for him and remove my hand from the phone. "Betty, you there?"

"I am." She exhales loudly. "Maybe I should just give Daniel half. After all, he's Willie's only blood relative, and I don't want to drag this out in court. What if this gets in the paper? That's going to ruin any chance I have at a career."

"No," Willie is adamant. "He will never touch my money."

I cover the phone again. "Think about Betty. Maybe if she gives him, like, five mil, he'll be happy and this won't have to go to court?"

"No."

What's five million when you have three hundred? But, it's not my decision. I release my hand from the phone. "Betty, if Willie wanted Daniel to have the money, he would have indicated as much in his will. You're married. This shouldn't be a problem. You need to file the paperwork today with the court."

"Did she order the autopsy?" Willie asks.

Oh, right. "Betty, did you order the autopsy?"

"No. Daniel called this morning and told me he would be taking care of Willie's remains and I have no right. When I brought up the autopsy, he said I was being ridiculous."

Willie and I share a look. He clasps his hands together as if he's about to pray. "Repeat after me," he says. "Drive down to the funeral home and demand an autopsy. You are executor of the will, you have every right to make the decisions."

I relay this message to Betty.

"But ... but ... what do I do about Daniel? Zoe, he's married with three children. He said his kids all adored their uncle Willie."

Willie's face goes puce. I think he's going to implode.

But before he does, I say, "Betty, if Daniel's kids adored

Willie, don't you think you would have seen them at least once over the last couple of months?"

There's a pause. I assume she's thinking.

"You're right," she says, her voice small. "You are so right. But—"

"No buts," I cut her off. "You are a strong, beautiful, good-hearted woman. Now it's time to fight for your husband, dammit." I slap my hand over my mouth. Oops. My mom would have a conniption if she heard me use that language. *Crude words trigger unnecessary stress*, she would say.

Except, this situation is already stressful, and she's not here. So I guess I can say whatever I want, dammit!

Willie urges me to keep talking.

"Right. Sorry about that." I clear my throat. "Go to the funeral home and order an autopsy. Get the death certificate. Then you must file the will with probate court."

"It's what Willie would want," she says, and I'm not sure if this is a statement or a question.

"You know it's what Willie wants."

"All right, I'll do it," she says with little conviction. "Can you come with me? I could really use the company."

"Errrr ..." I rub the back of my neck and look at Willie.

"Go with her," he urges.

"But how?" I mouth. *"I don't have a car."*

"She can pick you up."

Huh. That's not a bad idea. I check the time. It's not even noon. I still have five hours before I get off of "work." Why not? At least then I'll know it got done, and so will Willie.

"Can you pick me up at the Fernn Valley Library?" I ask Betty.

"I'll be right there." I can hear the smile in her voice.

We hang up, and I take a seat on the ground. The grass

scratches the exposed parts of my ankles, but I don't mind. The fresh air is a welcomed change from the muggy library quarters. I open my briefcase, grab the lunch Mom made me, and the copy of *Reaching the Other Side*.

"What do you think you're doing?" Willie asks.

I look at the book in one hand and the sandwich in the other. "Lunch break?"

Willie mutters under his breath and shoves his hands into his front pant pockets. I wish he weren't invisible, because he'd block the sun perfectly from where he's standing. I'm starting to get a headache, and the glare isn't helping.

I take a bite of my sandwich and flip open the book to *Chapter Ten: Unruly Spirits*.

Dark Spirits are ghosts, earthbounds, or entities who have walked away from the light and chosen to follow the dark path or transition to the dark underworld. Their presence can prove unsafe for your wellbeing. It's important to remember that if you want a Spirit (light or dark) to leave, all you have to do is ask with a sincere intent.

In order to determine if the Spirit is dark or light, ask yourself these questions:

When you're around your Spirit do you feel scared?

Has the Spirit made physical or emotional threats?

Do you have a sinking, unsettled feeling when your Spirit is around?

My answer would be *no* to all questions. Which is a sweet relief. Willie is grumpy, a bit intrusive, and oftentimes rude, but he's not evil. I guess I'm lucky?

However, I did ask Willie to leave multiple times, and he didn't. Perhaps there was a part of me that wanted him around.

It must be a small ... small ... *small* ... *minuscule* part.

There was also that unsettling feeling I got in his room. Could that have been a dark spirit?

"What's wrong with you?" Willie asks. "You're making a weird face."

"Nothing." I slam the book closed and poke the straw into my juice box. Willie tilts his hat back and takes in the surroundings. I forgot how handsome he is, probably because his good looks are masked by his personality.

"Were you married before Betty?" I ask.

"No."

"Were you ever close? Ever been *madly* in love?"

Willie frowns. "No time for that."

"Come on." I cross my legs and lean back on my hands. "There had to be *someone*."

He grunts. "There was one woman back in the forties, but it didn't work out."

Now we're getting somewhere. "Did you meet at one of those USO dances? Oh! Was she a nurse, and you were a wounded solider? Oh, wait, wait. I got it! She was your sweet, innocent, virginal secretary, and you were one of those hot millionaires who swept her away in your private jet."

"You need to get out more."

"Come on! I'm stealing cars, demanding autopsies, researching wills, and accusing people of murder. Give me something good here. I *need* it." Man do I need it. I haven't read a good romance novel in almost five days. Typically, I devour four books a week. My fictional characters are what keep me going ...

A sad reality when you think about it. Especially since I've momentarily replaced my fictional characters with a ghost.

"You're making that face again," Willie says.

"Oh, sorry." I take a sip of my juice in hopes it will get rid of the dismal feeling slithering around in my stomach. No such luck.

Whatever. This isn't about me. It's about Willie. "Tell me more about your one great love."

"I didn't say it was a great love."

"But it was love, and I want to hear."

Willie's face is motionless, but I can see his eyes flickering from me and away again. "I'll tell you once, and we never talk about it again. Agreed?"

"Agreed." I try not to appear too anxious, but I am dying to hear the details.

"Wipe that goofy grin off your face," he says. "It's not one of those trashy romance novels you have hidden in your closet."

"They're not trashy."

"One book is titled *Trashy* with a picture of a shirtless man on the cover holding a wastebasket."

"Because it's about a *trash* man who falls for ... you know what?" I throw my hands up. "It doesn't matter. We're talking about you. No goofy grin." I pretend to wipe the smile off my face. "I'm ready."

He switches his weight to one hip. "When I was about your age, there was a girl. Her family didn't approve, and that was that. I lived my life, and she lived hers."

I wait for more, but apparently that's all I'm gonna get. "What happened to her?"

He shrugs.

"Is she still alive?"

He shrugs.

"Why didn't her parents approve?"

He shrugs.

Seriously? That's it! Then I remember his comment about being in Mexico during World War II and put two and two together. "Did you go to Mexico to avoid the draft? Is that why her parents didn't approve?"

He shrugs.

I rest my elbows on my knees. "I read a book once about a man who went to Venezuela to avoid the Vietnam draft and fell in love with a woman there."

"How'd it end?"

"He went back to the United States, was arrested. She met someone else and had a baby."

"Some romance," Willie mutters.

"They reunited later in life. It was so romantic."

"Sounds stupid. For your information, I served in the Navy for a year."

"Then why were you living in Mexico?"

"It's not important."

"It is to me." I scratch my lower legs. The grass is giving me a rash, and I pull up my socks to protect my ankles.

"I had a good life, person. Don't worry about my past." Willie buttons his jacket and pulls out his cuffs. "Let's talk about your lack of social life instead."

"I'd rather eat dirt," I say. Oddly, my mouth tastes a bit like dirt. I take a sip of my juice to wet my palate. It doesn't help.

"You're sweet on the editor at *The Gazette*," Willie says. "But you're going about it all wrong."

"I don't remember asking you for advice."

"If you're going to dress like a Golden Girl, then you have to back it up with confidence. A self-assured woman is sexy as hell."

"Hey, I'm confident." I'm very confident. *I think.* Okay, maybe I'm not confident enough to walk around in a bikini like Betty. And maybe I'm not so sure about ... *anything.* "Just out of curiosity. How might one go about showing confidence?"

Willie smiles. "Stand up."

I stand.

"See, that right there is the problem. You're too compliant. Don't be afraid to push back."

Okay. Push back. I can do push back. So I sit down.

Willie gives an exasperated sigh. "Why are you sitting down?"

"Because you told me not to stand ..." Oh. I get it. But I don't know whether to stand or sit, so I rise to my knees.

He opens his mouth, then closes it, then opens it again, then snaps it shut. "I don't like the boundaries because I can't give it to you straight."

"You mean you can't be a jerk."

"What's the point of being an old man if I can't say what I want ..." His voice trails off, and he tilts his head to the side as if straining to hear a noise off in the distance.

"What's wrong?"

"Your newspaper guy is here."

"What? Where?" I turn around, and much to my horror, I can see Brian through the library window. He's standing at the computers talking to Rosa. "What is he doing here?" I ask Willie.

"He's probably looking for you."

"*Pfft.* No, he's not."

Just then, Rosa points out the window, and I can see her mouth make the words *Zoe is out there.*

Gah!

I crawl to the tree and take cover. What is Brian doing here? In all my years, I've never seen him in the library. I've never seen anyone in the library!

"He's coming," Willie says. "Remember to be confident."

I will myself to become one with the tree. I'm not ready to face Brian, not after I nearly maimed him with my briefcase then ran away like a lunatic. Also, there's the whole dead man hovering nearby. If I accidentally spoke to Willie in front of Brian, I'd be mortified.

I hear the side door open. *Crud.* I can hear footsteps in the grass. *Please don't see me, please don't see me, please don't see me.* Brian's shadow grows taller. *Gulp.*

"I've been looking for you," he says.

Willie gives me two thumbs-ups. I try to ignore him. "Wh-what can I do for you, Brian ... or *not* do for you ... um." This confidence thing is confusing.

"Were you at the MacIntoshes' house yesterday pretending to be a reporter writing an article on Willie's death?"

Oh.

I don't know how to answer. So I play dumb. "What makes you think I was there?"

"Betty MacIntosh said a reporter named Zoe stopped by yesterday to do an article on Willie."

"*Pfft.*" I stand and dust off the back of my pants. "There're lots of people around here with the name Zoe."

"Betty said the reporter was about five foot one with light brown hair, dark brown eyes, and wearing a blue pantsuit."

I shrug innocently. "That sounds like a lot of people."

"Subsequently, Old Man LeRoy was accused of being at the MacIntoshes' house yesterday. His car was seen outside. Both Betty and Old Man LeRoy deny he was there."

This is getting really hard to talk my way out of. I look to Willie for help. He's mouthing *abort, abort, abort.*

Good idea.

I step aside, and Brian moves with me, blocking my path. My stomach erupts in butterflies. If this were a novel, he'd kiss me right now. He'd grab me by the cheeks and plunge his tongue into my mouth. Our bodies would dance in sweet unison. Sparks would fly. His hands would be in my hair, on my face, on my ... oh, my.

I stare up at Brian, my chest pumping, my hands sweaty, my mind blank.

"You're drooling," Willie says.

Oops. I wipe my chin.

"Are you unwell?" Brian asks.

"I am perfectly fine," I say with, what I hope is, a confident smile.

"Why were you at the MacIntoshes' house?"

Smile gone. "I don't know what you're talking about. I don't know Betty MacIntosh."

A horn beeps in the distance. I know without having to look that it's Betty. Mostly because, *of course*, she shows up right now.

I turn around to verify.

Yep. Betty is sitting in a silver Escalade, waving at me.

"You don't know Betty MacIntosh?" Brian asks again with a wry smile.

So denial is no longer a viable option. Willie says men want confidence. Well, I'll give Brian confidence!

"As a matter of fact, I do know Betty MacIntosh. She's a friend. Now, I must be going." I grab my briefcase, and it pops open. *Reaching the Other Side* falls to the ground, and Brian picks it up.

"A guide to speaking to spirits?" he reads.

I yank the book out of his hands. "It's research for ... um ... a friend." I shove it back in my briefcase, and *Sizzling Hot Fireman* falls to the ground. Brian picks it up. This is not a fun game we're playing. Not fun at all.

"*Love has never been so hot?*" he reads from the back cover.

I yank it from his hands. "It's research for ... um ... a friend. Gotta go." I run as fast as I can to Betty's car, yank open the door, hop in, pull the seat belt over my shoulder, and say, "Go, go, go."

Betty doesn't ask questions and slams on the gas. Willie's in

MAKING A MEDIUM

the backseat, looking out the window. "We lost him," he says. "That boyfriend of yours is nosey."

"That's the guy from *The Gazette*," Betty says, checking her rearview mirror. "He was at my house earlier today." She takes a sharp turn, and I hold tight to the grab handle to keep from tipping over. "He asked questions about Old Man LeRoy. I don't know why everyone thinks LeRoy was at my house? Arnie next door said he saw LeRoy there as well. I swear I haven't spoken to him in weeks." She makes a sudden stop at a red light, and I put my arms up to keep from head-butting the dashboard.

"It's my fault," I admit. "I used LeRoy's car yesterday."

Betty looks at me, red in the cheeks. "Why did you have his car?"

"Errr ... I borrowed it."

The light turns green, and the back of my head slams against the headrest.

"How do you know LeRoy?"

"We ... um ... ran into each other?"

Willie laughs. "That's a good one."

"Well, that makes sense." Betty flips the visor to check her lipstick. "When that editor guy showed up, I thought he was there to ask about Willie. He invented a part of the fuel system for NASA," she says proudly. "Except all he asked about was LeRoy and you."

Oh, no. I'm scared to ask, but I have to know. "What exactly did you say?"

"I said LeRoy wasn't there, but he kept pressing and pressing and pressing." She shakes her head, agitated. "He was borderline rude. Anyway, I said the only person to come by was a reporter. Then he asked what paper. I said *The Paper*. He'd never heard of it. Then he asked for a description of the reporter, so I gave it to him. Then he asked if the reporters name was Zoe. I said yes. But don't worry, I didn't tell him about your gifts."

Oh, hell. Brian knows I pretended to be a reporter. I'm sure he'll figure out that I'm the one who stole LeRoy's car. I feel a bit dizzy, and I fear I'll vomit all over Betty's expensive-looking leather interior.

"Are you okay?" Betty asks.

I swallow a few times. "I'll be okay. Do you have the will?"

She nods and cocks a thumb toward Willie. "It's on the backseat."

I grab a blue folder labeled "Will" and look over the paperwork inside. The words blur, and I blink a few times to regain focus. After three hours of research this morning, I'm feeling like quite the expert. That is until I actually read through the pages. It's all a bunch of long words and fancy language. But it appears to be in order. I think. "We'll get the death certificate from the funeral home and file this at the recorder's office."

"Thank you for coming," she says, pouting her bottom lip. "I don't think I could do this alone. Not after what happened yesterday."

"I'm happy to help." I tuck the will into the folder and set it beside Willie. "Betty, can you tell me more about Willie's relationship with Ron MacDonald and ..." The name of the first person who wanted Willie dead escapes my mind.

"Arnie the neighbor," Willie says, as if reading my thoughts.

Right. Arnie.

"And Arnie," I say.

"Why do you want to know?" she asks.

"It seems Willie had arguments with the two prior to his death."

Betty fidgets with the stitching along the steering wheel for a little too long. "Arnie is our neighbor. I've never witnessed any arguments between him and Willie, but I know the two had a love-hate type relationship."

"Mostly hate," Willie adds.

I blow out a sigh. "Do you think he'd ever hurt Willie?"

She gives a slight shrug of her shoulders.

Not exactly helpful, but it's a start. "What about Ron MacDonald?"

Betty wets her lips. "Ron and Willie were golfing buddies."

I wait for more, but apparently that's all I'm going to get. "Did you wait on him when you worked at the golf club?" I ask, remembering what Willie said about Ron having a thing for Betty.

She nods her head. "LeRoy, Ron, Jackson, and Willie would play golf on Tuesdays and Thursdays. They'd come in after for drinks."

"Who is Jackson?" I ask.

"My lawyer buddy," Willie says from the backseat, and I suddenly remember. Yes, the ruthless attorney who has a terrible swing. Got it.

"Sorry, I know who Jackson is," I say to Betty. "Please continue. When was the last time you spoke with Ron?"

Betty twists her mouth to the side. "I don't remember."

She's lying.

I can feel it.

I can see it.

The slouch of her shoulders. The tightening of her grip on the steering wheel. The rapid rise and fall of her chest.

"You don't *remember* the last time you spoke to Ron MacDonald?" I press.

"Stop pestering her about Ron!" Willie grumbles. "Ask about Monday morning."

But ... *ugh* ... fine. "Tell me more about Monday morning," I say. "Do you *remember* seeing anything out of the ordinary when you returned home?"

Betty swerves onto the main highway toward Trucker. "No. Everything appeared normal. In the morning I went to Target, Anthropologie, and a few other places. Willie called and asked for his medicine. I was at the pharmacy for almost an hour. Then I came home. Went to my room to drop off a few bags. Came downstairs and found Willie." She frowns at the memory.

I can't help but feel a stab of sympathy for Betty. I can't imagine how traumatic it must have been to perform CPR on your own husband.

Unless you're the one who killed him.

Then it might not be so traumatic.

"Ask her if she went through the garage," Willie says.

Right. The key. "Did you come in through the garage?" I ask Betty.

"Nope." She flips on the blinker and swerves into the right lane. I notice, for the first time, the wedding band on her left ring finger. Based on Willie's wealth, I would have expected a fifteen-carat diamond encircled with rubies and emeralds and pearls, but this wedding ring is a plain silver band no thicker than an ant. "I don't ever go in the garage," she continues. "That's where Willie keeps all his cars."

"How many does he have?"

Betty counts on her fingers. "Six?"

Geez. That's a lot of cars. We should be borrowing one of those instead of LeRoy's land ark. "Do you know about the key broken in the garage door lock?"

"No." Betty wrinkles her nose. "I haven't gone out there yet. Willie must have done that."

I glance at Willie in the rearview mirror, but he's not there. Panicked, I turn around and find him still sitting on the backseat right where I left him. So you can't see ghosts in a mirror. Who knew?

"My keys are in my top dresser drawer with my wallet,"

Willie says. "I wouldn't have locked the door with a key ..." He makes a strangled sound and lurches forward. "Ask Betty if the hide-a-key is still under the second rock from the fence in the backyard."

"What are you looking at?" Betty veers off the road and nearly takes out a row of cyclists. "Is Willie here right now?"

"He is," I say, holding tight to the grab handle. "Please pay attention to the road."

Betty tears up. "Willie, where are you?"

"The road," I say. "You're driving on the shoulder. There's a deer!" I cover my eyes. *Please don't hit the deer. Please don't hit the deer. Please don't hit the deer.*

"I'm right here." Willie appears on the console between us. "Pay attention, Betty."

I peek one eye open. We're back on the main road again. Deer unscathed. *Phew.*

Betty turns to face me. "Is Willie in the car?"

"Yes, he's right beside you. But please pay attention to the road." I clutch the seat belt. This might very well be how *I* die. Betty's a worse driver than I am.

"But I don't feel anything," Betty says. "Why don't I feel anything?" She releases the steering wheel and clutches her face.

Ah!

I reach over and take hold of the wheel and keep us from veering off into the ditch alongside the highway. Betty's breathing becomes more rapid, and I try hard to keep my voice calm. "Betty, take a deep breath and pull over to the side of the road."

"I ... can't ... feel ... anything ..." she stutters out.

"Calm, Betty," I say again, still steering the car.

Finally, she takes back control of the car and eases to the shoulder. I grab Betty's hands, take a slow, deep breath, and encourage her to do the same. Her eyes lock on mine as she inhales and exhales in a steady rhythm.

"Good girl," I say with an encouraging smile.

"Why can't I feel Willie?" she asks between breaths.

I don't know the answer to that. I look to Willie for help, and he shrugs. "'Talk to her," I say. "Tell her something. Anything. Just try it."

Willie takes his hat off, holds it over his heart, and presses his mouth to Betty's ear. I think he's about to whisper sweet words of endearment. Instead, he says the lyrics to the *Friends* theme song.

Betty doesn't flinch. She doesn't bat an eye. Or give any sign she can hear Willie. So he says them louder, and louder, and louder until he's singing an off-key rendition of the song. It's quite unpleasant.

Slowly, a smile spreads across Betty's face, and her eyes gloss over as if she's in a trance. "We used to watch *Friends* together every night," she says. "At first Willie hated the show. He said the characters were too loud and had terrible style. But he eventually came around. We made it through seven seasons."

I'm speechless.

Watching Willie singing to Betty is a touching sight. It's hard to imagine him as a ninety-three-year-old man with saggy ears and a frowny face. Side-by-side, the two look as if they were made for each other. Like they could be one of those couples that come stock in picture frames. I feel a flash of jealously. Not because I want a dead husband to serenade me, but because I can feel the genuine affection the two have for each other. But it doesn't feel like a passionate, once-in-a-lifetime, all-consuming love. What Betty and Willie have is a deep friendship. And that, I realize, is something I've never had.

Betty wipes her eyes. "I feel better."

Me too, actually. Betty may be withholding information, but

I don't think she killed Willie. Which makes me feel better about helping her become a multimillionaire.

Willie retreats to the backseat, still humming the tune but, thankfully, not singing it.

"I'm glad," I say and check the time. It's almost one o'clock. "Should we get going now?"

CHAPTER NINE

The funeral home looks like a school house, with red siding, white trim, and a weather vane on top. Across the street are a florist, a Dress Barn, an estate attorney, a caterer, and the superior courthouse (where Betty needs to file her paperwork), making this corner of Trucker your one-stop-funeral-shop.

Betty parks beside a hearse, and the three of us exit the car. There must be a funeral going on because the parking lot is packed. Betty tugs at the bottom of her black shorts, which barely cover her butt, and holds tightly to her purse as if afraid someone might snatch it.

The funeral home smells of astringent, and there's melancholy music playing through the speakers. The chapel doors are open, and we can see an oak coffin with a spray of pink gladiolus, carnations, and asters on top. Floral wreaths are displayed around the altar, and every seat is filled with solemn-looking individuals.

I can't *feel* the presence of any spirits, which is odd given where we are. Even Willie is nowhere to be seen.

A man in a dark suit with chestnut-colored hair emerges from the chapel and slides the doors closed behind him. "Mrs.

MacIntosh," he greets Betty and kisses her on each cheek. Per the name tag pinned to his suit, this is Franklyn the Funeral Director.

Betty introduces me to Franklyn, and we step into his office—a small brown room with a large desk. It's oddly soothing in here. Or maybe it's Franklyn. He has the slightest lisp, a missing canine tooth, a servant's heart, and a calming spirit. I want to tell him all my secrets. But I probably shouldn't.

"What can I do for you, Mrs. MacIntosh?" Franklyn takes a seat behind his desk and folds his hands on his lap.

Betty gulps, still holding tightly to her purse. Her face pales and beads of sweat break out around her forehead.

"Are you okay?" I ask.

"It's a bit overwhelming," she says barely above a whisper and fans her face. "Maybe I should tell Daniel I'm here. I don't want to cause trouble."

Franklyn walks around from behind the desk and touches Betty's shoulder. "This is a difficult process, and we're here to do whatever we can. Take your time."

I check my watch. Problem is, we don't have *that* much time. I need to be back by five, and we still need to go to the courthouse. Who knows how long that will take.

Betty isn't talking, so I step in. "We're here to get Willie's death certificate, and Betty would like to inquire about an autopsy."

Franklyn nods. "I can get you the certificate, not a problem. If you'd like an autopsy, we can make the arrangements."

"I'm fine with that," Betty says with weak resolve. "It's what Willie wants."

Franklyn returns to his chair, flips through a Rolodex, and pulls out a business card. He picks up the phone then hangs it up almost immediately, distracted by a pink sticky note on his desk. "I'm sorry, Mrs. MacIntosh. I'm only just now seeing this.

It seems Daniel MacIntosh called earlier to inquire about having your husband moved to a different funeral home. Are you aware of this?"

Betty's shoulders fall, and she looks to me, desperately pleading with her eyes for help. "Betty is the executor of Willie's estate and his wife," I say, "which gives her the legal right to make all final decisions."

"Of course," Franklyn says, his words laced with compassion. "It's not a problem. I will arrange for the autopsy, and we can still have your husband's remains ready for pickup Friday, so long as the autopsy is finished in time."

Oh, sweet relief! I wish Willie were here, he'd be happy to know his autopsy has been ordered and he will have his answer by Friday. Which means I should be ghost-free by the weekend!

"It generally takes four to six weeks for the results," Franklyn says, and my head implodes.

"Four to six weeks!" I don't mean to yell, but, honestly. FOUR TO SIX WEEKS? "That's over a month!"

If Franklyn is taken aback by my outburst, he doesn't show it. "The preliminary results will be released about twenty-four hours after the autopsy is performed, but the full report takes longer."

Oh. Okay. Preliminary results should be good enough for Willie.

I hope.

Franklyn produces two copies of the death certificate. Betty chooses an urn, signs the papers for the autopsy, and bolts so fast you'd think the building were on fire. I hurry to catch up. There's still no sign of Willie, but I can't dwell on his whereabouts. He's around here somewhere. I'm just not exactly sure where or why he disappeared. So I escort Betty to the courthouse without him.

An hour later, the paperwork is filed, and I'm in desperate

need of two Advil, one nap, and the ability to teleport because I have twenty minutes to get back to Fernn Valley.

We hop in Betty's Escalade, and I jump when I see Willie sitting in the backseat. "Where have you been?" I mouth to him while Betty jerks the car into reverse and zooms out of the parking lot.

"Too much death. I didn't want to go in there."

"Is Willie still here?" Betty asks.

"He is," I assure her and check the time. "I don't want to rush you, but, um, can you hurry? I need to get home."

"Not a problem." She slams on the gas, and I feel a roller coaster lurch. "Can you ask Willie if he likes the urn I picked out?" Betty asks.

I turn around in my seat to face Willie. "It's a handsome, masculine metal urn with—"

"I don't want to know," Willie cuts me off and stares out the window.

With a sigh, I turn back around. Betty looks at me expectantly. "He says good job."

A smile creeps across her face. "I knew he'd like it. It reminded me of him. Strong and attractive."

I flinch a little when she refers to Willie as attractive. Just as I did at the courthouse when she told the county recorder that Willie was, and I quote, "a total beefcake." It's almost like she's trying too hard. As if she's justifying her marriage to others. Or perhaps she's trying to assure herself. Either way, it's uncomfortable. No one else sees the dashing thirty-something Willie I do. They see the long-eared, old man. Sure, he was a handsome old man. But he was no beefcake.

The phone rings, a local area code appears on the screen in her dashboard, and Betty presses a button on her steering wheel. "Hello?"

"Betty," a throaty voice blasts from the speakers. "It's Arnie.

You might want to get home. There's a car outside your house. I asked the gentleman what he was doing, and he said he's a detective for the Trucker County PD, and he's waiting for you to get home."

Betty's face goes pale. "Is that normal?" she asks me. "For a detective to come to your house after your husband dies?"

Um ... I have no idea. But I'm suspecting, no.

"Have her go home right now and tell the detective about the key in the door," Willie instructs. "Tell her! Tell her! Tell her! Tell her!" He's in my ear. "Go! Go! Go! Go!"

If Betty turns around and goes home, I will not beat my parents back to *The Gazette*, which will prompt a load of questions, forcing me to confesses that I lied about the job, which will raise another load of questions and, ultimately, a straightjacket.

On the other hand, this isn't about me.

This is about Willie.

"You better get home right now," I say, and Betty makes an illegal U-turn across two solid yellow lines.

CHAPTER TEN

"What do you mean you won't be home until after dark?" Mom asks.

I pace along the side yard of Willie's mansion, the gravel crunching under my pumps. Betty is inside speaking to a detective with the Trucker PD. I should be with her, but first I have to deal with Mom. When I called, Dad answered. I said I'd be late. He said okay. We hung up. A nanosecond later, Mom called wanting more answers.

"I have to work late, that's all," I say, which technically isn't a lie. Dealing with Willie has become a job.

A poorly paying job.

"When we drove past *The Gazette*, the lights were already off and no one appeared to be there," she says, her tone accusing. She's not buying this *I have to work late* excuse. Not one bit.

"That's because, um ... I'm in Trucker on assignment." Again, not technically a lie.

There's a long pause on the other end. "Does this have to do with Willie MacIntosh?"

"No. It's clerical ... stuff." Yeah, okay, that is a lie.

Willie appears in my pacing path. "Hurry up. I need you."

"I'm dealing with my mom," I mouth to him.

"Tell her you're allowed to be out past five o'clock by yourself and she's overbearing. Hurry up!"

Not a chance I'm saying that to my mother. "Mom, I have to work late, and I'll get there when I get there."

Mom exhales loudly. "How are you getting home?"

Good question. I suppose I can ask Betty for a ride, even if her driving makes me green. "I'll catch a ride with Be—*ttthhhh*. Beth!" I don't know anyone named Beth, but it's best to keep Betty and Willie out of the conversation.

"Oh," Mom perks. "Beth Wood? I heard she's thinking about listing her three-bedroom off Crawford Street."

"Um ... yeah, yeah. I heard that too." Another lie. This is becoming alarmingly too easy.

"Well, okay then. Put in a good word for us." You can always count on a real estate agent to jump at a good referral opportunity.

We hung up with a promise that I will call on my way home. "I'm probably going to hell for lying to my parents," I say to Willie as I slide my phone into my pocket.

"Trust me, kid. If I'm not going to hell, then there's no way you are. Now get to work!"

Turns out Willie wants me to sit with Betty and the detective—a serious-looking fellow with a long face and sunken cheekbones that goes by the name of Manfreed. They're in the living room. Daisy is back, sitting beside Betty with her front paws crossed. I sink into the chair Willie died in, feeling very much out of place.

"I didn't catch your name," Manfreed says to me.

That's because I didn't give it to him. When we drove up, the detective marched up to Betty and I made myself scarce, hoping to catch my parents before they drove to *The Gazette*.

I'm well aware they'll find out about my fake job. I just hope it's *after* Willie is gone.

I can only deal with so many disasters at once.

"My name is Zoe Lane. I'm a ... family friend."

"Zoe *Lane*?" The detective repeats and glances down at the tiny notepad in his hand. "You spoke with Sheriff Vance yesterday about Daniel MacIntosh."

Right. Forgot about that. Crud.

"I *may* have mentioned his name." I pick cat hair off my pants to avoid eye contact.

"You accused him of murder."

Betty gasps.

"Um," is about all I can come up with. What am I supposed to say? Yes, officer, I did accuse Daniel MacIntosh of murder. Even though I've never met Daniel. Even though I've known Betty fewer than forty-eight hours. Even though I've never met a living Willie.

"Why do you believe Daniel MacIntosh murdered his uncle?" Manfreed asks.

Betty gasps again.

The word murder seems to have that effect on people.

"The thing is ..." I say, again not exactly sure what the thing is. "Errr ..." Willie is at my side, muttering into my ear. "Daniel has been counting on his inheritance from Willie for years. When Betty entered the picture, he feared his fortune would be jeopardized. I believe he killed Willie before he and Betty could get married, or before Willie could alter his will to include Betty. But what Daniel didn't know was that he was too late. Fewer than twenty-four hours after Willie's death, Daniel had already made plans to sell the house. It sounds like a person desperate for money. It also sounds like he was a little too prepared if you ask me. You can stop talking now ... I mean ..."

Willie smacks his forehead. "You weren't supposed to say that last part out loud."

"Obviously," I say under my breath.

Detective Manfreed is just staring at me.

So is Betty.

"Tell him about the key," Willie says.

"Yes!" I jump to my feet. "Let me show you the broken key in the garage lock."

Even though I'm fairly certain this detective thinks I'm off my rocker, he follows me outside. Betty opens the four garage doors revealing a row of sparkly sports cars in every color of the rainbow.

"My babies!" Willie gives a red Porsche a hug. "I've missed you." He kisses the hood.

"I'll leave you two alone," I whisper as I walk past him, and past a green Lamborghini, and past a blue Maserati, and past a blocky-looking yellow car which appears too low to the ground to even move, and stop at the door leading to the house. "See," I point to the lock.

"What am I supposed to be looking at?" the detective asks.

"There's a key stuck ..." It's gone! There's no key stuck in the lock. I look at Willie for help, but he's too busy caressing a BMW to notice. I clear my throat loudly. "There's no key stuck in the door!"

Willie appears and examines the lock. "It was here yesterday. I'm sure of it."

I look at Betty for help this time. "I ... I ... I never come out. I didn't ..." She gives a desperate shrug of her shoulders.

"Check the rock!" Willie says.

Right. "The rock! There's supposed to be a spare key under the second or third rock from the back gate." I push past the detective, exit the garage and make a left, until Willie tells me to turn around and go right. I do as told and walk down the crunchy gravel along the side of the house and lift the second rock from the gate. No key. I lift the third rock, and first rock, and the fifth rock (and these rocks are more like boulders), and the sixth just to be sure. Still no key!

Unfortunately, this proves nothing.

Absolutely nothing.

Both Betty and Detective Manfreed are looking at me with polite smiles.

"There's the proof!" Willie almost cheers. "Someone stole my hide-a-key to enter my house and kill me! Tell them. Tell them." He's in my ear. "Tell them!"

"There's typically a key under the rock," I say, feeling a bit panicked.

The detective looks to Betty for confirmation. "It's possible there was a key there," she says. "I haven't lived here very long."

Well, she's of no help.

"Come on, Betty." Willie is now in her ear. "You know there's a key there. I told you I put a key there. Tell them there is supposed to be a key there!" Willie yells desperately and Betty's eyes flicker from the detective to the rock and back again. I can almost see the wheels in her head turning, but unfortunately, nothing comes out of her mouth.

"And you said your name is Zoe Lane, correct?" The detective asks me with a click of his pen, notepad out. "Spelled without a *y* at the end?"

Oh, geez.

"Correct," I squeak out.

"And what exactly was your relationship with Willie MacIntosh?"

My heart thunks into my gut. "Um ... I didn't exactly know Willie."

Manfreed regards me with an unreadable expression. "How

did you know about a key supposedly hidden under the rock in his yard?"

Oh, gosh. I think I may vomit. Um ...

"Tell him, Zoe," Betty urges. "You can tell him the truth."

Okay, I really am going to vomit now. I am not, under any circumstance, going to tell a detective for the Trucker Police Department that I'm conversing with Betty's dead husband. I can't do it. I won't do it. There is no way!

Unfortunately, Betty can, and she will, and she does.

"She's a medium," she says as if this explains everything. As if medium is a typical, humdrum, every day type job.

Willie grimaces.

I don't know how to respond. If I deny it, then I'll lose Betty's trust. If I confirm it, then I look like a complete nut-ball. So I say nothing.

"You are a medium by profession?" the detective finally asks.

"Not exactly by profession," I say. "It's more of a newfound ... *talent*." Oh gosh, he's going to arrest me. He's going throw a pair of cuffs around my wrists, shove me into the back of the squad car, and drop me at the nearest mental institute.

"She can see Willie," Betty says. "She knows things no one else does. She can also see my dog, Daisy, who passed away when I was seven. She's the real deal."

I'm sending mental messages to Betty, begging her to stop talking, but she's not getting them.

"My psychic told me Willie would send a sign, and he did." Betty wraps an arm around my shoulders and squeezes me tight. I want to melt into the ground.

The detective is staring at us with such an odd expression I don't know whether to laugh or cry.

"And you have reason to believe your husband was killed?" Manfreed asks Betty.

She looks at me. "Does Willie think so?"

"Yes!" Willie answers. "Whoever used the key under the third rock to enter *my* house, got the key stuck in the door, and returned today to remove the evidence. Tell him, Zoe! Tell him now!"

I can't believe I'm about do this. "Yes," I say, my voice barely above a whisper. "Willie believes the killer broke into his home using the hide-a-key."

"Tell him to check into Daniel!" Willie yells.

"And he thinks it might be Daniel," I repeat, my voice still low.

"Do you have any evidence?" the detective asks.

Evidence would be nice, but ... "No."

"We did order an autopsy," Betty says. "That should let us know if Willie was killed, right?"

The detective takes a step back, not hiding his surprise. "An autopsy would provide some answers, yes. The initial death report said he died of natural causes ..."

Betty and I share a look, neither of us knows if the detective is making a statement or asking a question.

Manfreed massages his temples. "I'll take this information back to the station and be in touch," he says with a shake of his head. He pushes open the side gate and stalks back to his car, which is parked at the end of the driveway.

My legs feel all shaky, and there's a slight chance that I've either soiled myself, or I'm just sweating profusely. This whole situation is out of control, and all I want to do is go back to last week when my days consisted of reading, and eating, and watching television.

Also, I have a headache.

"I don't think that went well," Betty says.

Ya think?

I turn around slowly to face her. "Why did you have to tell him I was a medium?"

"Because you are. I'm not going to lie to him."

Ugh. "What about the hide-a-key? Willie told you about the key under the rock. He told you multiple times."

Willie returns to Betty's ear. "Last week, you were in the kitchen making my lunch when I told you about the hide-a-key! Remember! Remember! Remember! Remember!"

Betty's eyes gloss over. "It sounds familiar."

"Then you should have told the detective!" I snap. I can't help myself. I've just inserted myself into a murder investigation and given the detective enough reason to think I should be a suspect.

"Don't yell at her!" Willie is in my face. "It's not her fault!"

"I'm not yelling!" I rise to the tips of my toes until we're nearly at eye level. "I'm talking loudly and, yes, it is her fault that she can't remember a conversation that happened last week!"

"You're right!!" Betty wrings her hands. "I just ... just ... I just ..."

Willie appears beside Betty and wraps a protective arm around her. "Now look what you've done. She's upset."

Oh, geez.

Betty's bottom lips quivers. "I just ... I just ... I just ... This whole thing has me completely freaked out! The will, Daniel, the detective, the key, and now murder! Everyone thinks I'm a gold digger, and it's just ... it's awful!"

Okay, now I feel bad for snapping. "I'm sorry," I say. "I shouldn't have yelled at you."

"Damn straight," Willie agrees.

I suppress an eye roll. "But I have to ask. When you married a ninety-three-year-old millionaire, did you honestly think no one would think of you as a gold digger?"

A mixture of pain and confusion flashes across her face. "I don't know. The thing is, Willie was arrogant, and grumpy, and intrusive, and—"

"Tell her to get to the point," Willie says.

"He sounded like he was trying to hide the fact that he was lonely." Betty goes back to wringing her hands. "My parents divorced when I was three, and my dad took off—"

"So you married a man to replace the hole your father left?" I interrupt, trying desperately to understand.

Willie grimaces.

"No! ... Yes? ... No!" Betty kicks at the gravel. "You don't understand; I never had siblings or any family around. Especially after my mom died. I know what it's like to be lonely, and I thought, perhaps, I could keep him company. We could keep each other company."

She's wrong.

I *do* understand.

I understand better than anyone else what it's like to be lonely, to be cooped up in your house all day by yourself, to have no one but your parents to converse with, to schedule your days around little excursions like the library, or the bakery, or even a drive around town. What it's like to pine over a man whose picture you see in the paper and to ... wait ... not about you, Zoe.

Back to Betty.

Anyway.

I understand what she's feeling, which is why I'm having a hard time believing her. "Betty, I'm here to help Willie and because he cared about you, I'm here to help you, too. But I need you to be honest with me." I think back to our conversation in the car. She's hiding something. What? I don't know. I don't think she killed Willie. Otherwise she wouldn't have ordered an autopsy. I do genuinely believe she cared for her husband. But I do think she knows more than she's saying. Or maybe she knows more than she realizes she does.

I take a step forward and place my hands on Betty's shoulders. She closes her eyes. "I need you to be honest with yourself,"

I say. "If you were lonely, that's fine. If you thought Willie was lonely and you wanted to keep him company, I get it. But you could have been friends with Willie, or even his roommate. You didn't have to marry him. That's what I don't understand. Was it the money?"

Her eyes flutter open. "Yes," she says in her raspy voice.

Willie doesn't appear shocked or upset by this news.

"But I didn't think it would be *that* big of a deal," Betty continues. "He doesn't have kids or a wife. He didn't like Daniel. So, I married him."

I nod my head, keeping my hands on her shoulders, encouraging her to keep going.

"I didn't think it would hurt anyone. I honestly thought we'd do more good than harm. I promise. But I really care about him," she says. "More than I thought I would. He is so funny, Zoe. Like I could be having the worst day, and he'd make me smile." She laughs at a memory. "He took care of me, and I took care of him." She pauses to regain her composure. "So, yeah, okay, maybe I married him for the money, but I think he married me to prove something to his friends. I'm not a total idiot. I know Willie, Jackson, and LeRoy all had a thing for me. They were great tippers. I know none of them were happy with Willie when the two of us got together, and I know that's part of the reason he asked me to marry him. So I think we're sorta even, right?"

Dang.

Betty is more insightful than I thought.

"What about Ron?" I ask.

Betty crinkles her nose. "Huh?"

"Ron MacDonald. You said LeRoy, Jackson, and Willie all had a *thing* for you. But I know Ron was in that group as well. Did he?"

"No," she says, drawing out the word. "He's the only one in the group that's married."

So Ron is married. Not sure how this matters, but it feels important. I open my mouth, about to inquire more about Ron MacDonald, when I'm interrupted.

"Yo, Betty?" A middle-aged man with thick, black hair and unruly eyebrows is peeking over the fence. "Everything okay?"

Betty steps away, and my arms fall to my sides. "Oh, hey, Arnie." She tucks a strand of hair behind her ear. "We're fine."

"Why were the cops here?"

Betty sighs. "We think Willie might have been k-i-l-l-e-d."

"That doesn't surprise me," Arnie says. "MacIntosh was an arrogant son of a—"

"You idiot!" Willie is on the other side of the fence now. "I'm not arrogant. I'm right! The judge said so!"

"Honestly, Betty," Arnie says, not at all affected by the ghost beside him. "I think you're better off."

"You're done, little man." I can only see the top of Willie's head over the fence, but I imagine he's rolling up his sleeves. "Punch this fool for me, Zoe."

Yeah, no.

"Oh, stop," Betty says with a wave of her hand. "You're such a flirt."

Willie walks through the fence. "Flirt? That's not flirting! He's an idiot!"

Seems every resident of Trucker County over the age of fifty has a *thing* for Betty MacIntosh. Why all these old men believe they have a shot with this thirty-year-old hottie is beyond me.

Arnie uses the bottom of the fence to hoist himself up so we can now see his nose. "If you're ready for a real man, I'm available."

"Gross," Willie and I say in unison.

"Excuse me?" Arnie raises his bushy brows. "Who are you?"

It takes me a moment to realize he's talking to me.

"This is my medium, Zoe," Betty says. "She sees Willie."

Every time she says this out loud, I cringe a little. It sounds so absurd and, yet, so true ... *wait, where is Willie?*

He's gone, and I have a sinking suspicion wherever he is, he's up to no good.

Arnie laughs. But not a *he-he-he* polite or someone told a joke type of laugh, more of a mocking laugh.

"There is no such thing as a medium." He reaches his hand over the fence and points a chubby finger at me. "You're a fraud and, based on your clothing, not a very good one."

Okay, now *I* want to punch him.

Willie reappears, speaking so fast I can barely keep up. "The man has a subscription to a hair club service, and there are fuzzy pink handcuffs in his nightstand! In the medicine cabinet is a prescription for Viagra! Say it, Zoe. Say it out loud. Say it! Say it! Say it! Say it!"

Awk, I can't say that.

"Say it! Say it! Say it! Say it!"

"Fine!" I shoo Willie away. "There is Viagra in your dresser drawer, and a hair piece in your cabinet, and fuzzy handcuffs in your nightstand."

Willie drops his head. "Well, you royally screwed up the delivery on that one, person." He clasps his hands together and speaks slower. "The Viagra is in the medicine cabinet. He has a hair piece subscription and fuzzy handcuffs in the nightstand."

Oh.

Oops.

Okay. I suck in a breath, prepared to try again, when I notice there's no need. The portion of Arnie's face that I can see has gone white.

"You're a liar," he says.

"No, I'm not," I say. "And I know it's a hair piece for men

subscription, and the medicine is in the cabinet, and the cuffs are in the nightstand." I feel vindication. Who is he calling a fraud now? Ha!

Arnie grumbles and jumps down from the fence. We can hear his back door slam shut.

Willie and I share an air high-five.

"Let me guess. That was Willie?" Betty asks trying, and failing, to keep a straight face.

"Yep."

She smiles. "That wasn't very nice of him to pick on Arnie like that."

Willie tips his hat back, pleased with himself.

"Well ..." Betty blows out a long breath. "Was Willie really killed?"

"Yes," Willie says. "I'm sure of it."

"He sure thinks so," I say. "And, honestly, I'm beginning to think he was as well."

"Finally!" Willie claps his hands together. "Now tell Betty to set the alarm whenever she's in the house. I don't want her hurt as well."

I relay this to Betty.

She screws her face into a giant question mark. "We have an alarm?"

"Yes, of course we have an alarm," Willie says with a shake of his head. "Go show her how to use it, person. The code is one-two-three-four."

CHAPTER ELEVEN

Betty gives me a ride, and I'm home by nine o'clock. Dad is already in bed, and Mom is sitting at the kitchen table wearing the same red paisley bathrobe she's had since I was a kid. Her hands are wrapped around a steaming mug of hot chocolate with a lipstick stain on the edge.

"It's about time," she greets me.

I drop my briefcase on the couch and take off my walking shoes—which I'd fortuitously grabbed from Betty's house.

"Sorry I'm late." I place my shoes in the rack beside the door and run my hands down my face. It's been a long, exhausting day. "Good-night," I say over my shoulder.

"Wait, Zoe." Mom grabs me by the elbow. "You can't go to bed again without dinner. You need more protein and iron in your diet. Now sit. I saved you a plate."

I'm too tired to argue. I take a seat at the table and rest my chin in my palm. Mom pulls a plate out of the microwave. Meatloaf, mashed potatoes, and corn. Not sure how iron-rich this meal is, but it smells divine. I don't realize I am hungry until I take a bite.

"That looks like hospital food," Willie says.

I ignore him. Mom makes the best meatloaf, and her mashed potatoes are creamy and soaked in butter—just how I like them.

"I had the pictures from your first day of work printed." Mom goes to her office and returns with a scrapbook, the same scrapbook I've had for as long as I remember. It holds all my childhood, adolescence, and adulthood photos of my most memorable events. Mom flips to the back page. I am smiling for the camera, holding the pen Dad gave me. It's so odd to think Willie was beside me in this picture, yet there's no visible trace of him. It's also odd that I didn't remember to grab the pen when I was at Betty's. I make a mental note to get it tomorrow.

"Thanks, Mom," I say and flip back a page. It's the day my high school diploma came in the mail. I'm standing by the mailbox with a paper cap on my head that my dad bought at the party store, smiling from ear to ear. "Mom, can I ask you a question?" I flip to the front of the book, a picture of my mom holding me as a newborn in the hospital. The next few pages are my first bath, first steps, first birthday, second birthday then the day we moved into this house, shortly after I turned seven.

"What is it?" Mom asks.

"I have no memories of my life before I'm seven, and even in this book there's nothing between my second birthday and my seventh. Why is that?"

"It was a busy time. We were moving, and you were quite the active toddler. There was no time to take pictures." Mom stands and rinses out her mug in the sink.

"I should have at least one memory," I say. "But there's this huge void."

"Most people don't remember anything before they're seven years old. Your brain isn't fully developed yet." Mom kisses the top of my head. "I'm going to bed. I'll see you in the morning." She is out of the room before I can say another word. Very unlike her.

Jabba jumps up onto the table and eats what's left of my meatloaf. I go to pet his head, and he snaps at me.

"That has got to be the ugliest cat ever created," Willie says.

Jabba narrows his golden eyes and hisses at him.

Willie puts his hands on his knees. "Can you see me?"

Jabba claws at his face, and Willie jumps back and falls through the wall.

My life is weird.

I flip through the scrapbook again. So many baby pictures then—*bam*—I'm seven. And every little event is documented from there on out. Losing a tooth. Playing baseball in the backyard with dad. The day Jabba showed up. There's an entire page dedicated to a time I found a snail in the backyard. A snail! Yet nothing between two and seven.

"It's just bizarre," I say out loud.

"What's bizarre is your mother." Willie is back, standing on the other side of the room, keeping his distance from Jabba. "And that cat."

I flip the book closed and run my hand along the vinyl cover. "I don't think my mom is bizarre. The situation is. I know she's hiding something, though. The question is, what?"

CHAPTER TWELVE

According to *Reaching the Other Side,* a spirit cannot make you do anything against your will. Which means deep down, *way* deep down, there must be a part of me okay with allowing Willie to give me a makeover. Nothing drastic. Of course. I'm wearing jeans and a white T-shirt.

"How is this any better than what I typically wear?" I ask.

Willie smiles. "Those clothes are too big on you. Too *old.* You're young, smart, and too pretty to hide behind brightly colored parachutes."

I tug at the bottom of my shirt. It's not awful, but it feels a bit too plain. "Did you spend this much time obsessing over fashion when you were alive?"

"No, but I don't have anything else do right now but stare at people, and even I—a grumpy old man—know you need a makeover." He circles me slowly, tapping his chin with his forefinger. "What other shoes do you have?"

"My pumps."

"You mean those slippers with a peg attached?"

"*No,* I mean my pumps. I also have my sneakers."

He shudders at the thought.

"You're getting on my last nerve, ghost." I cross my arms. "What would you suggest I wear?"

"Something without arch support. Something with a little more pizazz ... something ... youthful. Let's move on for now. We'll come back to the shoes. Take your hair out of the ponytail."

Okay, there's a request I can deal with. I yank the scrunchie out, and my hair falls below my shoulders.

"Do you have one of those ... shoot, what are they called?" Willie closes his eyes, as if the answer is written on the backside of his lids. "Straight iron! You need one of those to make your hair less ..." He puffs his cheeks and mimics an explosion.

"No, I don't." I sweep my hair up into a bun on the top of my head.

Willie whistles. "Even better. Your hair looks good off your neck, kid. Really good. Now I can *see* you."

My cheeks go red. I can't help myself.

Still, whether I look good or not, or whether I was hiding behind my clothes or not, this outfit feels too plain. "The jeans I can live with," I say; admittedly they look pretty good. I've had them in my closet for years. I'd found them in a hand-me-down bin outside the library, but I've never even tried them on. I'm not sure why. "But I'm not wearing this top."

"What? No," Willie grumbles. "That's the best part. You look your age."

"I'm not comfortable." I grab a pink blazer off the hanger.

"If you wear that, I'll vomit," Willie says.

"I'd like to see you try." I shrug into the blazer and leave the buttons undone. Much better. This is an outfit I can live with.

Mom, not so much.

I think her eyeballs are about to fall out of her head when I walk out to the living room. Dad spews his hot chocolate all over the table. Even Jabba is giving me the once-over.

Geez. It's not like I'm prancing around in a bikini.

"Pay no attention." Willie is behind me. "Your people don't know style. Is your mother wearing shoulder pads?"

"Boundaries," I remind Willie under my breath. "No making fun of my clothes or talking badly about my parents." I'd also added no accompanying me to the bathroom after I nearly chocked on toothpaste this morning when he appeared out of nowhere wanting to talk about my wardrobe.

Willie MacIntosh has a hard time adhering to boundaries.

I sit at the table, and Mom plops down a blueberry muffin, a cup of orange juice, and an iron pill. She's unusually quiet. It's because of last night, when I asked about my childhood. She's actively trying not to think about it by singing Bon Jovi songs in her head. Clearly, she's hiding something, but I have serious doubt I'll be able to crack her. My eyes slide to Dad, who is cleaning up his mess.

Dad I can break. It's just a matter of getting him alone so I can read his thoughts.

I'm struck with an idea. "Dad," I say while unwrapping my muffin. "Do you want to meet for ice cream after work, just you and me?"

Mom drops a plate in the kitchen.

"You okay in there?" I ask.

"A-okay." Mom grabs two potholders from a drawer and slams it shut with her hip. "Forgot the pan was still hot."

"What are you making?" I move to the kitchen. Mom has dropped a sheet of freshly baked chocolate chip cookies on the ground.

"That's unfortunate," Willie mutters.

I help Mom clean up the mess. "Are these for work?" Mom typically buys scones and donuts from Butter Bakery for their open houses.

"No." She drops a handful of mushed cookies into the sink

and wipes the chocolate off of her hands. "I made them for Brian Windsor."

I pause mid-chew (ten second rule). "Wh-wh-why are you making him cookies?" I ask in a panic. *Why? Why? Why?* My mom cannot talk to Brian. Also, who bakes their daughter's boss cookies? He's not my teacher. I'm socially awkward, and even I know that's weird.

Mom grabs a rag out of the sink. "As a thank you. Word around town is he was quite heroic when you were hit by Old Man LeRoy."

What in the what?

I look at Willie for confirmation, and he shrugs. "I wasn't paying attention."

"Why not?" I mouth.

"I'd just died. I needed a moment to figure out what the hell was going on!"

Fair enough.

Dad chimes in. "Everyone says Brian rushed to the scene and carried you to Dr. Karman's office."

"He carried me?" The thought is equal parts horrifying and thrilling. "I don't remember him being there at all."

"The story goes," Dad says, "that he dropped you in the office and ran to tend to his uncle."

"Who is his uncle?" Willie and I say in unison.

Mom is on her hands and knees, wiping the floor with more vigor than the situation requires. "Brian Windsor is LeRoy's great-nephew. Don't you know that?"

"Why would I know that?" I look at Willie. *"Why don't you know that?"* I mouth.

He pauses, struck by a memory. "Now that I think about, he did mention his nephew moved to town to run the paper."

I roll my eyes then realize Mom and Dad are staring at me. "What's wrong?"

"Who are you talking to?" Dad asks cautiously.

Oops. "I ... um ... wasn't talking to anyone." I shove another broken cookie into my mouth.

Mom slaps the rag onto the counter, and both Willie and I jump. "Yes, you were!"

"No, I was ... um, talking to Jabba." I hurry out of the kitchen, and Mom follows.

"I know you were not talking to that cat. You were talking to something else," Mom is adamant, and I'm scared to make eye contact.

"No, I wasn't!" I say to the ground and grab my sneakers.

"Not the ugly man shoes," Willie whines. "You'll ruin the whole youthful vibe of the outfit."

"Shut up!" I say out loud. Oops. *Gah*! I need to be more careful.

"Zoe Matilda Lane." Dad marches to the living room. "You don't tell your mother to shut up."

"She didn't, John." Mom crosses her arms. "She's talking to imaginary people. Is it the guy with the hat?"

"What? *Pffft*. No. I was talking to ... um ... you!" I cross *my* arms. "Yeah, you!"

"That's it," Mom seethes. "You're ... you're ... you're grounded!"

Willie takes a seat on the couch and laces his fingers behind his head. "This is getting good."

"No, it's—I mean." I blow out a breath and regain my composure. "I'm an adult," I say to Mom. "You can't ground me. And what are you going to ground me from? I don't touch the computer. I rarely use my cell phone. I never leave the house. I don't hang out with friends." I feel a sudden surge of anger and resentment. "You've prohibited me from living, and I'm sick of it! Get your own damn life and stay out of mine, woman!"

A tremor of shock passes over Mom's face. This is the

moment when I should feel guilty, except I don't feel guilty, which makes me feel guilty, and really I'd like to go back to a time when the only feelings I felt were my own. The S name is swimming around in Mom's head, and she narrows her eyes. "Zoe Matilda Lane, you are out of line."

"You are out of line!" I yell back.

"How about ice cream?" Dad offers, because in his book, any disagreement can be settled with dessert.

"Why aren't there pictures of me when I was a child?" I ask.

"I told you it was a busy time, Zoe!"

"What are you hiding from me?" I demand.

"Nothing!"

The doorbell rings, and we all freeze. Mom with her mouth wide open, me with my arms still crossed, Willie on the couch, enjoying the show. Then there's Dad, who is in the kitchen digging around in the freezer.

"I'll get it," I finally say and swing open the door. "Ah!" It's Brian. Brian Windsor is at my house, on my front doorstep, wearing a plaid blue shirt, jeans, and a smirk. I step outside and slam the door shut behind me. "What are you doing here?"

Willie appears and is studying Brian's face with intense scrutiny. "Now that you mention it, I can see the resemblance. He's got LeRoy's nose. Damn shame. LeRoy didn't age well."

Brian adjusts his glasses and clears his throat. "Every time I try to speak to you, you run away. I figured I'd catch you at home."

"Um." I look right, then left, feeling the urge to run again. But where do I go? If I go inside, I'll have to face Mom, and I don't want to. So I give up. "What can I do for you, Brian?"

"Make eye contact," Willie says. "You're not making eye contact."

I stare into Brian's eyes, and my stomach does an almighty flutter. They're gorgeous.

"Move closer," Willie says. "And take off the blazer."

Gah, this ghost is maddening.

I stand my ground and leave my outfit alone. Brain already appears uncomfortable enough with the direct eye contact. "I'm writing an article about your accident on Monday and would like a statement. I also wanted to see how you're doing."

Oh, an article. I, Zoe Lane, will be featured in *The Fernn Valley Gazette*. How exciting ... *wait a minute*. "Isn't it unethical or un-something to write about the accident when your uncle is the one who hit me?"

"I can be impartial." He pulls a notepad from his pocket and clicks a pen. I wish I could read his mind. I wish I could feel his feelings. I wonder if his heart thrums when I'm around. I wonder if he lies in bed and thinks of me like I've thought of him many times over the last year. Or if he's ever wondered what it would be like to kiss me.

I concentrate, hoping to catch a glimpse of his emotions the way I can with my mother. Hoping to feel something, or hear something, or see anything.

Brian takes a step back. "Are you unwell?"

"Stop being weird," Willie grunts.

So I can't read Brian.

What's the point of having gifts if you can't freely use them on whomever you want?

"Smile!" Willie is behind Brian, giving me an exaggerated grin. "Show your teeth."

I give a fleeting smile to appease him. "I feel good," I say, which is a lie. My back is killing me this morning. I was, after all, *hit* by a car.

Brian writes this down and looks up. "For your information, we packed up LeRoy's house and got him situated at MelBorne Assisted Living last night. So he's off the streets."

"What!" Willie shrieks so loud I flinch. "You put LeRoy in a nursing home? That old man doesn't need a nursing home!"

"Wh-why would you do that?" I ask Brian. "I didn't press charges. He said he'd stop driving. Was that necessary?"

"It was his idea," Brian says. "He hasn't been the same since the accident. He doesn't even remember driving to Betty MacIntosh's house the other day. Then I caught him in the car yesterday driving around. It's for the best."

Willie turns around slowly. "You broke the old man."

"I didn't break him! I was in the crosswalk."

"I'm not arguing that point," Brian says. "I witnessed the entire thing. It was one hundred percent LeRoy's fault."

"You witnessed it? Weren't you inside?"

"I had come after you," he says.

Brian came after me!

"I felt bad," he says. "About how our interview went. I was going to offer you an internship."

He came after me because he felt bad. I can live with that.

"Looks like you already have a job though," Brian says.

"I do?"

He makes a *V* with his brows. "Aren't you writing for another paper?"

Am I? I can't remember all the lies I've told over the last few days. I should probably write them down. "Sure?"

"Are you covering the Willie MacIntosh story?" He tilts his head. "There's a lot of talk about his wife Betty and a possible scam."

"Tell him he's being ridiculous, Zoe." Willie is in my ear. "Tell him!"

"That's ridiculous." I shoo Willie away. "There is no scam. The marriage is legal. The will is legal and was drafted by a sound-minded Willie. Your uncle was one of the witnesses ..." Crap. If LeRoy is not himself and he recently checked into a nursing home, will he be a credible witness if or when this goes to probate court?

"Stay here," Willie says and suddenly disappears.

Great. What's happening now?

"Are you okay?" Brian asks.

"No ... I mean, yes. I am." His face blurs into two, and I blink to focus. "I'm fine. I'm great! You can use that in your article," I say, distracted. It is odd that Mom hasn't stormed out here demanding to know who is at the door.

"I know that you're friends with Betty," Brian says. "But if you're writing an article, you need to see it from both sides. Willie MacIntosh was a well-known womanizing bachelor. Doesn't it strike you as odd that he married two weeks before his death and that he altered his will shortly before? When Daniel had been set to inherit his money for the last thirty-something years?"

"No to the marriage. Yes to the death. Not sure about the last question."

"I heard the police were at her house yesterday," Brian says.

"Are you trying to poach my article?" I ask, as if I'm actually writing a story. As if I actually have a job. As if I actually know how to craft an article even if I were asked to write one.

Brian doesn't answer. Instead, he returns the notepad to his pocket and gives me an incredulous look. "What paper did you say you were writing for again?"

"I'd rather not say."

Brian nods and backs away. "Then I guess I'm done. I'm glad you're doing well," he says. "I'll see you around." He strolls to his car, which is parked along the curb. A black sedan with tinted windows.

I'm trembling as I watch him drive away. The lying is getting to me. I can't live in this made-up world anymore. I can't pretend that I don't see Willie. I can't pretend I'm not devastated to learn that if I had waited outside *The Gazette* for ten more minutes, I wouldn't have been hit by a car, Old Man LeRoy wouldn't have checked himself into a nursing home, and I would have an internship. I feel horrible about LeRoy. I need to fix it. I don't know how. But I have to.

Willie appears. "How'd it go?"

"Terrible. We need to speak to LeRoy and clear this up."

"Agreed. But we've got a bigger mess inside."

I massage my temples. My head already hurts. "What's happening now?"

"Your parents are in their room arguing. Your dad wants to come clean. Your mom refuses. She said if your dad tells you, then she'll leave him."

I drop my hands. "That's serious."

"They won't say what it is that they're keeping from you. But they mentioned a fire."

"A fire?" I whisper in shock. "Did they say anything about a person with a name that starts with an S?"

Willie shakes his head. "But we're going to find out what's going on."

I take a seat on the step and pull my knees to my chest. "I'm not going to put my dad in a position where he needs to tell me. Not if it will break up my parents' marriage."

"You don't have to." Willie kneels beside me. "I found a safe in your parents' closet, and I have a feeling that whatever it is they're hiding is in there."

This is not news to me. I've seen the safe before. It's a twelve-inch black cube, sitting on the top shelf of my parents' closet. I once asked my mom what was in it, and she'd said it's where she kept her jewelry. Made sense to me, and I never inquired again.

"We'll walk back to your house after they drop us off," Willie says. "And we'll get inside the safe and find out what's going on."

"What about LeRoy, and Betty, and Daniel, and your will, and your autopsy, and the key, and the detective, and Ron, and Arnie, and—"

Willie shushes me. "That can wait. I also have some good news." He rubs his hands together with the goofiest grin on his face.

"What is it?" I could really use some good news right about now.

"When I was in the closet, I found a red box filled with lingerie, and your mom has a pair of black leather shoes."

I grimace. "That is the opposite of good news."

"They could look good with your outfit, or not, but it's worth a shot."

"*Gah!* Would you get off the shoes? Honestly. We have more important things to deal with." I stand, dust off the back of my pants, walk inside, slam the door, and make a mental note to never look inside a red box.

CHAPTER THIRTEEN

My house is eerily quiet. There's only the hum of the refrigerator and the ticking from the grandfather clock in the living room. I feel intrusive, almost criminal, and I don't know why. I've been home alone hundreds of times before—probably thousands. It could be because I had to climb in through the window. I realized after my parents had dropped me at *The Gazette* that I'd left the house key on my nightstand.

Smart move.

"Let's get this over with," I say to Willie and walk down the hallway. My parents' room looks exactly as it has my whole life. The walls are a peachy yellow, and an oil painting of a farmhouse is hung above the bed. The nightstands and headboard are a matching pine set, and the comforter is the same color as the walls. White bi-fold doors are all that stand between me and the black box in my parents' closet.

I rest my hands on the knobs. Do I even want to know what's in the safe?

Willie is staring at me. "Open the doors. Come on, person. We've got places to go, people to see, murders to solve. Open. Open. Open. Open."

Fine, I decide. I want to know who this mysterious S person is and why fire is associated with the name. This is my life, after all.

With newfound determination, I pull open the doors and spot the safe on the top self. It's next to the red box.

I'm too short, and the safe is too high. I drag a chair in from the kitchen table to give me a boost. The safe requires a code, and I start with my birthday.

Doesn't work.

I try my parents' wedding anniversary.

Nope.

My mom's birthday, Dad's birthday, the day Apollo 11 landed on the moon (per Willie's suggestion), D-Day, V-Day, one-two-three-four, four-three-two-one, Christmas, Fourth of July, and the first six numbers of our phone number ...

Nothing works.

Frustrated, I start to descend from the chair when I'm struck with an idea. "Can you stick your head in there and see what's inside?" I ask Willie.

He stares at me for a few moments before he dissolves into laughter.

Well, he's cracked.

I fold my arms, not finding the humor in this situation. "Are you just about done?"

He slaps his knee, hunched over in a soundless laughing fit.

"What is so funny?" I demand.

"It's the fact"—he wheezes out between laughs—"that we've spent the last hour trying to crack the code to the safe when all I have to do is put my face in there." He wipes non-existent tears from his eyes. "You have to admit, that's funny."

"Wasting time isn't funny. Now, stick your face in there. And hurry up before you wake Jabba."

"Okay, okay. No need to be so pushy." He puts his head

through the safe. It's unsettling to watch, and I turn away. "There's a manila envelope," he says once he emerges. "And there's also a pistol."

"No, there's not. My parents don't own a gun."

"I just shoved my head into a safe, and I'm telling you, your parents own a gun."

"Why would they need a gun? We live in Fernn Valley. The most criminal thing to happen around here is when someone changed Fernn to Sperm on the town's welcome sign."

"I don't know. But I have a feeling whatever you need to know is in that envelope."

Shoot! So close. Yet so far. I gnaw on my bottom lip and look around. There's got to be something else around here to give us a clue as to what is in the safe.

Willie and I search the room. I pull the mattress up, look through drawers, and under the bed. It would easier if we knew what we were looking for. In the end, all we find is a package of Little Debbie Donuts hidden in Dad's nightstand.

This mission is a total bust and a complete waste of time. I put the room back as I found it, and we go.

Next mission: Old Man LeRoy.

MelBorne Assisted Living is a somber-looking establishment. Single story with brown fascia, brown siding, brown doors, and windows with drawn, light brown curtains. Poorly kept shrubs line the walkway, and the cement is cracked and veiny.

Willie shakes his head. "I'd rather be dead than stuck in this place."

Agreed.

The automatic doors part, and I'm assaulted by a nauseating odor of urine and day-old cafeteria food. A woman in a blue nurse's uniform smiles at me. She looks to be in her thirties with jet-black hair slicked into a bun and thinly drawn-in eyebrows.

Per her name tag, this is Patricia. "Do you have an appointment?"

"I don't. I'm here to see Mr. ..." LeRoy's last name has escaped my mind, and Willie has wandered off. Then I remember where I live. Of course I don't need a last name. All I need to say is, "Old Man LeRoy." And the nurse knows exactly whom I'm talking about. Benefits of a small town.

"Come with me."

I follow Patricia down a linoleum-floored hall. Through a door I glimpse a few old men sitting in wheelchairs with knitted afghans on their laps, staring out a window with blank expressions on their faces. I don't feel the presence of any spirits, which doesn't strike me as odd. If I died here, I doubt I'd come back either.

"Are you related to LeRoy?" Patricia asks, showing me into to a reception area.

"No, I'm, um, a ... friend?"

"I'll need you to sign in." She steps behind a desk and hands me a clipboard. I write my name and hand it back to her.

Patricia scans the form. "Are you related to John and Mary Lane?"

"They're my parents."

Patricia's face lights up. "They put my house on the market Saturday, and I already have two offers."

"Is your last name Attwood?" I ask, trying to remember what listings my parents have right now.

"It is. I didn't even know the Lanes had children until I heard about what happened."

Oh, no. "What happened?"

"You got hit by a car?"

Oh, that.

"It's all everyone is talking about," she says. "Old Man LeRoy plowed you over, and Brian Windsor had to do CPR to bring you back to life. I heard you lost a leg." She peeks over the desk to verify that all my limbs are intact.

"I think the story *may* have been exaggerated," I say. "No CPR, no missing legs. I suffered a minor concussion, and that's all."

"Found him!" Willie appears, and I scream.

"Shhh, person. You want people to think you're crazy?"

Patricia rushes around the desk. "Are you okay?

"I'm fine." I clutch my chest and will my heart back to a normal rhythm.

"Come with me." Willie starts down the hallway.

"Thank you for your help," I say to Patricia. "I know where LeRoy's room is located." I chase after Willie, leaving a stunned-looking Patricia in the waiting area.

"Don't scare me like that again," I hiss.

"He's the last door on the left," he says, ignoring me.

As somber as MelBorne looks from the outside, it has nothing on the state of Old Man LeRoy's room. The walls are white and bare. The curtains are drawn, and the light is off. Boxes labeled *clothes, pictures, personal items* are stacked in the corner. A wilted potted plant is on the nightstand, and LeRoy is lying in a hospital bed with his arms at his sides and his eyes glued to the wall.

"Hey there, old pal." Willie crouches down and speaks to his friend. "What the hell are you doing in here? You don't belong in a nursing home."

LeRoy doesn't even flinch.

I clear my throat, hoping to grab his attention. Doesn't work. "LeRoy?" I try.

Still nothing.

"The man is hard of hearing. You're going to need to speak up," Willie says.

Oh. "LeRoy!" I yell, and he flops his head to the side.

"Who the hell are you?" he asks.

"My name is Zoe Lane."

He returns his attention back to the wall. "I don't want visitors."

I feel a stab of sympathy for the old man. This is no way to spend your final years. I grab a chair from the corner, drag it closer to the bed, and sit down with my hands in my lap. "LeRoy, if you're upset about the accident, please know that I'm fine and I don't harbor any ill will."

"Leave me alone," he groans.

"Tell him I'm here," Willie says. "Tell him to get his saggy butt out of bed and go back home."

"LeRoy," I reach to touch his hand, and he jerks away.

"Tell him I'm not mad," Willie says. "Tell him I know we fought the last time we were together, but it doesn't matter. There's too much history between us. I'm good."

"Willie says—"

"Also, tell him about how young I look." Willie straightens his tie. "Tell him I'm in my early thirties and when he dies, he'll be young too. He can go back to being my wingman."

"Willie is here, and he says—"

"Also tell him about being able to walk through walls."

"I will if you let me," I hiss out of the corner of my mouth and scoot my chair closer to LeRoy. "Willie is here, and he—"

LeRoy jolts upright and points to the door. "Get out!"

"But—"

"Out!"

Yikes. Okay. Okay. I retreat as fast as I can. This is not how I anticipated the visit going. "Has he always been so mean?" I ask Willie as we power walk down the hall towards the exit.

"Not usually."

"He did lose his freedom and his best friend all in the same week."

"So what? He needs to suck it up."

"You need to work on your compassion ..." my voice trails off as I realize every person we pass is glaring at me with an alarmed expression.

Oops.

I take out my cell phone and place it to my ear. "We need to tell him that I took his car."

"You heard him—he doesn't want visitors."

"But it's not right that he thinks he's lost his mind."

"Zoe?" A familiar voice hits my ear, and I turn around. It's Rosa from the library, holding a vase of sunflowers. "What in the world are you doing here?"

I snap my phone shut. "I came to visit someone. Are you here to see your mom?"

"I am, but it's fate that I ran into you." She thrusts the vase at me and digs through her purse, pulling out a ball of yarn, a wallet, ChapStick, a crossword puzzle, a cell phone, Tabasco sauce, and a stick of gum, until she finds what she's looking for. "Here you go." She hands me a crumbled flyer for a local authors event at the park. "A couple of your favorite authors will be there, including KR Tuss."

I gasp.

"Who is that?" Willie asks.

"She writes the Sizzling Firemen series," I reply in awe. I've read all her books, including *Hot Policemen*, *Hot Doctors*, and *Hot Baby Daddies*. The covers may have abs and pecs and smolders on them, and the language may be on the crude side, and my mother surely would be mortified if she knew what I was reading, but, *oh my*, can KR Tuss write a good romance. All her books end with happily ever afters, and I can't put them down until the heroine and hero have found each other—usually in an elevator, naked, but whatever.

Willie rolls his eyes. "You're kidding me, right?"

Rosa clenches her jaw and looks over her shoulder. "Did you hear that?"

Willie and I share a look. "Yes?" I say cautiously.

Willie goes up to Rosa and places his mouth directly at her ear. "Can you hear me?"

Rosa's eyes gloss over, and her arms erupt in tiny bumps. "Goodness me, I just got the chills. Anyway, I need a good turnout, so please plan to come."

"I'll be there." I hand Rosa back the flowers. "Have a good visit with your mom."

I walk out into the fresh air while reading the flyer. I've never met an author before. I'll have to make a list of questions for KR Truss. I open my briefcase and stick the flyer inside the *Reaching the Other Side* book.

"I can't believe people actually pay money to read that crap," Willie says.

"Which crap?"

"The medium book you're reading. You either see dead people or you don't. What's the point of a book?"

"Clearly there's a need. Not only do I love it, but someone has read it before me because pages have been dog-eared and multiple paragraphs are underlined with pencil."

"Yeah, yeah, yeah. I don't care. What time is it?"

I check my watch. "It's three thirty."

"Let's call Betty."

"Why don't we call her from home," I say with a yawn. "I'm tired."

"Yeah, I can tell. You look like crap."

"Thanks."

"You'd look better with cute shoes."

"Get off the shoes!"

CHAPTER FOURTEEN

"Six, seven, eight, five, four, eight," Willie says. He's lying on the ground of my parents' bedroom staring up at the ceiling.

I type in the numbers. "Denied access."

"Six, seven, eight, five, four, nine."

I type in the numbers. "Nope."

Willie spouts off another set of digits from the list. Over the last four days, we've tried three hundred numerical combinations. The autopsy results haven't been released, the detective hasn't been in contact, LeRoy put a "no visitors" sign on his door, and I called in sick to my imaginary job because today is Monday. Nothing happened over the weekend, and I want to be readily available if Betty receives the autopsy results or if Daniel files the appeal.

I type in the next set of numbers, blinking hard as the digital display blurs.

Access denied.

"I'm done for now." I drag the chair back to the table and curl up on the couch with a blanket.

"The results should be in today. Don't you think? It

shouldn't take this long. He said the preliminary should have been in by Friday."

"Mmmhmmm." I pull the blanket over my head.

"Let's go find Betty," Willie says. "I want to get out of this house. We've been in here too long."

"Let me take a power nap first." I roll to my side and close my eyes. Jabba jumps up on the couch and decides to lie on my head. Not exactly comfortable, but I'm too tired to care.

"You've already taken one nap today."

"I need another."

Willie grunts, and Jabba hisses at him.

"That cat is possessed," he says.

"This coming from a ghost wearing a homburg hat."

"What does my hat have to do with anything?"

"Don't know."

"All this waiting is getting to me. I've been doing a lot of thinking, and I've come up with more people who could have killed me. I need you to write them down and give the list to Betty so she can hand them over to the detective. He thinks you're crazy, so it's probably best that it comes from her."

"Mmhmmm." I've already tuned him out.

"Zoe! Get up!"

Ugh. I move Jabba (much to his disapproval) and shuffle to my bedroom to get a pen and paper. I unlock my briefcase, and suddenly it blurs into two. I blink a few times to focus and shake my head.

I return to the couch and my blanket, cross my legs, and click the pen. "Who wanted to kill you?"

"I'm up to fifty people."

"Fifty?"

"I'm starting in nineteen fifty-two."

"Fifty?"

"Are you going to start writing or not?"

"Yes, but *fifty*? I don't even know fifty people, and you have fifty people who you think could have killed you."

"Start with Jenny Clark. We dated for six weeks. I had to break up with her because she had terrible breath."

"Why would she want to kill you?"

"Because I told her she had terrible breath. Someone had to."

I start to write the name down. "Wait. Is that the same Jenny Clark who owns the salon?"

"Yes."

I scribble out the name.

"What are you doing?"

"She's a sweet old lady. She does my mom's hair."

"So she's blind with bad breath?"

"Boundaries," I remind him.

"Yeah, yeah," he grumbles.

There's a faint dinging sound, and I sit up straighter. "Do you hear that?"

Willie listens. "Sounds like a phone."

"Whose phone?"

"Probably *your* phone?"

Oh. Right. In my briefcase is my cell. It rarely rings, and I forgot what it sounds like. A blocked phone number flashes across the small screen, and I flip it open. "Hello?"

"You have a collect call from a Trucker County inmate. Do you accept these charges?"

"Who is it?" Willie appears.

"Someone from jail." I don't know any inmates, but I accept the call anyway.

"Zoe!" The line is staticky. "Zoe, it's Betty. I need your help."

"*It's Betty*," I mouth to Willie and put the call on speaker. "Betty, why are you at the jail?"

"I've been arrested."

"For what?"

"Killing Willie." I can hear the fear in her raspy voice.

I fall against the wall and slide down to my butt. She can't be serious. "*Did* you kill him?" I ask in shock.

"No! I swear I didn't. At least ... I don't think I did. But they're saying I did. I don't know. Did I?"

Willie disappears while I scramble to collect my thoughts. "Betty, when were you arrested?"

"This morning," she says, there's a commotion in the background, and I can barely hear her. "Detective Manfreed came to my door with cuffs and told me that I was under arrest for the murder of Willie MacIntosh."

"Without any warning? Did they question you after I left the other day?"

"They asked me to come down to the station on Saturday after the autopsy results came in."

"Why didn't you tell me?"

"Because I spent the entire day at the station. They were questioning me in this tiny room for hours, Zoe. Hours! I was hungry and tired and confused. They kept asking me why I wanted to fill Willie's blood pressure medication two weeks early. Then they searched the entire house."

They searched the house *before* they arrested Betty. That's not good. I wonder what they found. "What did the autopsy say?"

"You have one minute left," an automated operator says.

Crud!

"Can you ask Willie if I killed him?" Betty says. "I don't think I did, but maybe it was an accident."

"No, Betty. You didn't kill him." I don't think. But who knows. "Where exactly are you?"

"I'm at the East Trucker jail in the sheriff's building."

"I'll be right there. Hold tight. We'll figure this out."

I hang up and clamber to my feet ... *whoa*. The world tips to the side, and I grab ahold of the dresser to regain my balance. Right now is not a good time to be sick. "Willie!" I call out as I rummage through my closet. "Where are you?"

Willie appears, seething. "This is Daniel's doing. I know it."

"Where'd you go?" I peel off my nightgown and deposit it on the floor, not even carrying about Willie, not that he's paying any attention to me.

"I tried to leave, but I can't. I made it down the street before I reappeared here." He paces the room, rubbing his chin, muttering to himself.

I pull on a pair of black slacks and slip into a black sweater, grab my briefcase, and shove my shoes on. We're out the door and make it to the stop sign at the end of the street before I realize. "We can't walk to East Trucker. That will take us all day."

Willie throws his hands up in the air. "Why can't you have a license and a car like a normal person?"

"This is no time to argue." In my periphery I see our neighbors at the end of the street standing in their driveway holding grocery bags and staring at me. I give a friendly "Hello" and wave.

They continue to stare.

I press one finger to my ear. "Bluetooth," I say to them. "Sorry."

They exchange a look then nod their heads and walk into their house. The wife peeks out through the blinds. I need to buy a real Bluetooth and keep it in my ear at all times.

Anyway, back to Willie.

"I have an idea," he says.

"What is your—yeah, okay, I'm coming." Willie has already taken off down the street.

"Why are we at *The Gazette?*" I place my hands on my knees and gasp for air. It was hard keeping up with Willie.

"Ask Brian to give you a ride."

"That's a terrible idea."

"My girl is in trouble. You need to hurry up." He disappears into the building, and I take a moment to catch my breath.

Ghosts are fast.

I pull the door a few times before I remember to push. The work area looks exactly as it did the last time I was in here. Everyone is mindlessly at their computer but in different clothes. No one pays much attention to me, and I push open Brian's door, sending it crashing against the wall.

He spins around in his chair. "Zoe?"

"Betty MacIntosh has been arrested ..." I pause to suck in a breath. "And I need to get down to the jail right now."

It takes a minute for this to sink in. "Let's go." He grabs his coat on the way out.

CHAPTER FIFTEEN

Okay. Play it cool, Zoe. Sure, you're in Brian Windsor's car. But it's no big deal. He's simply giving you a ride because you burst into his office like a total maniac and asked for one. It's no big deal.

Don't. Get. Weird.

As we pull out of the *Gazette* parking lot, I feel almost convinced that I'm going to blurt out something stupid (like the unfortunate glandular comment last week). Oh, gosh. I'm going to accidentally confess my feelings for him, or talk to Willie out loud, or make a comment about how Brian smells like fall leaves and orange zest and it's the most delicious aroma I've ever encountered.

Oh no, I'm going to be weird.

I can feel it.

It's coming.

I bite my lip to keep from talking.

Brian's car is much like his office—clean, organized, and Lysolled. Not a piece of lint or a speck of dirt, and the passenger seat is at a ninety-degree angle, which is uncomfortable, but I'm afraid to recline because everything appears in perfect order.

Well, everything except for the sullen-looking ghost in the backseat.

Don't. Be. Weird.

We turn onto the highway toward Trucker, and Brian adjusts the rearview mirror. I catch a whiff of his intoxicating scent and dig my teeth into my bottom lip harder.

"Do you know the case specifics?" he asks.

I decide it's best to stick to the facts and avoid chitchat. "The autopsy results came back Saturday morning," I say. "I don't know what they determined to be the cause of death, but Betty mentioned blood pressure medication, so I'm assuming they found large traces of meds in Willie's system. She was brought in for questioning on Saturday, the house was searched Sunday, and Betty was arrested this morning, but she claims she didn't do anything."

"Call Jackson Anderson," Willie says from the backseat. "Tell him to get Betty out of jail right now."

Right. Lawyer. I pull out my cell phone. Willie rattles off the number while I dial. A deep voice answers on the third ring, "This is Jackson."

"Hi. My name is Zoe, and I'm a friend of ... um ... Betty MacIntosh. Um ... she's been arrested and needs legal help."

"What kind of legal help?" Jackson is pleasant but brisk and sounds like he could do voiceovers for movie trailers.

"Errr ... murder," I say.

"I'm on my way." He hangs up without asking for more details like, gee, I don't know, *who* did she murder, *when* was she arrested, *what* jail is she in, *who* are you? Seems like important details. But I'm a medium not a lawyer. So what do I know?

"Who was that?" Brian asks.

"A lawyer for Betty." I snap my phone closed and slide it into my pocket. "Do you happen to have something to drink in here?" I twist around to see if by some miracle there's a jug of water sitting on the backseat, because I'm parched and my mouth tastes like pennies.

"No, but we can stop and get you a drink if you want," Brian offers.

"There's no time!" Willie bellows into my ear. "Tell him to pass this horse trailer in front of us. We're not even going the speed limit!"

I should not be dishing out driving advice. The last time I was behind the wheel, I nearly rolled the car and took out a sprinkler.

"Tell him!" Willie is still at my ear. "This road turns into a single lane soon, and we'll be stuck. Tell him to pass the horse trailer! Tell him! Tell him! Tell him!"

Gah! Fine. "Can you please pass this horse trailer? We're kind of in a hurry."

"Yes." He flips the blinker, checks over his shoulder, and eases into the left lane, going a solid four MPH faster.

Willie attaches the F-word to a variety of creative nouns, kicking at the front seat. I can feel his angst bubbling over, and it's causing my palms to sweat.

I turn in my seat to face Brian. My gosh, he has a gorgeous profile.

Concentrate, Zoe.

"Brian, can you please drive faster?" I ask politely.

He taps the gas, and we're now going sixty-five in a sixty zone.

Willie claws at his neck and pulls his tie loose. I fidget with my fingers, eying the time displayed on the dashboard. It's been almost an hour since Betty called, and we haven't crossed the Fernn Valley city border yet.

"This boyfriend of yours is a ..." Willie moves his hands helplessly. "Moron!"

"*No, he's not,*" I mouth.

"What was that?" Brian asks.

"Nothing," I say with a smile. "Nothing at all."

Brian returns his eyes to the road, and I slump in my seat, which is hard to do given its perpendicular state. He turns on his blinker and glides into the slow lane. I crack my knuckles one at a time, anxiety thumping around in my throat, until I can't take it any longer.

"Floor it!" I blurt out before I can stop myself. "There's an innocent woman in jail!"

Without a word, he steps on the gas, and we lurch forward, zooming across the city line and officially into Trucker County.

"Finally!" Willie says, exasperated.

Brian has his hands at ten and two and checks the rearview mirror every few seconds. I can tell disobeying traffic laws makes him uneasy. Not a bad quality in a man.

"Why are you so sure Betty's innocent?" he asks.

"Because I know she didn't kill him."

"How do you *know*? What information do you have?"

"Well, for starters, she's the one who ordered the autopsy. Why would she do that if she's the one who killed Willie? She wasn't home Monday morning when Willie died, and she has no motive. Sure, if he dies she gets his fortune, but it's not like he had years left to live anyhow, and it's not like she had to perform wifely duties either." I feel a bit like Sherlock Holmes. All I need is a hat and a pipe and a Watson. "Daniel MacIntosh, on the other hand, did *not* want the autopsy. He did have a motive, and I believe he killed Willie ... or ... erm ... I suppose it could be an alarming number of other suspects." I think about Willie's fifty-person list.

"What was Daniel's motive?"

"I'm glad you asked," I say and launch into the CliffsNotes version of what I know about Daniel MacIntosh. I end with, "There was a key stuck in the garage door lock Tuesday afternoon, and when we went back on Wednesday, it was gone. So was the hide-a-key."

"And Daniel knew where the hide-a-key was?"

Good question. I turn around and confirm this with Willie. He shrugs. "I don't know."

"What are you looking at?" Brian asks.

"Um ... nothing." I shift in my seat. "So ... um ... I'm not sure if Daniel knew about the key or not." Okay, so maybe I'm not exactly Sherlock Holmes. "But ... um ... there are also several golfing buddies and one neighbor who made death threats to Willie shortly before he died."

"That doesn't surprise me. Did you know Willie MacIntosh?"

"No," I say, crossing my fingers. Which I suppose I don't need to do. Technically, I didn't *know* Willie—past tense.

I know him now.

"He was the most obnoxious person I've ever met," Brian says. "And I grew up in Portland. I've met a lot of obnoxious people."

I cough to cover a laugh. Mostly because Willie has the most hysterical expression on his face—like he's just swallowed a fly. "He's got a lot of nerve. I never even met this man!"

I work hard to keep a straight face. "When did you meet Willie?" I ask Brian.

"I had lunch with him and LeRoy three weeks ago at the country club."

I glance back at Willie. He's avoiding eye contact. "I forgot about that," he says, playing with the end of his tie.

"All he did was talk about himself," Brian says. "About his boat, and his house, and wife, and his invention, and about all the amazing things he's done in his life. Seemed to me he was compensating for the fact that he wasn't all that interesting of a person."

Willie grabs at his hair. "This coming from the editor-in-chief of the most boring paper in the world! Aren't you going to say something, Zoe?"

Nope.

I just admitted that I didn't know Willie. I can't very well argue against Brian's impression.

So I decide to change the subject. "LeRoy was one of the people who threatened Willie right before he died."

This news surprises Brian. "That doesn't sound like something LeRoy would do. He and Willie have known each other since they were kids. Hell, during World War Two, Willie and LeRoy drove to Mexico to hideout and dodge the draft together."

Aha! Willie did go to Mexico to avoid the draft. I knew it. "Did LeRoy ever mention a woman Willie met in Mexico while he was there?" I ask in a whisper, hoping Willie won't hear.

"Yes, a woman named ... *Isabel*. Her father owned a chicken farm where LeRoy and Willie worked. From what I know, Isabel and Willie had a fling, but her father was adamantly against the relationship and kicked them both out. Willie went back to the states, joined the Navy, while LeRoy went down to Guatemala to wait out the war."

"Did Willie go back for her?"

"Yes, I did," Willie says. "She'd moved on. Like I said, I don't want to talk about it."

What a sad ending. "How do you know so much about Isabel and Willie?" I ask Brian.

"I found a picture of LeRoy, Willie, and Isabel in one of my uncle's photo albums once, and he told me the story."

"Did LeRoy ever talk about Betty?" I ask.

"I know he thought she was sweet and pretty," he says with a hint of a smile. "Not that you can blame him. She's an attractive woman."

I feel a stab of irrational jealousy.

Then I remember that Betty is in jail for the murder of her husband, and there's no time for feelings right now.

I blow out a breath, making an involuntarily raspberry sound with my lips. "Did LeRoy tell you that he witnessed Willie's will?"

Brian narrows his eyes, still watching the road. "When did this happen?"

"The week before Willie died."

"Willie altered his will the week before he died?"

"Odd timing, right?"

He nods. "A terrible choice on Willie's part. LeRoy has been on a mental decline for a while now. Talking to himself, mixing up dates and times, having trouble recalling recent events. He shouldn't be signing any legal documents."

Well, crap.

"That's part of the reason I moved here," Brian says. "So he wouldn't be alone."

Willie pushes his hat back on his head with a grunt. "This kid doesn't know what he's talking about. LeRoy is still sharp as a tack. And he doesn't deserve to be at MelBorne, that's for sure. Tell him, Zoe. Tell him! Tell him!"

Gah. I need to add *no more screaming in my ear* to Willie's list of boundaries.

I shoo him away. "LeRoy shouldn't be at MelBorne. It's not a good fit for him."

Brian gives me a quizzical look. "I wasn't aware you were well-acquainted with my great-uncle."

"I'm not! It's just ... that place is depressing, and it ... um ... seems like he would do better at home?" I feel intrusive butting into his family affairs, but I also don't want LeRoy spending his last days in a dark room staring at a blank wall.

"I offered for him to come live with me, but he declined,"

Brian says. "Between Willie's death and the car accident, he's been having a hard time. Honestly, I don't know how much longer he has left."

This news has me equal parts sad and terrified.

Sad that LeRoy is in an assisted living home. Sad that he's not himself. Sad that Brian will lose his uncle. Yet I'm terrified LeRoy will visit me after he dies. I'm still a little bitter that he ran me over with his car.

Also, isn't one grumpy-old-man ghost enough for one lifetime?

Brian takes the East Road exit and turns right onto W Street. We pass by news van after news van after news van. All parked along the side of the road with their satellite antennas up. A crowd is gathered on the front steps of the sheriff's station, with cameras and microphones pointed at an unseen target.

"Did they arrest a celebrity?" I ask, trying to see through the group of reporters.

Brian slows and leans over to get a better view out my window. He's so close I could lick him. Not that I would. But I could. If I wanted to. But I won't.

Don't lick him, Zoe.

I need to lay off the erotic novels.

"There aren't any celebrities around here, though." Brian pulls over and parks in a red zone, leaving the car running.

"What are you doing?" I ask.

He opens the glove compartment and pulls out a press pass. "I'm going to find out what's going on." He smacks the hazard button to turn on his emergency lights and gets out of the car.

Um, okay.

I stumble outside with my briefcase in hand. Brian disappears into the crowd, and I snake around the reporters, trying to reach the entrance, but find myself at the front of the press line instead.

Much to my horror, standing behind a podium is Daniel MacIntosh with his weasel face and slicked red hair. To his right is a petite woman with dark skin, silky hair streaked with gray, and expensive looking shoes on. To his left is a short man with a lightbulb-shaped head and rimless glasses. Further off to the side is Detective Manfreed.

Willie appears behind Daniel. He steps forward with a feral look in his eyes.

Oh, no!

"On behalf of the family, we would like to thank the Trucker County PD for their swift action and superb investigation into my uncle's death," Daniel says, reading off a paper in front of him. The petite woman places a supportive hand on Daniel's back, and I assume she is his wife. "We understand this will not bring Willie back, but we're happy that justice will prevail."

Willie plunges forward in a snarling rush and goes right through his nephew and lands in the pit of reporters.

I crumble into childlike panic. Unsure of what to do or what to say or how to help, but before I can dwell too much on the implications, my hand shoots up in the air, and my mouth is moving. "Betty MacIntosh is innocent! Daniel MacIntosh is the murderer!"

Everyone swivels their attention to me. Seven microphones appear an inch from my mouth. *Oops.*

Both Daniel and his wife appear to be in a complete state of shock. Until Detective Manfreed leans in and whispers something into Daniel's ear. I'm not sure what he said, but Daniel meets my gaze, and there's a murderous look in his eyes.

Gulp.

I barely notice the reporters firing off questions. *What's your name? How do you know Mrs. MacIntosh? How are you acquainted with the family? What makes you think Daniel MacIntosh murdered his uncle?*

"Everyone, calm down." Detective Manfreed has taken over the podium. "Calm down! I can assure you that we thoroughly vetted Mr. Daniel MacIntosh and are confident he had nothing to do with the murder of Willie MacIntosh."

"I have a question! I have a question!" a familiar voice yells from the crowd. I crane my neck to see who is talking. Brian steps forward with his hand raised. "Brian Windsor, *The Fernn Valley Gazette*. When did this interview with Daniel MacIntosh take place if the autopsy came back Saturday morning and you immediately brought Betty MacIntosh in for questioning and spent all day Sunday searching the MacIntosh home? Can you thoroughly investigate anything in such a short amount of time?"

Willie appears at my side. "I'm liking your boyfriend more now."

"According to my sources, there was a high amount of blood pressure medication found during the autopsy," Brian goes on. "Given the advance age of Willie, isn't it possible he accidentally took the medication?"

"Never mind," Willie says.

"The results of Willie MacIntosh's autopsy are classified," Manfreed says. "I don't know where you're getting your information."

"Isn't it true Betty MacIntosh was the one who ordered the autopsy and you, Daniel, were against it?"

My mouth drops open. Brian is repeating the information I gave him in the car!

"And isn't it true, Daniel MacIntosh, that you had no idea Betty and Willie were married? And that the day after Willie died, you tried to list his house for sale?"

Daniel starts to go after Brian. The man with the lightbulb head holds him back and leans into the microphone. "These allegations are absurd, and my client has no comment."

"A reliable source told me there were several death threats made to Willie MacIntosh over the last couple of weeks, yet I know you didn't interview these individuals."

Yeah, okay, I need to be careful about what I say to Brian. I cannot believe he's repeating everything I told him!

Manfreed grips the podium. "I don't know who your source is, but they're wrong. We are confident in our case against Betty MacIntosh. We will take no further questions."

The lightbulb-head guy grabs Daniel MacIntosh by the shoulders and directs him through a side door into the building.

Well ... that happened.

"We need to go to Betty," Willie says.

Right. Betty.

The reporters disperse to their various news vans, leaving a clear path to the door, and I run inside before anyone can question me about my allegations.

The lobby is beige, square, and gloomy. The linoleum floors are scuffed and faded, and the walls are chipped and smudged with dirt. There are a few professional-looking individuals scattered around the room, talking on their phones, but no one is in line. I walk right up to Window One and tap on the plexiglass. A policewoman with big bangs and dry lips slides open the window and stares at me as if she's already bored with our conversation.

"I'm here to see Betty MacIntosh," I say.

"You and every other person in the city."

"She probably put you on the visitors list," Willie says.

Good call. "I should be on the visitors list."

The policewoman grabs a clipboard. "Name?"

"Zoe Lane. Spelled without a *y*."

"You're Zoe?" a deep voice asks.

I jerk my head up and—

Holy moly!

A tall hunk of a man with a square jaw, dark skin, luscious black hair, piercing hazel eyes, and pouty lips is standing in front of me, and I forget how to speak.

"Great, Jackson is here. Let's get my girl out," Willie says and walks through the metal detector toward the guarded door.

Here's what I know about Jackson Anderson: he could be an underwear model.

I was expecting someone around Willie's age, but Jackson can't be much older than thirty—if that. And he could easily grace the cover of *Sizzling Fireman IV*, or any romance novel for that matter.

We shake hands, and he flinches at my touch—my fingers are numb, which tells me there are more spirits here, but the only one I see is Willie.

"Betty wanted to wait for you before we proceed," Jackson says. "Sign in, get your sticker, and we'll go back and see her."

I do as I'm told. I'm patted down by two officers wearing blue gloves. My briefcase is thoroughly searched, and I walk through the metal detector—twice—because I forgot to take off my watch the first time. I'm deemed safe and am escorted down a long hallway with hazy florescent lighting. Jackson follows. I have no idea where Willie is, but I suspect he's already with Betty. My suspicion is confirmed when the police officer opens the door to a small room and there's Betty sitting at the table in a blue jumpsuit, her hands clasped in her lap, face plagued with distress, and Willie sitting beside her.

"Zoe, you're here." Betty stands and opens her arms until the guard barks at her to sit down and not to touch anyone.

Geez.

"I got here as quick as I could." I take a seat on one of two chairs across from Betty. Willie is quiet and retreats to the corner with his hands shoved into the front pockets of his slacks.

Jackson plops his briefcase onto the table and pulls out a

leather-bound folder. "We're going to get you out of here," he says.

"Thank you," Betty sighs. "I can't believe this has happened. I'm ruined. Completely ruined. They're never going to let me back at the Teen Center. I'll never get a job with the county doing social work. I have a big paper due next week." Her breathing quickens.

I want to tell her she doesn't have to worry about any papers due, because likely she'll still be jail next week, but I don't think that will help.

"I should have just given Daniel all the money and walked away!" Betty slams the table.

"What reason do they have for arresting you?" I ask.

Jackson unbuttons his suit jacket and takes a seat, opens his folder, and clicks his pen. He moves with such precision that I wonder if he served time in the military. "There was a lethal amount of blood pressure medication found in Willie's system," Jackson says. "When they searched the house, they found the medication had been smashed and mixed in with a container of overnight oats in the refrigerator."

"Which is the last thing Willie ate before he died," I say, remembering out loud. "And what you made him every night." I look at Betty. "It's also how your psychic said he died."

Dang, I really do need her number.

"But I didn't put his pills in there!" she cries out.

"We could argue that you put the pills in there because Willie refused to take them on his own," Jackson says, writing this down on his paper.

"But I didn't put his pills in there!"

"They claim you were at the pharmacy Monday morning causing a commotion about needing to refill Willie's medication," Jackson says.

Betty fumbles with her fingers and takes a deep breath.

"Like I told Detective Manfreed, the reason I was upset at the pharmacy was because they wouldn't give me the medication. They had to call the doctor because it was too early for a refill. The doctor wasn't in and his front office staff wouldn't agree to refill it! Willie had just recently changed his blood pressure medication, and the doctor said it was vital that it be taken properly. Why would I put it in his oatmeal? He's not a dog or a child I needed to trick into taking medication. The truth is that I did not do it. Tell him, Zoe. Tell him what Willie said."

Jackson slides his gaze to me.

Please don't say it, Betty. Please don't say it, Betty.

"She's a medium," Betty blurts out despite my mental pleas. "She sees Willie. What is he saying right now, Zoe?"

I can feel Jackson's eyes beating into the side of my head. "Not much, actually," I say, mostly to the ground because I refuse to make eye contact with Jackson.

"A medium?" Jackson doesn't hide the skepticism from his voice.

Willie walks through the wall and disappears, which isn't like him. Makes me wonder if he questions Betty's innocence. Makes me wonder if I should question Betty's innocence.

Jackson clasps his hands together, appearing as if he's about to lead us all in prayer but silently studies Betty instead. "I've known you and Willie for a while. I know Willie was arrogant and outspoken, but I also know that he adored you, which is why I want to help. But I need you to be completely honest with me, because once I start digging, I will find the truth."

Betty stares him straight in the eyes. "I did not kill my husband," she says, unyielding.

Jackson picks up his pen. "Then who did?"

"Have you looked into Daniel?" I ask. "He had a clear motive."

"The police say he has a rock-solid alibi, but I haven't seen a transcription of his interview yet," Jackson says.

"There's also the key," I say. "The hide-a-key is missing, and on Tuesday it was broken in the garage door lock."

Jackson pauses with his pen poised and ready, his brow furrowed. "I don't recall seeing a broken key on the list of evidence the police recovered from the MacIntosh home." He looks to Betty, and she looks to me, and I look to Willie who is still nowhere to be seen.

"So ... um ... here's the thing. Someone came back and removed the key between Tuesday afternoon and Wednesday evening. So the police didn't have a chance to see it."

"But you did?" Jackson asks me.

"Well ... um ... here's the thing. I didn't actually see it, but I know it was there."

Jackson slides his chair back. "Can I talk to you in private?" He must be speaking to me since he's headed toward the door and Betty isn't permitted to leave.

So I follow.

We step outside, and Jackson closes his eyes, as if mentally composing himself, and I wait for him to finish.

"I don't know who you really are," he finally says, his voice measured. "But there is no such thing as a medium, and what you're doing to Betty is unacceptable. I know she believes in psychics and all that other bull, but Willie didn't, and I don't. You're nothing but an opportunist looking for fame and money. You are not allowed near my client. Do you understand me?"

"B-b-but Betty wants me here," I say.

"Because she believes you see her dead husband," he says as if he's explaining something very simple to someone very stupid. "I have zero tolerance for frauds. Do you think that you're the first person I've run into who sees *dead people?*" He hooks his fingers into air quotes. "Now, wait here."

I'm too shocked to protest. Jackson slips inside and returns with my briefcase, holding it between his forefinger and thumb like it's contagious.

"Take this," he says, and I do.

He steps back inside and closes the door behind him. I stand there, trembling in outrage. I'm tired of people calling me a fraud. I *can* see dead people, and I can prove it! I'm not sure how, but there's got to be a way!

Feeling indignant and determined, I grab ahold of the door handle, ready to burst in and give Jackson Anderson and his beautiful mug a piece of my mind, but an officer barks at me to leave, and I do as I'm told.

I mean, it's not worth being arrested over.

"How'd it go?" Brian asks as soon as I step into the lobby. At first, I'm pleasantly surprised he waited for me, but then I remember with a crash of my ego that I'm his informant on the case, so of course he wants to know about my visit with Betty.

"I'm not talking to you." I step around him and set my sights on the exit when suddenly the door blurs into two and I'm struck with a whoosh of vertigo.

"Zoe?" Brian grabs ahold of my arm.

I look around for Willie, but he's gone. "I-I-I'm fine," I say and close my eyes, attempting to regain my balance.

"Let's sit down," Brian says.

Good idea.

Brian ushers me to a row of chairs lining the side wall, and I plop down with my head in my hands.

"Water?" Brian asks, and I give a feeble nod.

He returns with a Dixie Cup of room-temp water. I'm not sure what has come over me. It must be the stress of the situation. My body isn't used to this much excitement.

I take a deep breath in through my nose and blow it out

slowly through my mouth. Inhale ... exhale ... inhale ... exhale ... inhale ... exhale ...

"Are you practicing Lamaze?" Comes a familiar voice, and I can't help but smile.

Willie is back.

I polish off the last of the water. The vertigo is gone, and I'm feeling better. "Thank you for your help, Brian. But I need to get going." I stand without assistance. Willie and I stride side by side toward the exit when I suddenly remember. "Um ..." I smooth out my sweater. "Can ... um ... you give me a ride?"

Brian grins, and my stomach does that fluttery thing, even though I'm upset with him. Stupid stomach.

"I'd be happy to." Brian spins his keys around his finger.

"But I'm not divulging anymore information about Betty MacIntosh." I pretend to zip my lips close.

"Fair enough." He holds open the door. "After you."

"I don't mind if I do," Willie says and steps ahead of me.

CHAPTER SIXTEEN

The car ride back to Fernn Valley is quiet. I'm too preoccupied for chitchat, which is good because Brian appears lost in thought anyway. Willie stares straight ahead with his hands on his kneecaps, feet planted on the floor, and back straight, like he's Forrest Gump waiting for bus number nine.

When we reach *The Gazette*, I see our van parked out front. Great.

"Why do your parents drop you off here every day?" Brian asks as he pulls into a parking spot.

I unbuckle my seat belt. "They think I work here," I say, because my brain is incapable of producing any more lies.

"Why do they think that?" Brian asks.

I give a relenting sigh. "Because I needed a job to get out of the house, but don't worry, I'll tell them the truth."

"So you're not working for another paper?"

I shake my head no, feeling hot in the cheeks and completely humiliated.

"Does Betty MacIntosh still think you're a reporter?" he asks.

I shake my head no and reach for the car handle.

"The internship is still open," Brian says.

I let go of the handle and gape at him. "Really? You want me to work at *The Gazette* ... Wait, is it just so I can give you inside information about Betty?" Admittedly, I'd still say yes even if it was. Not that I'd tell him anything. Lesson learned. But I'd love a job. Except ... I'm fairly certain "intern" is code for free employee, but at least it would be a step in the right direction.

"I don't expect you to give me any information unless you want to." He pauses and runs his finger along the stitching of the steering wheel. "I'm sorry about today. I thought the information you provided was on the record."

"Well, it wasn't." I hug my briefcase.

"I misread the situation, and I apologize." His tone is husky, and I feel a bit flustered.

"It's ... um ... well ... good. I mean, it's fine." I can't concentrate on what I'm saying. My heart starts beating more quickly, and I'm suddenly aware of every movement I'm making.

"Okay," he says.

"Okay."

"Good."

"Good."

"All right."

"All right."

Neither of us makes an attempt to exit the car. Instead, we sit there, side by side, eyes forward. There's a dumpster in front of us. It's a faded green color with the Fernn Valley Disposal logo stamped across the lid and trash bags piled to the top. Not exactly a lovely view, yet Brian and I are staring at it as if it's the most interesting thing we've ever seen.

I sigh.

He sighs.

We do this for a while until Brian gives a short laugh and leans on the console between us.

Willie slides to the middle seat in the back. "Hot damn! This fool wants to kiss you," he says, but even his commentary can't spoil the moment.

I meet Brian's gaze and tuck a loose strand of hair behind my ear. His eyes are glossed over, almost as if he's in a trance, but I know it's not Willie because he's still in the backseat, biting at his fingernails, watching with wide eyes. So perhaps it's me. He's entranced by me.

Brian puts a hand up to my chin and cups it for a moment, as if deciding what to do with it.

Okay, so I've never been kissed before. But I've read a lot of romance novels, so I know how it goes. I know that he will gently pull my face up to meet his, and our lips will touch, and our tongues will dance, and my insides will shrivel into a giant ball of passion, and my heart will explode into a billion pieces.

Except in my books the heroine's mother doesn't knock on the window and ask what's taking so long.

Which is exactly what happens.

Mom is standing outside, peering in, telling me to hurry up.

Willie covers his eyes and falls to his side. "We were so close!"

Yes, yes we were.

If looks could kill—my mother would be dead.

But she pays no attention to my death glare and pulls open the car door. "We're in a hurry, dear. Let's go." She grabs my briefcase off my lap. "Come, come."

My cheeks are burning red, and I can't seem to move. Like my butt has attached itself to the seat.

"Hi, Mrs. Lane." Brian gets out of the car. "How are you doing?"

Mom forces a smile. "We're doing well, thank you." She bends down. "Zoe?"

I feel so stupid but force my legs to move anyway. I step out of the car and yank my briefcase from my mother's grasp.

"I'll talk to you later," Brian says.

I'm too embarrassed to speak, so I give him a thumbs-up and stalk toward the van.

"Wait for me, dear." Mom has on a black pencil skirt and is having a hard time catching up. Dad isn't in the van, and I fling open the front passenger side door, toss in my briefcase, and jump in. Willie appears in the seat behind me, with his legs crossed.

"It's time to cut the cord," he says.

Agreed.

Mom slides into the driver's seat and locks the doors. "How was your day?"

I don't want to speak to her. There's no point. So I pull my seat belt on and keep my mouth shut. Mom doesn't press for more details and starts the van.

"We sold the Attwood house," she says in an effort to start conversation.

I don't respond.

"It was a hard sell, too. Only has *one* bathroom and the kitchen was outdated, but we managed to find the perfect buyer." She smiles at me, but I keep my focus on my shoes.

Mom continues to go on and on about the Attwood listing as if I care, when in reality, I don't. I'm too busy plotting how I can break free from her tightly wound parental cord and start living my own life. Kiss boys and go to work. Even drive!

Note to self: go the DMV this week and start the necessary steps to obtain a driver's license. Also, find out what the cost of living is in Fernn Valley.

"May Day. May Day. May Day," Willie is chanting. "Houston, we have a problem!"

I peer up and notice we're nowhere near home but on a bumpy back road that I've never seen before. "Where are we going?" I ask.

"We're running a quick errand," Mom says with a forced smile.

She's lying. I can feel it. The S name is flashing in her head, and panic rises inside of me.

"Tell me where we are going," I demand.

Behind a bend in the road, I see a two-story Victorian-style building with a sign out front: *Fernn Valley Mental Care*.

"Stop the car!" I unlock the door, and Mom locks it again, her finger on the button, ready to strike.

"It's nothing to be upset about, Zoe," Mom says. "I did a tour this weekend, and it's a lovely place."

I press unlock, and Mom locks it again.

We do this for a while. Unlock. Lock. Unlock. Lock. Unlock. Lock.

Curse you, stupid automatic locks!

"You're not well, sweetie," Mom says. "We know everything. We know that you've been going around town talking to yourself. We know about the press conference today, and when I contacted Beth to talk about her possible listing, she told us you didn't have a job at *The Gazette*. Honey, it's not your fault, but you must let us help you."

This is not happening. This is *not* happening!

Even though it's proven to be a futile exercise, I press *unlock* again, and Mom quickly locks the door. I'm trapped! The panic rises up inside of me, and I unbuckle my seat belt, unsure of what to do. "Does Dad know?" I ask. Surely he wouldn't be okay with my mother taking me hostage.

Mom's mouth pinches tight which answers my question. He doesn't know. "There are counselors here that can help you," she says, her voice laced with concern. I realize she's doing what she thinks is best for me, but I cannot go to a hospital. Not now. Not when Betty is in jail.

Not ever!

"We need to get out of here!" Willie is outside the van pulling at the handle to no avail.

"Stop the car and unlock the door," I demand.

"No."

I break out into a sweat, my heart slamming against my chest, and I search the car, looking for something—anything—to help me escape. There's a water bottle in the cup holder. That will have to do, I decide. I grab the bottle and throw it toward my mother. It bounces off her forehead. She swerves off the road and is distracted enough for me to unlock the door, push it open, and fall out of the car. I roll down a slight embankment and land in a freaking rose bush.

Ouch!

"Let's go!" Willie says. "Get up!"

I scramble to my feet and take off toward the woods. Mom shuffles after me with her legs still stuck together by her tight skirt, which works to my favor because we lose her quickly but keep going for good measure. I want to put as much distance between that hospital and me as I can.

When we reach the main road, I grab ahold of a tree and stop to catch my breath.

"That was a close one," Willie says. "That woman is crazy."

"She's not crazy," I say between gasps for air. "She just thinks I am."

"What are we going to do now?" he asks.

I have no idea. I can't go home. I'm not going to call my dad for help and pit my parents against each other either.

"Keep going, I guess." I swallow a few times, take a few breaths, and let go of the tree. We follow the road but stay hidden among the trees in case my mother drives by.

What a mess.

Just when I think my life has spiraled out of control—it spirals even more. And I have no idea what to do. My briefcase is in the van along with my wallet. I have my phone on me but no one to call.

Willie kicks at the dirt. "You okay, kid?"

"No." I pull a twig out of my hair. "Are *you* okay? You've been awfully quiet since we arrived at the courthouse."

"I've been thinking, that's all."

"About what?"

"Life," he says reflectively. He's taking the news of his murder much better than I thought he would.

But then again, since the moment he arrived he's maintained that there was nothing natural about the way he died. He's known all along he was murdered, and I'm the one who refused to believe him.

Lesson learned.

"Do you think Betty did it?" I ask him.

"I don't think so," he says. He's so calm and soft spoken. It's very un-Willie-like, and frankly, it's freaking me out.

Or perhaps I'm freaked because the sun has set and I'm walking through the woods with a ghost.

The leaves crunch under my shoes, and I can hear an owl's "hoo-hooo" in the distance. I jump when a small creature darts from under a bush and scurries across the ground and up a tree. Likely a squirrel, but my mind conjures up all kinds of paranormal possibilities, and I know the only way I'm going to get through this night trek is if we keep talking.

Unfortunately, Willie is not up for conversation.

"Do you think it was Daniel?" I ask.

"Not sure."

"Do you want to talk about the list of fifty people? We can ... um ... go through each name and why ... you um ...think it's them ..." Another small creature darts in front of me, and I nearly soil myself.

"It's none of them," Willie says.

"How do you know?"

He doesn't reply.

"Willie?" I ask. "Do you know who killed you?"

He runs a hand down his face. "I'm working it out."

I don't know what this means, so I say, "I don't know what you mean."

He lets out a relenting sigh. "I always liked puzzles."

"Okay?" I'm not a fan of his newfound ambiguity. "If you know who killed you, then you need to tell me. I could relay the information to Jackson Anderson, even if he thinks I'm nuts. What's with him, anyway? Do you only surround yourself with beautiful people?"

Willie laughs.

"It's not funny," I say. "He called me a fraud and told me to stay away from Betty."

Willie shrugs like this is of little importance.

"How can I help Betty if I'm not allowed near her?" I say.

"You'll figure it out. You always do."

"Since when did you become so ... so ..." I search for the right word. "So casual."

"I'm getting tired, kid. That's all."

"That's *all*," I repeat. "What do you mean? Can ghosts even get tired?" I'm struck with a horrid thought. Is this Willie's way of saying he's ready to go? Ready to cross to the other side? The thought brings on a wave of despair. Even though he has been a royal pain on multiple occasions, and even though I've found myself smack dab in the middle of a murder investigation, and even though he screams in my ear and curses and has way too many opinions on what I wear—I'll miss him terribly when he leaves.

"We're here, now what?" Willie says.

I look around. We've made it into town. The streets are bare, and the buildings are shut down. Fernn Valley doesn't exactly have a nightlife. Most places close at seven.

"I know where we can go," Willie says.

"Are you thinking about sleeping behind Butter Bakery? Because that's what I'm thinking." Mr. and Mrs. Muffin (when your last name *is* a baked good, you sort of have no choice but to own a bakery) throw out all day-old items before they close shop. Normally, I wouldn't eat out of a trashcan, but I'm starving.

"Nope." Willie points straight ahead to the only building with a light on—*The Gazette*.

CHAPTER SEVENTEEN

Banging on someone's window at night, while wearing all black, with twigs and leaves sticking out of your hair, and dirt smeared on your face, is perhaps not the best idea.

Unfortunately, I didn't realize that until *after* I had banged on the window, while wearing all black, with twigs and leaves sticking out of my hair, and dirt smeared on my face.

So I can't really blame Brian for calling the police.

"And you said you had car trouble?" Sheriff Vance confirms. The blue and red lights alternate across his face as he talks, making him look a hundred times scarier than he actually is.

"Um ... yes," I say, hoping he doesn't ask for more specifics because I don't have any—neither do I have a car nor a license.

Really, I should have come up with a better lie.

"I'm sorry, Vance," Brian says. "I didn't realize it was Zoe, otherwise I wouldn't have called."

Sheriff Vance rubs his protruding belly in slow, rhythmic circles. Like he's about to birth his donut any moment now.

It's unnerving.

"Okay," he finally says and gives me the once-over. "Are you working on the MacIntosh story?"

"We are," Brian says. "We've got a tight deadline."

Sheriff Vance nods his head but doesn't move. "What kind of car trouble did you say you had?" he asks me.

My stomach does an almighty flip.

"There ... um ... was ... a ..."

"Flat tire," Willie says. "Tell him you had a flat tire, but you were in such a hurry to get back that you didn't have time to change your clothes."

I relay this story to the sheriff. I'm not sure if he's buying it or not, but at least he's inching toward his car now.

"Have a good night," Brian says with a wave.

"You too." Sheriff Vance turns around and saunters back to his car, stealing one last glance our way before driving off.

"What's his problem?" Willie asks.

I have no clue.

"And your boyfriend is a sissy," he says, sounding more like himself. "If there was a crazed person pounding on my window, I'd handle it like a man." Willie closes one eye and holds a pretend rifle up and fires two shots.

Oh, geez.

"Sorry about that," Brian says. "You scared me, but I'm glad you're here." He opens the door for me. "You have to see what I found."

I follow him through the workspace and into his office. It looks exactly the same as the last time I was here, except for the large chalkboard in the middle of the room with notes scribbled in barely legible writing. It looks like some sort of family tree made with circles and connecting lines. Willie's name is written in the middle circle with lines and smaller circles coming off of it. Betty, Jackson, LeRoy, Daniel, Ron, and a big question mark fill the smaller circles.

"Wow, you've been busy." I plop down on the chair and resist a moan. My legs, back, neck, and head are throbbing, and I would kill for a hot bath, four Advil, a cheeseburger, and a two-week nap.

Brian grabs a piece of chalk. "There hasn't been a murder in Trucker County since two-thousand-and-three. This is big news. Tomorrow's paper is already printed, but I can print a special edition."

That's a long time without a murder. "When was the last time there was a murder in Fernn Valley?" I ask, curious.

"Over fifteen years ago."

"Let's concentrate on my murder, please." Willie studies the board with his hands on his hips. "What's with the question mark?"

Not sure. I ask Brian.

"You said a neighbor made a death threat, but I don't have the neighbor's name," he says. "You also said Willie's golfing buddies had made death threats." He points to each circle as he speaks. "LeRoy, Ron, and Jackson played golf with Willie at least twice a week. Then there's Betty and Daniel."

"Arnie," I say. "His neighbor's name is Arnie."

Brian erases the question mark and writes Arnie in all caps. "I've been on the phone for hours with various contacts at the police station and friends of the suspects." Brian returns to his desk and shuffles through a pile of papers. "According to my sources, Daniel and his family were in Mammoth all weekend."

"But that doesn't mean anything," I say. "He could have hired someone to kill Willie."

"Exactly."

"Zoe!" Willie hollers over his shoulder. He's still studying the board. "Come here."

I do as told. Willie points to Daniel's bubble. "Why does it say boat under his name?"

Good question. I ask Brian.

"According to Daniel's friends and neighbors, Daniel has

been making big purchases lately. Bought a boat, motorhome, remodeled his kitchen, and is currently getting bids for a new pool. And he's been telling everyone about his big inheritance that is coming soon."

What a weasel. I'm liking Daniel less and less. Who spends their inheritance while the person they'll be inheriting it from is still alive? It's just poor manners. "Is this *friend* going to tell the police?" I ask.

"No, but I'm printing it. The jury of public opinion, especially in a small community like this, can hold more weight than anything the police say." He talks with such childlike excitement I can't help but smile. This is a far cry from the potholes, new trees, and "Squirrel of the Month" articles typically printed in *The Gazette*. He did say he wanted to "shake things up" around here.

Murder *is* a big shake-up.

"There's still so much to do before we go to print," Brian says. "I haven't been able to come up with plausible motives for Ron and LeRoy." He slides his gaze to me. "You never told me *why* they made a threat. Care to share now?"

"I thought the internship was mine whether I gave you details or not."

"It is. But if you know how to connect a few of these dots, it could make for one compelling story." He smiles, showing his teeth, and what nice teeth they are.

Fine.

Problem is, though, that I don't remember why LeRoy and Ron were angry with Willie.

I'm hungry.

I have a hard time thinking when I'm hungry.

Good thing I have Willie here to recall the details. "Ron and Willie got in an argument about Betty," Willie is whispering into my ear, and I repeat out loud. "He didn't approve of our relationship ... I mean ... of Betty and Willie's relationship. Not that I gave a damn ... I mean ... not that *Willie* gave a damn."

Brian writes this down under Ron's name.

"You need to speak in third person," I mutter under my breath to Willie.

"What was that?" Brian asks.

"Nothing. Nothing at all. I was just thinking about Jackson, you wrote down that he might have been in love with Betty. Therefore he had a motive to kill Willie. I observed Jackson and Betty together today, and I don't think he has strong feelings for her. I mean, it's possible." Since every able-bodied man in the area seems to be in love with her. "But he could have killed Willie because they were both jerks."

"Being a jerk isn't a good reason to kill," Brian says.

"Is *any* reason a good reason to kill?"

"Touché." He writes *jerk* beside Jackson's name.

Willie shakes his head. "Jackson Anderson is a terrible golfer but a decent human. You're getting this all wrong."

"We can probably take LeRoy off this list." Brian draws a big X over his name. "Which leaves us with Arnie, Betty, Daniel, Jackson, and Ron."

"I don't think you can completely dismiss LeRoy," I say. "He *did* threaten to kill Willie." And he ran me over with his car.

"I suppose you're right." Brian erases the X and rewrites LeRoy's name. "We have Betty, Daniel, Ron, Jackson, LeRoy, and Arnie. Really, Betty is the main suspect here."

I feel like saying, *no duh*! Betty is obviously the main suspect—she's in jail pending trial for the crime! But *duh* isn't a very intelligent answer, and I don't want to insult him.

"According to sources, she accompanied him to every doctor's appointment." Brian is tossing a piece of chalk up in the air as he talks. "She made the oatmeal he ate. Do you know where she was Monday morning?"

"Running errands and trying to fill Willie's blood pressure medication," I say.

Brian writes this down. His chalk is down to nothing but a pebble, but he keeps going.

Willie takes a wide stance and strokes his chin, studying the board. There's something new troubling him—I can feel it—but I can't ask in front of Brian. I need to get Brian out of here.

For lack of a better idea, I start coughing. But Brian doesn't notice. So I cough louder, adding in theatrical gasps for air.

"Are you okay?" he asks.

"Water," I rasp out. "Need water."

Brian reaches under his desk and produces a plastic water bottle. "Here you go."

Crud.

"Um ... do you have ... ice?" I pause to cough into the crook of my elbow. "It helps ... *cough, cough* ... my ... *cough, cough* ... throat."

"Ice water?" he repeats.

I fold over in a coughing fit.

"Okay, I'll get you ice." He hurries out of the room, and I turn to Willie.

"What's wrong?" I ask.

He's still stroking his chin. "It's sad to think that I spent a great deal of my time with the names on this board, and yet, there's a good chance one of them killed me. Except Arnie, I didn't spend much time with him. He's an idiot."

"Do you have a hunch as to who it might be?"

"I've always known that it wasn't Betty," he says, his voice low.

I want to ask him if he's sure, but he was sure about being killed, and I decide to trust him.

Brian returns with a cup of ice water in a red Solo cup, and I remember to cough.

"*Cough ... cough ...* thank you." I take a sip. The water goes down the wrong tube, and I hunch over in a real coughing fit.

"Seriously, person," Willie grumbles. "This guy is never going to kiss you if you're spitting everywhere."

I pound my chest with my fist, take a few more sips of water, cough twice more, and I'm good to go.

Hold on.

... cough ... cough ...

Okay, now I'm good to go.

Brian and I spend the next hour combing the internet, looking for more information on Daniel, Betty, and Ron. We find out that not only is Ron married, but he was just named chiropractor of the year for Trucker County. Not exactly a huge accomplishment given there are three chiropractors in the county, but it's still something. The most concerning information is that he was born in 1984, which means his parents were well aware they were naming their child after a burger chain. We're having a hard time linking Ron to the murder. Sure, he was angry with Willie, but did he have a motive?

We put a big question mark next to his name.

The hardest part is the key. Who knew about it? Who could get in the gate? This points to Arnie, Betty, Daniel, LeRoy, but then Willie thinks he may have given Ron the code to his home before, and it's possible he knew about the key.

The computer screen is getting fuzzy, and my eyelids droop. I'm exhausted.

"Why don't I give you a ride home," Brian says.

Home.

Right.

I'd almost forgotten about my mother's attempt to commit me. I can't go home. But where else can I go?

At the very least I should call my dad to let him know that

I'm alive. I don't want him worrying. My cell is still in my pocket, and check to see if he's called.

I have ten voicemails.

TEN!

Nine of which are from my mother, which I don't bother listening to. But the tenth one is from a number I recognize.

I press play. "Zoe, it's Betty. I'm home now. Can you please come over right away when you get this? It's important."

The message was left fifteen minutes ago.

Jackson is a good lawyer if he managed to get Betty out of jail. I thought for sure they'd deny her bail based on many factors. One of which is that they believe she is a *murderer*.

"Who was that?" Brian asks.

"You up for another ride to Trucker?"

CHAPTER EIGHTEEN

Betty walks in from the kitchen carrying a tray piled high with enough food to feed a small army. She's wearing gray sweatpants and an oversized pink sweatshirt. Her nose is red and raw, eyes are blood shot, and her blonde hair is in a loose ponytail.

She looks equal parts terrible and beautiful.

"You don't have to feed us," I say, and snatch several grapes before she's even set the tray down on the coffee table. Betty knows how to put on quite the spread—blocks of cheese, crackers with bits of fruit in them, deli meat draped into thirds, apricot jam, and candied walnuts.

Brian politely declines, claiming he's not hungry.

I understand why he's hesitant to eat food provided by a woman who is currently awaiting trial for poisoning her husband's breakfast, but if Willie says Betty didn't do then—*bon appétit!*

"It's the least I could do. I appreciate you coming over. It's been an awful day, and I don't want to be alone right now." Betty curls into a ball on the couch and pulls her sweatshirt over her legs. Daisy is there, panting at her side. "Plus I like feeding people ... *oh*." She grimaces. "I guess I shouldn't say that in court! What a mess!"

I'd comfort her, but my mouth is full.

Willie is outside, pacing along the back walkway, mumbling to himself while stroking his chin. He's working through something. What? I don't know. We haven't been alone long enough for me to find out.

"How are you holding up?" I shove another cracker into my mouth.

"Jail is just so awful," she says. "They made me stay in this small room with glass walls. And I was all by myself. There's no private toilet, and the guards have to watch ..." She looks so appalled and defeated that I feel bad I'm sitting over here stuffing my face.

I slide my plate onto the coffee table and wipe the corners of my mouth with a napkin.

"It's called The Bubble," Brian says. "It's a jail within a jail, specifically for dangerous or high-profile inmates."

"Whatever it's called, it's horrible! I don't ever want to go ... back ..." A single tear slides down her face. "I seriously didn't kill my husband. I wouldn't even think to put his medication in his oatmeal. I'm not smart enough to come up with something like that!"

I move to the couch. "Sure you are, Betty ... I mean ..." Oh, geez. That didn't sound right. Never mind. "Jackson will figure this out. We've been working on it as well."

Betty pulls the sweatshirt over her hand and uses it as a Kleenex. "You have?" Her blue eyes are wide and hopeful.

"Mmmhmmm, we've come up with a number of possible suspects. Haven't we, Brian?" I look to him for reassurance.

He moves to the edge of the chair Willie died in and clasps his hands. "If you didn't do it, then who did?" He asks, and I shoot him a look.

On the car ride over, I was quite specific when I said he could come inside so long as he promised to keep this visit off the record and not ask too many questions. I don't want my ghost-seeing abilities to come up, and the last thing Betty needs right now is another interrogation.

Except ... I still have Betty by the hand, and I can feel her pulse quicken.

"Do you know who did it?" I ask.

"No, of course not." She yanks her hand free and starts cleaning up, grabbing my empty plate and scooting off to the kitchen.

She's lying.

If she knows who did it, then why wouldn't she just say so?

Unless she's protecting someone she cares about. Which would discredit the Daniel theory. Betty doesn't like Daniel. She told me multiple times when we were filing the paperwork last week.

Unless she's being blackmailed.

Although, if Daniel had something on Betty, I'm sure he would have played that card by now. He's counting on Willie's money. Who else would blackmail her?

I'm so deep in thought that I don't realize Brian is talking to me.

"Huh?" I ask.

"I said, what do you suppose that is?" He points to a porcelain sculpture thing on the coffee table. It looks like a blob, but is probably worth six-figures.

"If you squint your eyes, it kind of looks like an elephant."

Brian picks up the art and examines it under the light. "It has a hole in the top. It could be a glorified pen cup?"

Oh, pen!

That reminds me.

"What are you doing now?" Brian asks.

I'm on my hands and knees, searching under the couch. Then I shove my hands along the sides of the cushions. "I'm looking for a silver pen. I left it here the other day."

"What does it look like?"

I give him a look. "It's silver, and it's a pen."

"Right. I'm tired."

Me too. I check my watch. It's nearly midnight.

I move to the chair and lift the cushion. Voilà!

"Found it," I say as I put the chair back together.

"Check this out," Brian says. He's looking under the chair Willie died in, using his phone as a flashlight.

I drop to the floor. Stuck to the upholstery netting is what looks like a small, silver golf ball. I grab it and sit up. Upon further examination, I determine it's a cufflink.

"This must have been Willie's." I show it to Brian. "This is the chair he died in."

Brian shines his light on the cufflink. "You'd think the police would have found it if they searched the house."

"They obviously didn't search the chair."

"That's mine!" Willie yells, and I scream in fright.

"What's wrong?" Brian touches my arm gently. "What happened?"

Betty runs in from the kitchen, drops to her knees, and grabs my face, holding it tight between her hands. "Are you hurt?"

"I'm fine." I hold up Willie's cufflink like it's a trophy. "I've found this!"

Betty grabs the cufflink, her brows knitted together. "Thanks," she draws out the words, as if not sure what to make of my discovery. Then she folds into the fetal position and sobs.

Um ...

Brian taps my shoulder. *"We should go,"* he mouths.

I can't leave Betty now, not in this state. That wouldn't be right. I can't go home either.

Hmmm ...

"This is my favorite guest room." Betty flips on the light—and not just any light—a dramatic crystal chandelier, which hangs above a queen-sized bed covered in more pillows than I can count. All cream and gold with long tassels. The room is lovely and romantic. If only Brian hadn't decided to go home and leave me here, we could have picked up where we left off in the car. Maybe on that chaise lounge at the foot of the bed.

Hey. Hey.

"Wipe that goofy grin off of your face," Willie says. "And be grateful she's letting you stay here. That bed has never been slept in."

"Why not?" I ask him when Betty moves to the attached bathroom.

Willie shrugs. "Never had too many guests."

"Then why have this beautiful room *for* guests?"

Willie shrugs again. "I'm rich."

Oddly enough, this feels like a perfectly reasonable explanation.

Betty returns with a bathrobe and two towels. "Here you go." She drapes them over the side of the lounge chair. "If you need anything else, please don't hesitate to ask me. I'm two doors down on the right."

"This is great, thank you."

"No, thank *you*." She *boops* my nose with the tip of her finger. "I wouldn't have been able to do this without you."

This is true.

But not in the way she thinks.

If I hadn't interfered, the police wouldn't have had a reason to look into Willie's death, Betty wouldn't have ordered the autopsy, she wouldn't have been arrested, and she wouldn't be out on bail right now awaiting trial for murder. At worst, she would have lost half her fortune to Daniel and be forced to live the rest of her life on a tight one-hundred-and-fifty-million-dollar budget.

Betty and I say goodnight, and I close the door behind her. "What now?" Willie asks.

"Is sleep not an option?"

"I guess." He rolls his eyes.

I grab the towel and burry my face in the soft fabric and inhale the sweet, calming scent.

"Are you smelling my towels?" Willie asks.

"They smell like I'm standing in a field of lavender and," I take another whiff, "yet it also smells like I'm standing on the beach with my toes in the sand and the ocean breeze on my face."

"You're weird."

"Mmmhmmm." My towels smell like Tide and the fabric is rough and scratchy from years of being tossed around in our old washing machine.

"Seriously, person. Step away from the towel. We need to go check on something."

"Fine." I take one more whiff with my eyes closed. Man, how I wish I were on a beach right now. I let out a sigh. "Okay. Where are we going?"

CHAPTER NINETEEN

I follow Willie down the long staircase, past the library, and past the office, and past a powder room, and past a closet, and into his bedroom. It looks exactly as it did the last time I was in here. Same bed. Same worn recliner. Same deer head staring at me. Same bad feeling.

Someone with a dark spirit was here. My eyes slide to the pills lined up on his nightstand. The blood pressure medication is gone. The police must have taken it. Whoever killed Willie was in here messing with his pill bottles. Which is why I had the bad feeling the first time I came in here.

I'm momentarily paralyzed, in awe of how powerful this gift I have is. Now I just have to figure out how to use it properly.

"What are you doing?" Willie asks.

"Nothing ..." He already knows he died of an overdose of medication. Why state the obvious? "What are we doing in here?"

"This way." He waves for me to follow him into his closet. I flip on the light, and they come on one by one, illuminating his impressive suit collection.

"Did you wear all these?"

"No."

"Then why have them?"

"Because I'm rich."

"Yeah, okay. What are we looking for?"

"Pull that open." He points to the third drawer under his shoe rack.

I do as I'm told and reveal a long tray of cufflinks in every shape, size, color, and some look like they have *real* diamonds in them.

Wow.

"This is impressive," I say. "And I'm guessing we're looking for a golf ball?"

"Exactly."

I scan the drawer, and my eyes land on the small golf ball identical to the one I found under the chair. Except there are two.

"Dammit!" Willie punches the air. "Dammit! Dammit! Dammit! Dammit!" He rips the hat off his head and slams it on the ground.

I feel like I'm missing something here. But I wait for him to finish before I ask.

"I died on a Monday," he replies, as if this explains everything.

"I'm not following."

"Don't you see ..." he jerks his hands around. "I wear those to the club. I don't go to the club on Mondays. I wasn't wearing cufflinks when I died."

"Okay."

"So there's no way this fell off of me when I died."

"Still not getting it. Sorry."

Willie grunts. "Listen to me, person. I don't lose things. Never have. Never will. That right there"—he points to a pair of small gold cufflinks—"I've had those since nineteen fifty-five.

Look!" He pulls his cuffs out of his jacket and shows me the same cufflinks. "They're the first pair I bought."

I'm trying, really, really, *really* hard to understand where he's going with this. "Are you saying that the golf ball cufflink didn't belong to you?"

"Yes!"

"B-but, you have golf ball cufflinks."

"I have two!"

"Betty could have put it back after she left my room."

"No, she didn't."

"But you said it was yours," I remind him. "You yelled it into my ear."

"That was before I thought about it. I have these golf ball cufflinks, but so do several other people."

Oh! Okay, now I'm getting it. He's saying this cufflink fell off the person who killed him. Which seems like a long shot, but I'm going to trust Willie's instincts. "Like who?"

He directs his gaze to the ground. "My golfing buddies. I bought a pair for Ron, Jackson, and LeRoy last year for Christmas. Right before Betty started working at the club."

Willie's anguish is palpable, and I wish I could give him a hug.

"But couldn't it have fallen off one of them when they were here for a visit?" I ask.

"No," he says curtly. Anger rising up inside of him. "No, it couldn't have because none of those ungrateful pieces of crap have been to my house since Betty moved in. And Betty is the one who ordered those damn chairs!" He's up pacing again.

Okay, this is bad.

It would be far easier for Willie to accept that Daniel, who he never liked, who was desperate for money, who Willie never trusted, killed him. It's going to be difficult for him to accept the fact he was killed by a man he called his friend.

"No," I say. "I'm not giving up hope. There has to be a reasonable explanation as to why there was a cufflink under the chair." I close the drawer and hurry out of the closet, up the stairs, down the hall, past the guest room, and find Betty's door.

I grab the handle and jerk it open an inch, to make sure Betty's decent before I barge in. She's at the foot of her bed, sitting with her legs crisscrossed, talking on the phone.

"It was under the chair," she says.

The room is a mess, and there are bags on the floor. One from the pharmacy, two from Target, and a drawstring laundry bag from a place called Newsgate House. Betty said that she had gone to the pharmacy the morning Willie died and that she'd brought the bags up to her room before she went to check on him. So it's safe to say she went to Newsgate House that morning as well. I've never heard of it. Not sure it's relevant.

But what is relevant is the fact that the golf ball cufflink is sitting on the dresser near the door and *not* in Willie's closet.

"It could only be one then," Betty says. "You're right. But ... okay ... I will ... I love you, too."

My breath hitches in my throat. *I love you, too.*

She could be talking to her family about the cufflink *under* the chair.

Although, she did say that she didn't have any family.

"I'm coming," Willie says from the end of the hallway. "I am approaching you, and giving you plenty of warning, so you won't scream."

I carefully reach in and grab the cufflink. Betty doesn't notice, and I close the door and slowly release the handle.

"What are you doing?" Willie asks.

"Um ..."

"What happened? Where's Betty?" He disappears through the wall and returns. "She just turned on the shower. Go speak to her now."

"Um ..."

"Come on, person!" He walks through the wall again and reappears several moments later. "I don't see the cufflink, maybe you're right." His face bewildered. "She could have put it back. Go ask her. Ask her! Ask her! Ask her!"

I fold my hand tightly around the cufflink. "I'll wait until she's out of the shower."

"She's not going to take *that* long," Willie huffs as I walk toward my room. I close the door and lock it, the cufflink still hidden in my grasp.

"My head hurts." Which isn't a lie, it does hurt. Quite badly, actually. It's also past midnight. "I'm going to bed now." I push the mound of pillows off the bed and slip in, pulling the comforter up to my nose.

"You're not even going to shower first?" Willie says in disgust. "I'm sure you stink and are covered in cat hair. That's my brand-new bed."

"Betty's," I say. "This, all of this, now belongs to Betty."

"Tomato, *tomahto*. Who cares?"

I close my eyes and deepen my breath. Willie puts his face right up to mine, and I breathe deeper.

"There's no way you fell asleep that quickly."

My legs go cold, and I know he's sitting on them.

"Person! Wake up! This is important!"

I concentrate on my breathing and even add in a little snort for effect.

Willie finally gives up and stalks to the other side of the room. "Falling asleep while my murderer is out there," he mutters to himself.

If only I could fall asleep. I'm too afraid to let go of the cufflink, and my mind is too busy crafting a plan to find its owner.

CHAPTER TWENTY

For a while I can't even move. I lie there, dazed, and stare at the chandelier hanging above the bed. The early morning sun reflects off the teardrop crystals, making a mesmerizing rainbow on the ceiling. Sweat trickles down my forehead, and a spasm runs through my body. I close my eyes and breathe through the pain.

There is a chapter in *Reaching the Other Side* that talks about the physical toll communicating with spirits takes on you: headache, exhaustion, and even shivers. But nowhere does it mention hot flashes and body spasms. Nor does it say anything about blurred vision and nausea.

It could be the stress.

You know what, yes!

Of course it's the stress.

There's a key piece of evidence clasped in my hand, and I'm almost convinced Betty is having an affair. I think about Willie's face when he realized it was likely one of his friends who'd killed him. News of Betty's involvement will *crush* him. Which is why he can't find out. At least not until I know the details. Not until I know for sure.

The problem is wherever I go, he goes.

Case in point: I roll upright and sit on the side of the bed, waiting for my equilibrium to catch up, and there is Willie. Standing in front of me with arms crossed, foot tapping, mouth set to a line.

"Go talk to Betty now," he says.

I check the clock. It's six a.m. "I'm sure she's still asleep."

"Then wake her up!"

"Give me a minute." I shuffle to the bathroom, grabbing one of the towels on my way, and shut the door. Willie impatiently waits outside.

No bathroom—it's one of our boundaries.

I stand at the sink and stare at the mirror. Oh, geez. I look terrible. My face is pale, my eyes red-rimmed, my hair ... *oh, my hair* ... it looks like a poorly constructed beehive with ... what the heck? ... I yank a little twig out.

Ugh.

I should have taken a shower last night. There are probably fancy smelling shampoos and soaps waiting for me.

I check.

Yep.

A cherry blossom bath and shower gel made by a company I can't even pronounce—L'Occitane—which means it's probably worth more than my shoes. I pop open the cap and take a whiff. *Oh, my.*

Can you wash your face with shower gel?

Probably not a great idea.

But I do it anyway.

I tame my hair into a bun on the top of my head. My clothes are wrinkled, and I wet my hands and use them as a makeshift iron.

Better.

"Okay," I whisper to myself in the mirror. "Time to put on

your big girl panties and get to work. You can do this. You *will* do this."

My pants lack pockets. I guess this is when having jeans would come in handy. I slide the cufflink into my bra for safekeeping.

I suck in a breath and blow it out slowly. I do this a few times because for one, it feels good and two, I'm procrastinating. But if I don't leave soon, I'll lose the chance.

As soon as I swing open the door, Willie appears. "Took you long enough. Let's go talk to Betty." He starts for the door.

"No," I say, my feet planted.

Willie turns around slowly, weighted by shock. "What do you mean, no? This is your job. Go talk to her."

"No."

Willie is in my ear. "Go talk to her! Go talk to her! Go talk to her!"

I close my eyes and picture myself on the beach with my toes in the sand, ocean breeze on my face, and zero ghosts screaming in my ear.

Willie gives up and steps back, a tremor of shock passes across his face. "What is wrong with you?"

"I want you to leave."

He looks as though I've slapped him across the face. "Why?"

"I *want* you to leave," I say, my voice low and stern. It takes everything in me not to cry. But the truth is, I *do* want him to leave. I *need* him to leave for his own good.

Willie flickers slightly, as if he is shorting out. He appears so hurt and angry that I can't even look at him. I grab my cell phone and leave, knowing without having to check that Willie isn't following me. For the first time in over a week, I'm alone.

The silence is deafening.

But there's no time to dwell. I race downstairs, turn off the alarm (one-two-three-four), open the garage door, and flip on the lights. The sight of Willie's car collection causes my heart to plunge into my gut.

I can't believe I'm doing this.

Borrowing LeRoy's old, dirty clunker of a car was one thing; borrowing a Lamborghini is another.

The keys are proudly displayed on hooks above the light switch. I decide on the copper colored BMW i8. Out of all the cars, it's the only name I can confidently pronounce (should I need to defend myself in court). I grab the key—except it isn't a key. It's a fob with a touchscreen—and when I get in the car, I'm super confused on how to start the thing (never mind that it took me ten minutes to figure out how to get in the car, since the doors slide up—*Back to the Future*-style).

This car is way out of my league. It's muscular and digital, and there is *no* keyhole. None! There is, however, a button on the center console that says *Push to Start*. So I push it and ... nothing. The dashboard lights up, but I don't hear the engine. I press it again, and the dashboard turns off.

Well, this is frustrating.

I slam the brake pedal down and push the button. The dashboard lights up, but I don't hear the engine. I'm exactly three seconds away from throwing the stupid fancy fob out the window, except the window doesn't even roll down all the way!

"Okay, be smarter than the car," I chant to myself. "Smarter than the car."

I press the button once more. The dashboard lights up, but the engine remains silent. On the gearshift there is an option for *Eco* or *Sport*. Eco sounds safer, and the dashboard turns white. Okay, so maybe the engine starts when I put the car into drive?

Doesn't make sense, but I'm desperate.

Why can't Willie drive a freaking Honda?

I put the car into reverse and tap on the gas.

Aha!

I'm moving backwards ... wait. Wait! I slam on the brake and search the visor for the garage door opener. Found it. The garage door rolls open, and I try it again. I've managed to make it out of the garage, which feels like a small victory. Car in drive and ... *holy hell!*

I zoom down the driveway, pass all the mansions, and reach the community gate in less than thirty seconds. Wow. This thing is dangerous.

But hella fun!

With a big goofy grin on my face, I look over at the passenger seat, waiting for Willie's reaction when it hits me. He's not here.

I blow out a sigh and wait for the community gate to open. I ever so lightly tap on the gas, and I'm on my way. First stop is Newsgate House. I've never been there before, and I have no idea where it is. I'm sure there's a feature on this futuristic dashboard that would happily point me in the right direction (heck, it might even drive me there), but I don't have time to figure out how to use it. A quick stop at the gas station for directions and fifteen minutes later, I'm at Newsgate House—a bed and breakfast.

"Crud. I was hoping I'd be wrong," I say out loud and instinctually look at the passenger seat.

He's not there.

"This is for Willie," I say, out loud, again. A habit I'm really going to need to break.

Newsgate House is a yellow cottage with a cobblestone walkway, dormer windows, and jasmine growing on the white picket fence. I fall out of the car (there's no graceful way to enter or exit this thing) and pull the door closed.

"You've got this," I remind myself and pat my bra, where the cufflink is.

A bell attached to the door announces my arrival. The

inside of Newsgate is a jumble of several different styles—country chic, Victorian, there's a lamp in the corner that has a modern vibe to it, and the rugs are Persian. It's like the owners shopped estate sales and grabbed whatever furnishings were viable.

A tall, slender man wearing a cardigan with elbow patches and a pink bow tie emerges from the sitting area. "Welcome to Newsgate House. Can I help you?"

"Do you happen to have a gift shop here?" I ask.

Bow Tie Man shakes his head. "No gift shop, but there is a market around the corner."

My heart thunders. No gift shop means Betty wasn't here picking out a gift or buying new towels.

"Did you want to make a reservation?" Bow Tie Man returns to the sitting area and grabs a thick reservation book, licks his fingertip, and flips through several pages. "We had a cancellation for next week if you're interested."

"Um ... actually." I clear my throat. "My friend was here last week and ... well ... she sent me here because she left a ... um ... notebook. Yes, a notebook in the room and wanted me to get it. Her name is Betty MacIntosh."

Bow Tie Guy doesn't fall for it. "If a guest left a notebook, I would have found it. Sorry."

Right. Time for Plan B: the truth.

"Look, I need to see if Betty MacIntosh was here Sunday night or early Monday morning, and if she was, I need to know who she was staying with. She's currently awaiting trial for the murder of her husband, and I need this information."

Anyway.

So that didn't work.

After being asked to leave, I take a seat behind a bush across the street and wait for Bow Tie Guy to leave. Not exactly a great plan, but it's all I've got.

Finally, Bow Tie Guy emerges with a watering can, which he fills using the spigot on the side of the house. He's rhythmically tapping his foot and swaying his hips, and it appears there are earbuds in his ears. And once he pushes open the back gate, I realize this is my chance.

I cross the street—checking both ways for a car—and open the front door, using a stick to hold the bell up so it won't announce my arrival to anyone else who might be in the house.

Coast is clear.

I tiptoe to the living room and grab the reservation book. This thing goes all the way back to the 90s. I start at the end and flip backwards until I get to last Sunday and run my finger down the list of reservations until a name screams out at me.

Ronald McDonald checked in on Thursday and checked out Tuesday morning.

"Ronald Freaking McDonald!" I slap my hand over my mouth and listen for footsteps.

Nothing but silence.

Phew.

I return the book and tiptoe back to the door, using the same stick to hold the bell, and hurry down the cobblestone walkway back to Willie's car.

Ron lives in Trucker. What would be the point of staying in a hotel—more specifically, a romantic B&B—in the town you live in? And if Ron is married, why would he be staying by himself? Where is his wife? More importantly, why did Betty have a laundry bag from Newsgate Monday morning?

I don't have a definitive answer to any of these questions. All I have are assumptions.

And I'm assuming the answer is this: Betty stayed with Ron the night before Willie was murdered.

CHAPTER TWENTY-ONE

If Betty and Ron were having an affair, then both of them had motive to kill Willie. My gut still tells me Betty didn't do it, but my gut also told me to steal a hundred-thousand-dollar car, so I'm not sure how trustworthy my gut is this morning.

But I need more information on Ron, specifically, where he lives and where his office is. And while I don't know where he works, I do know where he plays golf on Tuesdays, and that seems like a good start.

The country club is located near the lake and looks like your average country club. Single-story building with vines growing up the sides. Clean landscaping and golf carts scattered everywhere. I'm fairly certain you need a membership to enter, which is problematic since I don't have one. Instead, I wait near the entrance for someone to walk in.

If Willie were here, no doubt he'd be impressed with my spying abilities. I'm practically James Bond. I mean, I've got the car.

Two older men with silver hair, each one wearing beige pants and a white-collared shirt, shuffle toward the entrance.

"Hello!" I jump up, and both men grab their chests.

Okay, so maybe I shouldn't have been quite so energetic.

"Oh ... um ... gosh ... I'm sorry," I say.

The first old man pounds his chest, while the second old man folds over into a dry, hacking, coughing fit.

I pat Man Two's back. "Should I go get help?"

Neither answer. Man One is still giving himself chest compressions while Man Two is too busy hacking up a lung. I guide them both over to the nearest bench, one on each arm. My plan was to strike up a conversation and casually follow them in—not to kill them.

Some James Bond I am.

"Now ... um ... stay here. I'll go get help." I run to the entrance and yank on the door. It's locked. I cup my hands around the window and see a man wearing beige pants and a white-collared shirt walking by. "Hello!" I pound on the glass. "Hello!"

The man stops and looks around, unsure of where the noise is coming from.

"Help!" I yell even louder and suddenly the door swings open.

The man is around mid-thirties, black hair, dark eyes, small nose, impressive cheekbones, and nice eyebrows, which are currently squished together.

"These two men out here need medical attention," I say breathlessly.

The man rolls his eyes. "Arthur and Bernard are here," he hollers over his shoulder.

Another man in beige pants and a white-collared shirt—I'm sensing a pattern here—pokes his head around the corner and does the same eye roll. "Let's go take them home," he says, and the two start toward my dying duo, leaving me enough room to slip in behind them. I feel guilty leaving the elderly men, but it's not like I can offer much help, at least not until *after* they die.

The club's entryway looks like an upscale hotel lobby: it has cherrywood floors, beautiful sprays of brightly colored flowers adorn the console tables, a red oriental rug the size of a swimming pool is splayed out on the ground, and the curtains are long and velvet.

Lucky for me it doesn't appear to be busy, and I follow the signs pointing toward the bar without being stopped.

The bar is closed, which makes sense, it's not even eight o'clock. The chairs are still upside down on top of the tables, the floors are shiny and wet, and the lights are dim. The television is on behind the bar, and there's a woman watching the news while drying glasses.

I carefully walk across the clean floor and slide onto a bar stool. The woman is engrossed in what's on the television screen. As am I. It's footage from yesterday. Betty walking down the front steps of the sheriff's station with Jackson cautioning reporters to back away.

"Oh, Betty," the bartender sighs. She's in her fifties, with dirty blonde hair twisted into a clip, and a smoker's voice. "How'd you get yourself mixed up in all this?"

I clear my throat.

The woman turns around and swings the towel over her shoulder. "We don't open till ten, doll."

"I'm not here for a drink," I say. "I came looking for someone, but maybe you can help me. Do you know Betty?"

The woman places a glass on the shelf behind the bar and grabs a wet one from the peg tray. "I ain't talking to any reporters."

"I'm not a reporter," I say. "I'm a friend of Betty's."

"Oh, yeah," the woman's not buying it. "Then what's your name?"

"Zoe."

The woman frowns and shakes her head. "Yeah, I heard of

you. Betty told me. You're the one who claims to be seeing Willie."

Oh, geez.

I wonder how many people Betty has told?

"I am a ... medium, actually." It's still hard admitting this out loud—it sounds absurd.

"My mom used to go to a medium all the time," the woman says. "Claimed she once got a message from John Lennon."

"Who?"

The woman gives me a look. "He was one of the Beatles."

"Pffft. Oh, yeah. Of course." I pretend like this isn't new information.

"As far as I see it, if talking to you helps Betty deal with the death of Willie, then it doesn't matter if you're real or fake. You ain't charging her money. That's my take on it." She puts down the glass and extends a friendly hand. "The name is Lin."

I place my hand into hers. "Nice to meet you."

"Dang, girl. Your hands are freezing. You should see a doctor about that. My great-aunt Gertty's hands were always cold. Then one day"—she snaps her fingers—"she dropped dead. Blood clot in the brain or something like that. Messed with her circulation."

Well, that's a pleasant thought.

"Um ... I'll keep that in mind. Thanks. Actually, I'm here looking for Ron McDonald." Seems too early to golf, but I don't play golf, so what do I know?

"Yeah, I seen him this morning."

"Do you know where he is now?"

"I seen him five minutes ago. He was here for the membership meeting this morning. You must have passed him on your way in. You know what he looks like?"

"No," I admit. There weren't any pictures of him on the internet.

"He's got dark hair, and he's about this high." She holds her hand about an inch above her head. So around five feet eleven. "Mid-thirties, and he's got great eyebrows."

"I did see him! He was going to help two elderly men who were having a hard time living."

"Ah, yes." Lin nods. "Arthur and Bernard. Now that Willie's gone, and LeRoy ain't coming around anymore, them two are our oldest members."

Shoot. Ron said he was going to take them home. I walk to the other end of the bar and peek through the window. I can just barely see the benches where I left Arthur and Bernard—which are now vacant. No Ron in sight.

I go back to the bar. "You don't happen to know where Arthur and Bernard live, do you?"

"Not a damn clue." Lin drops a napkin in front of me. "Pick your poison. On the house."

"Oh ... um ... Sprite." I'm not experienced enough to know what poison I like. Also, I'm driving a car worth more than the house we live in.

"Sprite it is." She uses a soda gun to fill up a glass and places it on top of the napkin.

"Thanks. Do you think Ron will come back here?"

"Not a damn clue." She drops a straw into my cup.

Darn it. I'm on a tight schedule.

I take a sip. "I'm assuming you worked here with Betty, right?"

"Girl, I've been here thirty years."

So that's a yes. "Were you around when Betty waited on Willie?"

She lets out a short laugh. "I witnessed the whole thing. They'd sit over there." She points to the table in the corner. "Willie, LeRoy, Ron, and Jackson. They'd have a fifty-dollar tab and give her a fifty-dollar tip, every time. When Betty told me about the offer Willie made, I told her, I says, 'Honey, if that rich fool wants to make you a millionaire, take it.'" She shakes her head and wipes the counter in slow, rhythmic motions. "I would have told her to run if I'd known it was going to turn into this." She gestures to the television—a commercial for the local carpet cleaners—but I get what she means.

"Do you think she did it?" I ask, cautiously. I don't want to upset Lin for multiple reasons. One being that I'm a little afraid of her. Not sure why. Could be the voice.

"Doll, I'm as sure of her innocence as I am that I'm standing here. Betty couldn't hurt a fly, even if she tried. You know what that girl did?" She doesn't wait for an answer. "Two weeks ago my boy, Billy, was in the hospital with a bursting appendix. And I was stressing out. We don't have good insurance, and if I don't work, I don't get a check. That damn fool of a girl *paid* for my son's hospital bill. Then she showed up here with her apron on and covered my shifts, even if she ain't technically an employee anymore. Gave me her tips and paycheck for the days she worked. Does that sound like a killer to you?"

No. No, it doesn't.

"What do you know about Ron?"

"Aside from the fact he's named after a burger place?" She slaps the towel back over her shoulder and leans in, folding her arms on the counter. "He's a chiropractor. Has an office off K Street. Let's see ... he joined the club two years ago. Willie took him in right away. That Willie MacIntosh, he was like the quarterback of this place." She laughs. "An arrogant son of a gun, talked a lot about his money and how many women he'd been with over his life, and he'd take certain men under his wing. Always footed the bill. It's quiet around here without him. It's a damn shame he didn't make it to the celebration."

"What celebration?"

"He was named the club's man of the century, and they were

having a big party Monday morning to surprise him. But he never showed up."

I choke on my Sprite. "They were having a surprise party here, for Willie, on Monday morning?"

"Sure were. We were all waiting for him when we got the call."

"When you say *we all*, who exactly do you mean?"

"I mean everyone at the club."

A Monday morning surprise celebration for Willie means that's likely where LeRoy was headed to when he hit me.

"Did Betty know about it?" I ask.

"You know what? I don't know if she did or not. I assumed one of Willie's guys told her."

It seems like something she would have mentioned.

"Was Ron here?"

"I don't remember," she says.

Shoot.

"Do you know anything else about Ron?" I ask.

"Let me see ... what else about Ron?" She clicks her tongue while she thinks. "I know he's going through a divorce."

"Wait, what?"

"He left his wife a couple of weeks ago," she says, and my head implodes.

I stand up. "Did he say why he left his wife?"

"Couldn't tell ya. I do know he had a thing for Betty."

"Did she have a thing back?"

"Couldn't tell ya."

This is huge! If Ron left his wife because he was in love with Betty, then there's his motive. Now I just need to verify that Ron is missing a cufflink, and I can turn this information over to ... crap. Who I can I give this information to? Not Manfreed. I don't trust him, and I think the feeling is mutual. Jackson thinks I'm a fraud ...

Brian.

I'll turn the information over to Brian.

"Where are you going?" Lin calls after me.

"I'm going to K Street," I say over my shoulder as I run out the door.

CHAPTER TWENTY-TWO

McDonald Family Chiropractic is in a strip mall on K Street, wedged between a dry cleaner and a shoe repair store, about a block from the funeral home. It's 8:45, and Ron's there. I can see him through the window, sitting at the receptionist's desk, talking on the phone. By process of elimination, I decide his car is the silver Mercedes parked out front. The vanity plate *BCKMAN*—as in Back Man (it took a minute to get it)—and the frame saying *I'd rather be golfing*, gave it away.

The bad news is the office doesn't open until noon.

I knock on the front door, but he doesn't hear me. I could tap on the window, but last time I did that, the sheriff was called. I don't feel like being arrested, so I decide to wait until Ron gets off the phone. Until that happens, I'm sitting in a stolen car, with a key piece of evidence shoved in my cleavage, stalking him.

It would make for an entertaining police report.

All signs point to Ron and Betty having an affair. He left his wife. Argued with Willie the week before he died, accused Willie of enticing Betty with his money, which was right before he threatened to kill Willie. Sounds like a furious lover, if you ask me. And I would know. I read the entire Furious Lovers series by KR Tush. So I'm basically an expert.

This has lover's vendetta written all over it.

Ron is *still* on the phone, and I rest my forehead on the steering wheel and continue to watch. My head beats in time with my heart, and I feel a bit shaky all over. Could be the anemia. Mom wasn't around this morning to shove a pill down my throat, and my body is running low on iron.

My thoughts return to yesterday—the treatment center, rolling out of the car, running away, the forty-two missed calls currently on my phone. I know Mom is desperately trying to do what she believes is right. But that doesn't change the fact that she's hiding something from me. I can't trust her, not until she comes clean.

I *deserve* to know the truth.

Finally, Ron hangs up the phone, grabs a notepad, and jots something down. He's left-handed, which doesn't mean much to the case, except for the fact that I'm left-handed, and I feel a sense of solidarity. He crosses the main waiting area with the note in hand.

It's go time!

I will confront Ron, tell him that I know he was involved in Willie's death, and force him to come clean for Betty's sake. And if he refuses, I'll show him the cufflink, and if that doesn't work, I'll call Brian and give him the story.

I cross the parking lot. It's not busy and I—*Aghk!*

CHAPTER TWENTY-THREE

Before I have time to process what is happening, my back is against a dumpster and I'm staring at my mother, who has a death grip on my arms.

She looks terrible: her eyes are cradled in yesterday's mascara, her hair's the size of Montana, and she's still wearing the pencil skirt.

"Zoe Matilda Lane." She spits as she talks. "Do you know what you've put me through?"

I yank my arms free. "Do you know what you've put me through? You tried to have me committed," I say in outrage.

"That's because you're not well, Zoe."

I roll my eyes. I'm not having this conversation again. I can't! There's no time. "Good-bye."

"You're not leaving." Mom pins me against the dumpster. She's deceptively strong and blindly irate. "We've been worried sick. Your father and I have been looking for you all night."

Great, a sliver of guilt worms its way into my subconscious. I don't have time to feel guilty right now. But perhaps I should have, at the very least, called Dad's cell to tell him I was alive, unharmed, and sane. It must have been awful to spend the night searching for your mentally unstable child.

"I'm sorry," I say.

Mom's eyes soften. "I only want what's best for you." She sweeps a strand of hair off my forehead.

"Then tell me who has a name that starts with an S, and when was there a fire?"

Mom's frozen, like someone has come up behind her and pressed *pause*.

I wave a hand in front of her face, and she doesn't flinch.

Well, she's cracked.

"I ... I ..." she says, stuttering. "I don't know what you're talking about."

"Sure you don't." I wrangle out of her grasp and back away. "When you're ready to tell me the whole truth, I'll be here. Until then, leave me alone."

"Wait, Zoe." Mom fumbles with the pockets of her blazer. "You forgot to take your iron."

"You can't be serious."

Oh, but she is. Resting in her palm is an iron pill. Has she been carrying it around all night? "You're anemic, Zoe. Remember?"

How could I forget?

But I don't want anything from her.

But then again, it's not like I have the funds to buy my own supplements.

Fine, I decide. Only because it's doctor's orders and I feel awful.

I reach my arm out, keeping my feet firm on the ground, afraid she's using the iron as a trick to lure me into a trap, and I snatch the pill out of her palm.

Aha!

What the … I examine the pill in the light of the day. "Why does this have an *H*, one, zero, *G* engraved on it?"

Okay, so most my knowledge on the elements comes from Bill Nye the Science Guy's videos from the library, but even I know the symbol for iron is FE.

Oh … crap.

My mind scrambles to put the pieces together as I stare down at the pill in horror. No. She wouldn't … would she?

No!

I gaze up at my mother, and she forces a smile.

Oh, hell. She would!

My mother is trying to slip me some kind of antipsychotic medication! Now she's gone too far.

"Have a good life, Mother." I drop the pill to the ground and smash it with my heel for added effect.

"Where are you going?" Mom asks, following me. "Let's talk about this."

I come to an abrupt stop and whirl around. "Was that an iron pill?"

"Okay." Mom is clasping her head. "Okay. Just listen to me. Don't get mad." *Too late.* "You threw yourself in front of a car and said you saw a man in a hat, Zoe. You've been walking around town talking to yourself. We saw you at the press conference calling our client a murderer—for the second time. And Mrs. Attwood said you were at the assisted living facility last week threatening Old Man LeRoy. You're not yourself. I … I … I didn't have a choice."

"For the last time … I. Was. In. The. Crosswalk!" I start striding across the parking lot, not exactly sure where I'm going. Ron's office is the opposite way, and Willie's car is parked on the other end of the lot, since it doesn't seem like the kind of car you park beside other vehicles.

"Zoe, sweetie, the ER doctor prescribed it," Mom says, struggling to keep up. "He said it has very few side effects."

Hold on. I come to a sudden stop, and Mom runs into the back of me. "You've been slipping me these meds since I was released from the hospital." Which explains everything. The headaches, blurred vision, feeling extra shaky today, not being on top of things —it all makes sense. These were side effects of a medication that I don't need. "You poisoned me!" My voice rises to a shriek.

People walking by are nudging each other and pointing, but I don't care.

"I'm sorry," Mom says in a panic. "I should have told you first, but I didn't think you'd take it if I did."

"No! I wouldn't have. It's my body, and I get to say what will and will not go inside of it."

"That's what she said," a teenager snarkily murmurs as he passes by.

Oh, geez.

"I'm sorry," Mom says again.

"Sorry isn't good enough!"

"You're right, sweetie." Mom gives me a strange look. "Just come home with me, and we can work this out."

She's got to be out of her hairspray-lovin' mind. I'm not going anywhere with her. Last time I did, she tried to have me committed. I scan the parking lot, looking for our van. There's no way Dad is okay with this plan. Except I don't see our car anywhere. "Where's Dad?" I ask.

"He's searching Fernn, while I've been looking in Trucker."

"How?" We only have the one car.

"Daniel MacIntosh gave me a ride." Mom makes a sweeping gesture with her arm, and I see the Black 4-Runner with Daniel at the helm, watching us through a pair of mirrored aviators.

I've lost the ability to speak.

"Everyone is worried about you, Zoe," Mom says. "Daniel, Dad, me, and Brian."

"Y-you spoke to Brian?" I feel a renewed surge of outrage. "Why would you talk to Brian?"

"He called my cell this morning asking for you. He said he didn't have your number."

"What did you say to him?" I take a step forward.

Mom recoils. "I told him that we had been looking for you all night."

"And he told you were I was?" I ask, feeling a bit betrayed. Not that Brian was aware of what had happened with my mom, so it wasn't like he was ratting me out. But still.

"He said he hadn't spoken to you since I picked you up from *The Gazette*."

Oh. My mood lifts—*slightly*.

I shake my head. "Mom, look, I'm not going anywhere with you. I'm not taking any pills. I'm not going to any hospital. But you need to stay away from Daniel MacIntosh."

Mom crosses her arms. "Zoe, the police already interviewed him, and he has an alibi. Daniel had nothing to do with Willie's death."

"Maybe he didn't kill Willie, but he's not exactly a saint either." I spot a coffee house down the street. "Call Dad. Then go grab a hot chocolate and wait for him. I'm sure Daniel has better things to do." Like spend his disinherited fortune.

"He's the one that offered," Mom says. "And I was desperate."

Gah! I don't have time to deal with this. "Call Dad. Hot Chocolate. I'm done." I wrap my arms around my waist and continue toward the sidewalk. I can't very well confront Ron in front of Daniel or my mother.

"Where are you going?" Mom calls after me.

"None of your business."

"When will you be home?"

I turn around and walk backwards. "Never, unless you ditch Daniel MacIntosh." I'm feeling like I have the upper hand in this argument, until I ram into a light pole, fall into the street, and scrape my hands on the asphalt.

Smooth, Zoe.

Real smooth.

I wait for Mom to rush over, but she doesn't. She's standing at Daniel's 4-Runner, talking to him through the passenger side window. The two interact for a few moments before he starts the car and drives away. Mom brings her cell to her ear and crosses the street to the coffee shop.

She listened to me.

I can hardly believe it.

Ha!

I stand and wipe my hands off. Tires slowly approach, and I look up in enough time to see Daniel coming right for me. I jump onto the curb, because being hit by a car once is enough for me to learn that I don't want to do it again. Daniel screeches to a stop and rolls down his window. He pulls down his glasses, revealing his beady eyes. "Don't get involved in things that are none of your business, or else."

He pushes his glasses back on and zooms away.

CHAPTER TWENTY-FOUR

"Or else what?" Brian asks.

"He didn't say." I trace the BMW symbol on the steering wheel. I'm parked in Willie's garage and had called Brian to get his opinion on what I should do about Ron, and Betty, and crazy Daniel. "He looked really mad, though," I say.

"He doesn't seem like the type of person you'd want as an enemy."

"No, he doesn't. Do you think he'd hurt my parents?"

"I don't know," Brian says, which is of zero comfort.

I massage my temples; my head still hurts. But knowing why I feel so crummy actually makes me feel better, as odd as that sounds. "So I have the cufflink, and I have the information on Ron. Can you run the story?"

"I'll need at least one more reliable source. Why don't you call Trucker PD?"

"Because there's no chance they'll listen to me."

"Why?"

"Um ... because Manfreed thinks I'm not credible."

"Why?"

Geez. He asks a lot of questions that I don't want to answer.

"Can't you just run the story anyway?"

"No, it could damage Ron's career, unless I have a little more proof. Tell Jackson Anderson."

"Um ... I can't."

"Why?

"He doesn't think I'm credible."

"Seems like every person but the accused has a problem with your credibility. Which makes me think you're onto something."

"Sure." Let's go with that.

"I'll do a little more research on my end, and I'll contact the PD for a comment. I'll reach out to Ron as well. I have his number around here somewhere. And I'll call Jackson."

"No!" The last thing I want is for Jackson to tell Brian about my *fraudulent* gift. Brian is the only one who has any trust in my ability to function as an adult.

Well, he and Willie.

Willie ...

I half expected him to be waiting in the garage, livid that I'd taken one of his babies out for a joy ride. But he isn't here.

"Why can't I call Jackson?" Brian asks.

"Errr ... because I'll tell him."

Maybe.

Probably not.

Perhaps I'll write him a note.

I hang up with Brian, return the key to the hook, and go inside.

"Hello?" I whisper, expecting Willie to be standing there with his arms crossed, foot taping, jaw set. But he's nowhere to be seen. He must still be in the guest room.

"Zoooeeee? Is that you?" Betty calls out from the kitchen.

"It is. I'll be right there." I go up the stairs, taking two at a time, my hand gliding along the handrail. "Willie?" I whisper.

Still nothing.

I walk into the guest room, close the door behind me, and just stand there for a few moments. "Willie?" I whisper. "Are you here?" I can feel the presence of a spirit, but I don't see anyone. "Willie, I'm sorry. There was an errand that I had to run by myself." I check in the bathroom, the closet, and under the bed. "I didn't mean to hurt your feelings. Please, speak to me. Willie?"

Nothing.

"You know what?" I wipe my eyes. "Fine. Don't speak. I just found out my mother has been drugging me, and I've been threatened by your nutso nephew, and, oh yeah, I took your car. The BMW with the butterfly doors. There was a dent on the rear fender before, right?" I say, hoping to aggravate him into appearing.

No such luck.

"I know you're here, Willie. I can feel you ..." At least, I *think* I can feel him. Perhaps the spirit I'm feeling isn't Willie but someone else. Someone not ready to show themselves and Willie really is gone.

But he can't be.

Not yet.

We didn't even say a proper good-bye. His killer isn't behind bars. Betty is out on bail. Justice hasn't been served. He can't transition when everything is still a mess.

Right?

I check the hallway, his bedroom, the garage, and every room in between—and there are a lot of rooms.

Willie is gone.

"Zoooeeee?" Betty calls again from kitchen. "Are you here?"

My legs feel like water, and I swallow a few times, trying not to panic, and make my way to Betty.

The kitchen has black cabinets with glass fronts, white

marble counters, multiple ovens, two grills, three sinks, and no Willie. I find Betty wrapped in a terrycloth robe, standing in front of a griddle with a spatula in her hand, a two-feet high stack of steaming pancakes on the counter.

"Hi, Betty," I say, trying to read her expression. She doesn't appear mad. To be honest, she doesn't appear to be anything. She stares mindlessly at the griddle as if hypnotized.

She reaches into the pocket of her robe and pulls out a wadded tissue and wipes at her nose.

"How did you sleep?" I ask as I sink into a barstool across from her.

"Wellss enough." Betty adds two pancakes to her tower. That's a lot of pancakes.

"Are you expecting company?" I ask.

"Nope." She pours batter on the griddle into four even circles. "Do you want"—she pauses to belch into her fist—"pancakes?"

"Not right now."

"Coming right up." She grabs a plate from the cabinet and flips one ... two ... three ... four ... five ... six ... ten pancakes on top!

"Um ... I really don't want any right now, thank you."

Betty drizzles the pancakes with syrup, making small circles until they're swimming in maple. Then she opens a drawer, pulls out a butcher knife, slices the butter in half, and drops it on top.

"Er ... *thanks.*" I take the plate, trying not to spill syrup onto the counter. I want to ask Betty about Ron, but this doesn't feel like the right time. Not when there's a large knife within arm's reach.

"Is Willie here?" She looks up, her eyelids appear heavy. "I need to speak to him."

"Not right now." I cut through the stack of pancakes with my fork and move mushy pieces of dough around my plate, to give the appearance that I'm eating.

Betty opens her mouth then closes it and clutches the edge of the counter so hard her knuckles turn white.

I place my silverware down and wait, positive she's about to confess about Ron.

But instead she blurts out, her cheeks flushed, "I lost his cufflink! I don't know where it went. It was on my nightstand, and I went to put it away this morning, and it wasn't there. I moved everything in my room, but I can't find it." She teeters to the right.

"Betty?"

"Mmmhmmm."

"Have you been drinking?"

She holds her thumb and forefinger together. "Just a wee bit," she says with another burp. "I tried this scotch Willie had." She makes a face. "It wasn't very good, but it did make me feellls a bits better."

Okay, Betty is completely bashed (read that in a novel once). I have no idea what to do with her ... except.

Well, I might as well ask her. "What's your relationship with Ron?"

Before she can answer, the doorbell chimes. Daisy darts from the wall and starts barking.

Gah!

My life is weird.

"I thought you weren't expecting company ... *Betty?*" She appears to have fallen asleep standing up. "Betty?" I come around to the other side of the counter and shake her by the shoulders until her eyelids pop open.

"What happen ... sss ... ed?"

"Are you expecting someone?"

"You're cute." She says with a lazy smile and *boops* my nose.

"Your style is a bit"—she waves her spatula at me—"off. Buts it's endearing."

"Thanks. There's someone at the door."

She puffs out her cheeks.

"Betty?"

"Huh?"

Ah! This is painful. "The door."

"What about the door?" She stumbles forward, and I catch her before she falls.

The bell rings again.

"There's someone ... *here*," I huff out. Betty drapes herself over me, and I turn around, using my back to bear her weight (which isn't much, thank goodness). "How much scotch did you drink?"

"I love pancakes. My mom used to make me pancakes when I was sad. I'm feeling sad. My life is ruined. Allsss I wanted to do was help."

There goes the bell again. Whoever is here is not going away.

"Let's answer the door, okay?" I shuffle forward with Betty on my back, making it all the way to the fridge before I give up. "Never mind." I drop her onto a chair. "Wait here and ... um ..." I yank the spatula form her death grip. "No more pancakes or going near hot things." I turn off the griddle first then hurry to the door.

Daisy beats me there and is barking frantically, racing back and forth and jumping up and down.

"Calm down," I say.

There's one of those old-fashioned peepholes on the door, the kind you have to flip open to see out. Not exactly discrete, but it's better than nothing.

I grab the little knob and ... okay, so the old-fashioned peephole is just for looks. Great.

The doorbell sounds off again.

Fine!

I open the darn thing and, crap. It's Jackson. He scrunches his masculine face at me in disbelief. "I thought I told you to stay away from my client."

Feeling irritated, I put a hand on my hip. "She asked me to come here because she didn't want to be alone last night."

Jackson doesn't wait for a formal invitation and walks right in, swinging a briefcase at his side. And Willie said those were not in style. Ha!

"Where is she?" Jackson asks.

"She's indisposed."

"What's that supposed to mean?"

"It means she's drunk."

His eyeballs nearly explode out of his head. "You got my client drunk!"

"There's no need to yell at me! It's not my fault. She got into Willie's scotch."

He points to the door. "Leave."

This man has a lot of nerve. "I'm not going anywhere. You leave."

"I'm the person that's going to keep Betty from serving a life sentence. Who do think needs to be here more? The ghost lady or the lawyer?"

I open my mouth, ready to spit out a witty retort, but nothing comes out. The witty part of my brain must be broken.

Or I'm intimidated by Jackson.

Probably both.

Jackson narrows his eyes. "Betty may think you see Willie, but she's in a delicate and vulnerable state of mind right now. I'm not." He takes a step closer, and I instinctually back up until I hit the wall. "You're an opportunist. Nothing more. I have it figured out: You read the article printed in *The Gazette* last month about Willie and the work he did for the space program. He bragged about his wealth, as he usually did, and you realized this multimillionaire was on death's door and decided to insert yourself into his life."

I'm baffled. "There was never an article about Willie in *The Gazette*."

Jackson reaches into his briefcase, pulls out a copy of the paper, and opens it to page six. "Right there." He points to the article circled in red.

I grab it from his grasp and scan down the page. It's a complete bio of Willie, detailing his time in the Navy, his work within the space program, love of cross-country skiing and boating. How he still played golf at the country club every Tuesday and Thursday, and it ends with a quote, "*Sure, I've had a great life. Made a lot of money, lived in many places, met a lot of beautiful women, but I'm happy. Trucker County is the best place to retire.*" And below the article is a picture of Willie in his thirties, wearing the homburg hat, suit, and tie. The same ensemble he's worn since he appeared.

The article was written by Brian. He'd said that he met with Willie, but he didn't say why.

How had I missed this? It was published right below "The Squirrel of the Month."

"Part of my defense is to provide a number of suspects who had reasonable motive to kill Willie," Jackson says. "And I've been doing research on the girl from Fernn Valley who claims to see dead people. And do you know what I found, *Zoe?*" He hooks his fingers into quotation marks when he says Zoe, and I don't know why. "It's like you don't exist. So, *Zoe.*" Again with the air quotes. "What is your real name?"

Now he's gone and ticked me off. "You don't get to talk to me like that, got it?" I poke him with my finger and *ouch!*

Gah! This hurts.

Jackson appears amused. "You okay?"

"Yes." *Noooo!*

I think I broke my finger. Is his chest made of titanium?

Jackson doesn't let up. "John and Mary Lane have one child, born October thirty-first, nineteen ninety-six."

"Right?" I say, holding my finger, not sure where he's going with this.

"A daughter by the name of Samantha Lane," he says. "No other children. So my question for you is, once again, who *are* you?"

My mind grabs ahold of one detail. "Samantha?" I ask at a whisper. "Did you say Samantha with an S?"

"Yes, *Samantha* Lane." He produces a file from his briefcase and flips it open. "Samantha Lane, born—"

I snatch the file. It's nothing but handwritten notes. *Samantha Lane* circled several times with a question mark. *Los Angeles. House fire? No driver's license. No bank accounts.*

I lift my eyes. "Why does it say fire?"

Jackson studies me with an intense gaze.

"*Why* does it say fire?" I press.

"John and Mary's house burned down in nineteen ninety-nine," he says, still studying me. "All articles say it was started by their child. But there's no record of a Samantha Lane after that. Your parents applied for a rental home when they first moved to Fernn Valley in two thousand three, and they claimed it would only be the two of them occupying the residence. Which makes me question where exactly you came from."

I don't know what to say. Samantha with an S and a house fire. Willie's article in *The Gazette*. I feel a bit dizzy and out of breath. Jackson is speaking to me, but I can't make sense of his words. The room is spinning around and around, as I mush this all together.

S and fire.

CHAPTER TWENTY-FIVE

It feels like someone has wrapped my head in cellophane, and I barely register Betty who has stumbled into the foyer slurring her words or Jackson who is still talking to me as if I were caught lying under oath.

Samantha, the fire, no memories of my life prior to seven. Even worse, the article on Willie ...

I knew Willie wasn't a figment of my imagination because I had never seen nor heard of him before. But that can't be true. I read that issue of *The Gazette*. I remember that squirrel!

Mom was right.

I don't see dead people.

I don't feel other people's feelings.

I'm sick.

With a clear brain scan and normal blood count, it means physiologically there's something wrong with me. My brain has manifested everything. *Everything!* None of it can be real.

I need to get out of here.

Ignoring both Jackson who is calling after me and the neighbors outside of their mansions watching me go by, I run down the street like I'm being chased. I'm able to slip through the gate when a car enters. I get as far as the frontage road before my lungs stage a protest and I collapse to my hands and knees.

The cufflink falls out of my shirt and lands in the dirt beneath my hands. I pick it up and fall back onto my legs. Is this real? If someone were to walk up to me right now, would they even see it? But Betty saw it. So did Brian.

Are they real?

Am I real?

Is this dirt real?

Is the little spider crawling up my arm real?

It feels real, but so did Willie.

I shove the cufflink back into my bra and bury my head into my hands, too freaked out to even cry. My mind is desperately trying to grasp the situation.

Roughly six minutes into my nervous breakdown, a car pulls over and rolls down the window. A bearded man in a pale blue shirt leans out of the car and asks if I'm all right.

I stare at him.

Is *this* guy real?

"Do you need help?" the man asks, giving me a pitiful look. Like I'm crazy, like I'm a charity case, like I'm one of those transient people who walk along the highway. Speaking of which, a man with a bushy beard and a Davy Crockett hat on his head stomps by, muttering something about vases and cigarettes. I reach out my arm, and my hand brushes against his pant leg, but he doesn't notice and keeps on walking. I think *he's* real, and wowza, his odor lingers. Blah!

"Can I call someone?" the man in the car asks, and I hear the unmistakable *click* of car doors being locked.

My cell phone is at Betty's, and I don't have my wallet or any way of getting anywhere.

Looks like I'm left with no other option.

MAKING A MEDIUM

When my dad arrives, I'm still sitting on the side of the road, hugging my knees. I asked him to come alone. I'm not ready to face Mom, because even though I have clearly hit rock bottom (quite literally, there are several rocks digging into my bottom), I still have a sliver of pride left (a very small sliver). And my pride doesn't want to hear, "I told you so."

Dad exits the car and walks toward me with his hands shoved into the front pockets of his pants. "Hey, Pumpkin." He extends a hand and helps me to my feet.

"Hi, Dad," I say to the ground. If I look at him, I will cry.

I slink into the passenger seat of the van and pull on my seat belt. My briefcase is sitting on the floor between the two captain's chairs in the back. Dad slides into the driver's seat and follows my gaze.

"I thought you might need that," he says.

"No." I shake my head. "I won't need it where I'm going."

"And where is that?"

I steal a glance at him. If he's concerned about my current mental state, he's not showing it. "You need to take me to a hospital," I say, feeling a little annoyed. Isn't it obvious? Does he not communicate with his wife? "I'm *seeing* imaginary people who claim to be dead."

"Is that so?" Dad shoves the key in the ignition and Jabba jumps up on the center console.

"Ah!" I grab my chest. "Why'd you bring the cat?"

"He followed me out to the car and jumped in. I tried to get him out." Dad pulls the sleeve of his shirt up, revealing red claw marks.

"Oh." Maybe Willie is right. Jabba is possessed. Except Willie isn't real. So he can't be right. Jabba is just a cat, and I've manifested the entire conversation.

Ugh.

I drop my head into my hands.

"How about ice cream?"

I peer up at my dad. This man is as crazy as I am. "No! I don't want *ice cream*. Did you hear what I said? I *see* people, Dad. People who don't exist. People like Willie MacIntosh, the multimillionaire who died in Trucker. The man whose house you want to sell. That's who I'm seeing." I stare straight ahead. "Now, hospital."

"Is he here now?" Dad looks around. "Willie?"

"*Nooo,* he's not." Geez. Getting committed is harder than I thought it would be. Maybe I should have called Mom.

"Why not?" Dad asks.

"I asked him to leave," I say, feeling frustrated. Does he not understand the gravity of this situation? "But it doesn't matter, because he's not real."

"Hmm."

"What do you mean, *hmmm.*"

"We need ice cream." Dad starts the car and takes off down the highway, toward East Trucker.

"Dad, trust me. Ice cream cannot fix this situation. Please turn around and take me to the mental hospital in Fernn Valley. I'm sure they're expecting me."

"Ice cream fixes everything." He takes the J Street exit and stops at an old-fashioned ice cream parlor, complete with pink and white awnings above the windows and a seven-foot-tall chocolate sundae statue out front.

"I'll be right back," Dad says before I can protest. I can see him through the window, pointing out his flavors to the girl working behind the counter.

Maybe the hospital has a two-for-one special.

I lean my head back and stare up at the ceiling, feeling completely dejected when Jabba paws at my leg.

"What do you want?" I ask, half expecting him to respond. I have made-up conversations with rich dead people. Why not pets?

Jabba scratches at my leg again then leaps down to the floor and lands on a copy of *The Gazette* beneath my shoe.

Of course, it's Tuesday.

I hadn't noticed it was there. The paper is still rolled and fastened with a rubber band, but I can see the front-page headline: "Pedestrian Struck on Main Street."

Great.

I snap off the band and unfurl the paper, leaving my fingertips black from the bleeding ink.

A woman was struck by a vehicle on Main Street early Monday morning ... LeRoy ... no charges filed ... yada-yada-yada ... article continued on page 4.

I unfold the paper and flip to the fourth page ... Ahhh!

There's a picture.

Not just any picture.

A full-page display of the accident! There's LeRoy standing beside his car with his hands over his mouth wearing the country club attire, beige pants and white-collared shirt. The driver's side door of his car is wide open, and my briefcase is lying in the middle of the crosswalk.

What I find horrifying is Brian, who is walking toward the doctor's office with me in his arms. My head is flung back and my mouth is open, while Brian's cheeks are puffed and, even though the picture is in black and white, you can tell his face is flushed. Like he's hauling a 200-pound bag of cement.

Gah!

This day just keeps getting better and better.

"Thanks," I say to Jabba. "This is exactly what I needed right now." I throw the paper on the ground.

Dad returns with an ice cream cone in each hand. Oh, for heaven's sake.

I open the door for him.

"Thank you, Pumpkin." He gets in and licks an escaped dribble of mint chip slithering down the side of the cone. "Here you go." He holds out a double scoop of vanilla with a cherry on top, and I give him a look. "What?"

"I don't want ice cream, Dad. I'm not seven. But I am sick."

"More for me." He shrugs.

"Fine." I yank the cone from his hand and take a small bite. Admittedly, he's right. I feel a tiny bit better. But that's only because my stomach is empty and the calories are a welcomed addition. "Can we go now?"

"No." Dad reclines his chair, like he's planning to stay for a while. "We need to have a chat. There are things your mother and I have been keeping from you."

I think about Samantha and the fire and why I wasn't with them when they first moved to Fernn Valley. I'm not sure I *want* to know the truth anymore. Honestly, I'd like to go back to being blissfully unaware.

"It started when you were three," Dad says. "You had imaginary friends. At first, we didn't think too much of it. You were young. But your friends weren't typical for a three-year-old. One friend was named Jose Luis Francisco, and he'd recently died on death row after being charged for the murder of his nephew."

I drop the ice cream onto my lap.

"Here you go." Dad hands me a napkin, not skipping a beat, and I clean up the mess, feeling numb. I've been crazy since I was three!

"We put you in therapy," Dad continues. "You told the therapist that Jose was wrongly accused, and it was your job to clear his name."

This sounds slightly familiar.

"Your mother freaked out."

That too sounds slightly familiar.

"And you told everyone about Jose," Dad says. "Teachers, strangers, neighbors, and even Santa Claus." A smile creeps on his face at the memory. "You sat on his lap and said all you wanted for Christmas was a plane ticket to Mexico so you could visit the Francisco family and tell them Jose was innocent. Then you showed him how to make a shiv out of a candy cane." He pauses to take a bite of mint chip. "It was right before your fourth birthday when the house burned down. You were making bacon for Jose at midnight and started a grease fire."

Sadly, this also sounds familiar. I can pull up a vague image of a man with dark brown hair, golden eyes, and a silver tooth telling me about how he was denied his last meal—which was bacon.

Oh, hell.

"We had no choice but to put you on medication," Dad says, his easy-breezy *let's eat our feelings* tone has faded. "You stopped talking to Jose, but the problem was, you stopped talking to everyone. Even us. You were tired all the time. It was a struggle to get you to eat. You said food didn't taste good anymore. You missed Jose. Kids wouldn't play with you. Their parents wouldn't allow it ... And that was our life until you were seven."

"So that explains why I don't remember anything before we came to Fernn Valley, because I was drugged."

"It does." Dad wipes the corners of his mouth with a napkin. "We decided to move to a place where no one knew us or you. We even went so far as to change your name, paranoid you'd somehow hear about the fire, or someone from Los Angeles would look you up. When we got here, we took you off all medication, and you appeared to be fine."

"But Mom put me back on it without my knowledge," I say.

"I didn't know about that," Dad says. "But, you have to

understand, your mother would do anything for you. She wants so badly to protect you, and she can sometimes overstep."

Ya think?

"We've spent a great deal of effort to make sure you were never too excited or exposed to anything that could trigger an episode. No internet. No caffeine. Your mom read that profanity caused stress and banned us all from using it. We found jobs which would allow us the flexibility to be around more."

So this is it—I've had another episode. Why now? I feel terrible for my parents. I had no idea they had gone through so much just to keep me sane.

"The thing is, Zoe, about a month ago, I was watching an episode of 20/20, and they ran a story about a man named Jose Luis Francisco who was killed on death row for the murder of his nephew. But new DNA evidence had come to light which exonerated him." He shakes his head. "When I saw the picture of Jose, a man with golden eyes and a silver tooth, just as you said, I yelled for your mother. She watched the episode but refused to believe it. This is where she and I differ." Dad stares straight at me. "Zoe, you can see ghosts. There's no way you could have known about Jose at three years old. We didn't even have cable back then. And I started doing research. The book in your briefcase, *Reaching the Other Side,* I'd read it when I'd take you to the library."

I bring my hand to my mouth. "You're the one who marked it up?"

Dad nods. "You have a gift, Zoe. Use it."

I can hardly believe what I'm hearing.

"B-but what about Mom?"

"I love your mother, and when you love someone, you'll do everything in your power to protect them. She doesn't handle paranormal stuff well. So for her sake *and* yours, we should keep this a secret for a while."

"Good call," I say, still not quite convinced this isn't all a psychotic meltdown. "But I read about Willie MacIntosh before he showed up. It was in *The Gazette* two weeks ago, right above 'The Squirrel of the Month.'"

"No, you didn't see the article because Mom took the page out. I clipped 'The Squirrel of the Month' for you."

He's right.

I'd completely forgotten about that. He'd told me Mom had cut out an article for work. But, "Why did she save the bio on Willie?"

"To convince me we should expand our business to Trucker because there were wealthier people there and we could sell bigger homes than we do here."

"Oh," is all I can say.

"I think you're going to do great things, Zoe."

I'm not so sure about that, but I appreciate his confidence in me. "What about the safe?" I ask. "The one in your closet. What's in there?"

"We have your health records and birth certificate."

"And a gun."

Dad nods slightly. "Once I realized my daughter sees dead ex-convicts, it seemed like a good idea to have some form of protection."

I laugh. I can't help myself. "I don't think a gun is going to protect you from a spirit."

"No, but it will protect me from the spirit's alive friends."

This is true.

Dad starts the car. "Where are we off to now?"

"I don't even know." I let out a sigh and think about the cufflink buried in my bra. Five hours ago, I was convinced Ron killed Willie. But something my dad said casts doubt on my theory. *If you love someone, you'll do everything in your power to protect them.* Why wouldn't Ron come forward and protect Betty? Why wasn't he at her house last night so she wouldn't be alone?

Perhaps I have Ron all wrong.

But then why would Betty have a clothing bag from the bed and breakfast?

No, the two are involved somehow.

I think ...

If they weren't, what would be Ron's motive to kill Willie? It's not like he'd get money.

Whoever killed Willie is missing a cufflink. Which means it can't be the nosey and obnoxious neighbor, Arnie. It was Ron, or it could be Jackson, or it could be both. They killed Willie before he could attend the Member of the Year surprise party Monday morning ... except ...

My eyes slide to *The Gazette* on the ground. Jabba is sitting on the paper with his paw positioned over the picture, staring up at me with his *golden* eyes. There's something strikingly familiar about his gold eyes that I'd never noticed before, probably because the crazy cat would never allow us to look him straight on. But for the first time, I feel an odd, familiar connection.

Jabba hisses and circles around the paper, which brings me back to Willie.

Specifically, Monday morning.

Monday.

Morning.

Monday morning.

MONDAY MORNING!

I sit up. It's like someone has stuck a flash drive into my brain and all this new information is downloading ... the cufflink; the day I met Willie; Ron, Jackson, LeRoy, Arnie; Brian;

Betty; the rock; the key; the accident; LeRoy's car; the missing broken key; Isabel ... and suddenly I know where I need to be.

"Dad, do you have *The Gazette's* number on hand?"

"Sure, why?"

"I need to borrow your phone."

CHAPTER TWENTY-SIX

Dad peers over the steering wheel. "MelBorne Assisted Living. Are you here to drum up business?"

"I don't think that's how it works."

Dad strokes his mustache. "Do you get some sort of warning when people are about to die? Like an alarm? Because if you do, your mother and I can make their acquaintance before they pass. We could build a relationship and list their home after they're gone."

"Dad! Seriously? After everything that's happened today, after everything we've talked about, that's what you come up with?"

"It's hard being in a business built entirely off of referrals," he says.

I pause, struck with a thought. "Were you and Mom real estate agents before we moved here?" My parents never talked about our life prior to living in Fernn Valley. Now I know why. Before Jackson's notes, I wasn't even aware we lived in Los Angeles.

Dad shakes his head. "I worked in finance and your mother owned a consignment shop."

My mother in a consignment shop? It's hard to imagine her doing anything other than real estate, but somehow, her in a shop filled with old clothes makes total sense. I'd venture to say most of her wardrobe came from her consignment days. "What made you become real estate agents, and why Fernn Valley?" I ask.

"We heard about it through a friend of a friend who grew up here. It sounded like a nice, tranquil place. After we moved here, we learned the only real estate agent in town had died. Which left an opening."

Oh, geez. They'd completely flipped their lives upside down for me. "Dad? Who is Phil?" I ask, remembering Phil was associated with the S and the fire.

"He was your therapist."

"Like Dr. Phil?"

"Yes, but not *that* Dr. Phil."

"Good to know." I still have so many questions, but there is a pressing *need* to get this over with. "Thank you for the ride, Dad." I pat Jabba on the head and grab my briefcase. "And thank you for ..." I search for the right words to adequately describe what a freeing feeling it is to have his support, to know I'm not crazy, to know the pieces of my past—but there aren't any.

Dad gives my arm a reassuring squeeze. "Remember, the less Mom knows, the better."

"But you won't let her drug me again, right?"

"How about you don't take any pills that anyone gives you. It's a good life practice anyway."

He's right.

When I step outside, a gust of wind nearly knocks me over, and I hold down my hair to keep it in place. It's then that I notice the dirt smudges on my knees, the ice cream stain on my thigh. My sweater is wrinkled, and there's an unidentified green dribble down the front. Looks like bird poop. Not sure when a bird pooped on me, but it seems right considering the day I've had. Who knows what's happening with my hair or if that spider from earlier is still crawling around on me. The thought makes me shudder. I want to go home and clean up, but there's no time.

I take a deep breath and go.

Dad rolls down the window. "Remember what I said? We could really use the referrals," he hollers after me.

I hold up my hand as an acknowledgement. He obviously doesn't understand how this works. There are no alarms that go off when someone is on death's door. At least I don't think there are. That would be a cool feature, though.

As I approach the building, the automatic doors part, and I'm assaulted by the same urine and day-old cafeteria food odor. A man in a blue nurse's uniform walks by without acknowledging my presence.

Good.

What's not good is that Patricia Attwood, the nurse from the first time I visited, is sitting behind the counter on the phone. I grab a magazine off a side table in the waiting area, some tabloid with Jennifer Aniston on the cover, and use it to cover my face while I pass the nurses' station. When I make it to the end of the hall, I discard Jennifer into a bin and duck into an alcove with a chair and telephone. I take a seat, open my briefcase, and pull out *Reaching the Other Side*.

I remember there being a section on reconnecting with spirits. After scanning through the table of contents, I find it.

There's no time to read all thirty-eight pages dedicated to the subject, and I skim through, picking up the basics.

First I must close my eyes. Then I must ... shoot. I open one eye and check the book, forgetting the second step.

Right.

Got it.

MAKING A MEDIUM

Take a deep, calming breath and picture a door surrounded by white light. I'm not exactly sure what I'm supposed to do with the door ... knock? Open it? Tap to the rhythm of "Shave and a Haircut"?

"Hello, there," comes a crackly voice, and my eyes pop open. An old woman with blue hair and a multicolored afghan wrapped around her frail shoulders is talking to me. She's using a walker with pink tennis balls attached to the bottom. "Are you lost?" she asks.

"Um ... no."

"Then what are you doing?"

"I'm ... waiting to visit ... a friend."

"Who is your friend?"

"Um ... Ttttammmbra." I pull a name out of my butt, assuming Tambra is an actual name.

The woman's face lights up. "I know Tambra!"

Okay, so I guess it is a real name. Who knew?

"She's not in her room right now," the old woman says. "It's Tuesday, Bingo in the community area. I can take you to her."

I open my mouth to respond but am interrupted by a high-pitched beeping sound.

Holy crap. I do hear alarms!

I stand and lean my ear closer to the woman. The alarm grows louder, and a group of men and women in blue uniforms turn the corner and run down the hall into a bedroom, one pushing a resuscitation cart.

The woman peers up at me. "Hello, there. Are you lost?"

"Um ... no."

"Then what are you doing?"

"Dammit, person!" Willie thunders into my eardrum, and I fall back into the phone. The receiver falls and dangles by the cord while I scramble to my feet.

I can't believe it.

He's back.

Willie is back!

He's standing there in the same fitted tan suit, dark tie, shiny black shoes, and a vintage homburg hat, looking as irritated as ever. My heart explodes in my chest, and I instinctually go to hug him, forgetting he's invisible, and end up stumbling over the chair and ramming my face into the wall.

"Security!" The blue-haired woman starts shuffling down the hall. "Security, there's a maniac on the loose!" Her yell is an octave louder than her speaking voice, and no one can hear her, not over the alarm. "Security! We have a mad woman here! Security!"

"Now look what you've done," Willie huffs.

"Where have you been?" I ask.

"What do you mean *where have you been?*" he repeats in a nasally mocking voice. "I've been here with you." He points his finger at my nose. "It took a great deal of self-control to not say something when you took my favorite car for a joyride."

"Wait ... you were with me then?"

He looks at me as if I'm an idiot. "I told you, I can't stay away. No matter how much I want to. You were gone for maybe twenty minutes, and then suddenly I was in the backseat of my car. If I weren't already dead, watching you drive my baby would have killed me."

"You saw everything? At the bed and breakfast, and the club, and at ..." I bring my hand to my mouth. He must know about Ron and Betty. "I'm sorry," I say, my voice low.

"What are you sorry about?"

"I'm sorry about Betty and ... you know."

"You don't know anything. Their affair has not been confirmed."

"But Betty had a laundry bag from Newsgate House, which is where Ron was staying."

"So?"

"And Ron recently split with his wife."

"Because she had an affair with their tax attorney! Just because Ron and his wife are separated, that doesn't mean anything."

"Willie," I say and take a step closer. "It's time to come to terms with the fact that Ron and Betty are having an affair."

"No, they aren't."

"*Yes*, they are."

Willie crosses his arms. "Then what are we doing here?"

"If you've been with me the whole time, then you know why I'm here. You saw *The Gazette*," I say and check down the hall. The blue-haired woman has shuffled three feet since I last checked. We have a little time before she makes it to the nurses' station.

Unless a nurse finds her first.

We'd better hurry.

I don't bother knocking on LeRoy's door. It's not like he'd give me permission to enter anyway. The curtains are drawn, and the lights are off. A quick glance at my watch says it's his nap time.

Unfortunate timing.

I grab the chair from the corner of the room and drag it closer to his bed. He stirs and wipes at his nose but doesn't wake.

"LeRoy." I shake him by the shoulders. "LeRoy!"

He smacks his lips, squinting one eye open.

"It's Zoe," I say. "Zoe Lane. The girl you ran over with your car."

LeRoy frowns and squeezes his eyes shut. "Get out of my room."

"No." I scoot to the end of the chair. "We need to speak."

"No, we don't."

"Yes, we do. I've been communicating with Willie."

LeRoy blows out a breath and laughs. "You're as nutty as your parents." He reaches for the call button, and I grab his arm.

"Don't do that. This is important. See, I've been doing a lot of thinking this past week, and there are a few things gnawing at me. I've met Betty. She's beautiful, and kind, and she has a good heart. Yes, her decisions do cause pause, but I know you were fond of her."

"No, I wasn't," he says too quickly.

"I think the answer to that is yes." I take a moment to regroup. "I *know* the answer to that is yes."

He mumbles under his breath.

"I know Willie only proposed to Betty to prove to you all that he could. Makes sense. He's arrogant, wealthy, a royal pain in the—"

"Get to the point!" Willie crosses the room.

I suppress an eye roll. "Betty has been arrested for the death of Willie MacIntosh," I say.

LeRoy waves his hand, as if this is of little consequence.

Not the reaction I had hoped for.

"Willie was poisoned," I continue, hoping to draw a reasonable reaction from him. "Someone snuck into his house Monday morning, using the hide-a-key in the backyard, and took his medication. They crushed it up and sprinkled it into his overnight oats. Betty wasn't there because she was at a bed and breakfast with Ron. It doesn't look good for her."

LeRoy shrugs.

He's as frustrating as his former best friend.

I let go of his arm and slide onto the foot of his bed. "There are a few pieces of information only you can help us with, LeRoy. First, I have to admit that I borrowed your car last Tuesday morning."

Leroy glares at me but doesn't say a word.

"I drove it to Betty's house, but I parked it around the corner, out of sight. But what I just realized was that Arnie, Willie's next-door neighbor, said he'd seen someone at Willie's house and that it was you. At the time, Willie and I assumed that he *had* seen your car at Willie's. But Arnie couldn't have seen your car—it was parked around the corner—and he can't see over his ugly fortress of bushes which are clearly a violation of the HOA terms and conditions, section One-A and section Five-B ..." Willie is in my ear, and I shoot Willie a *stay on topic* glance.

"Yeah, yeah, yeah," he says and puts his mouth to my ear.

"But he can see into Willie's backyard, specifically, his side yard." I shoo Willie away, wanting to use my own thoughts. "I never thought about the timing of everything until recently. I thought it was all a wild coincidence. But perhaps there is no coincidence. We view life as some big complicated mess, when in reality we're all pieces to a bigger puzzle that fit perfectly together to make—"

"If you start getting philosophical on me, I'm going to vomit," Willie moans.

I ignore him.

"You knew Willie's gate code. You knew where the hide-a-key was. Monday morning, you ran me over while I was crossing the street *in* the pedestrian lane. I don't remember much, but I was told that you were badly shaken up. Which I attributed to your hitting me, but the pictures at the scene have me questioning something." There's a shift in the air. Every hair on my body stands to attention. "You and Willie were best friends, but maybe not best friends as much as oldest friends. You'd known each other since childhood, and he had a tendency to take what was yours. Starting with Isabel and ending with Betty."

LeRoy sits up with the aid of his adjustable bed. His eyes are almost black. I reach into my bra and grab the cufflink, keeping it grasped in my hand.

"That morning, your car was facing south, but if you were on your way to Trucker it should have been facing north. You were wearing tan pants, a white shirt, and these." I uncurl my hand and show him the cufflink. "You dropped this one when you snuck into Willie's house to kill him."

LeRoy's face remains unmoved.

"You were on your way to the club for the gentlemen's meeting, where Willie was about to be named Member of the Century, but you made a detour to Willie's house."

"That's enough!" Brian is in the doorway. He crosses the room in one stride, slams the pictures I'd asked him to bring onto the bed, and grabs his uncle's hands.

LeRoy slouches, like he's fallen asleep.

"You need to leave, Zoe," Brian says.

"No." I stand my ground. Well … I sit my ground. My butt is still perched on LeRoy's bed.

Brian shakes his head, looking betrayed. "Leave, please."

"No, thank you."

"Zoe, stop it. I'd appreciate it if you left."

"I understand, but I do have to speak with your uncle."

Willie moans. "This is the most polite argument I've witnessed."

"Then I'll get the nurse." Brian leaves, and I grab the pictures and quickly flip through them. Willie is looking over my shoulder.

First picture: LeRoy is holding the driver's side door. He's wearing the beige pants and white shirt, but his right sleeve is down, and if I squint and turn my head to the side, I can see a single cufflink.

The next picture: Brian is carrying me. It's an even more unflattering angle than the one printed. I look pregnant!

The third picture is of LeRoy sitting on the curb, his face in

MAKING A MEDIUM

his hands, and his left sleeve is not buttoned. There is no cufflink.

Aha!

LeRoy was on his way home from killing Willie, as I suspected. Which is exactly why I asked Brian to bring the pictures. If he were going to Trucker, he'd be going north. But his car is facing south. If I hadn't been walking (legally) *in* the crosswalk, he would have made it home.

"You killed Willie. You took the key, broke into his home, and when you went to lock it on your way out, you were so frazzle that you broke the key. Then you went there to get the key out of the lock before you asked to be admitted here! You never fully forgave him for Isabel. It's not his fault she chose him. It's not his fault that she found someone else. It's not his fault Betty didn't want anything to do with you either. You killed me!" I stand up. "You selfish son of a bastard. You put the pills in my meal to teach me a lesson, but you didn't think it would kill me. I remember now. You tried to resuscitate me, but it didn't work, because of your damn arthritis. I told you to go see the rheumatologist! I remember everything."

Willie has taken over my body, and I don't know which way is up or down, and my legs feel like goo. I grab ahold of the bed rail and struggle to catch my breath, and then suddenly I'm on the ground. My hand goes to my forehead, and I stare at the crimson covering my fingertips. LeRoy blurs into two, his arms above his heads with a potted plant in all his hands.

Willie throws punch after punch after punch, growing more frustrated as his fists go straight through LeRoy.

"He wasn't supposed to die," LeRoy chokes out. "He was just supposed to have diarrhea!"

"You grabbed the wrong medicine, you fool!" Willie screams. "I died because you never got your damn cataract surgery!"

Between the head contusion and the lack of energy, I'm paralyzed.

LeRoy slams the plant down onto my head. My face is covered in soil and pieces of ceramic pot.

"I told you to leave me alone!" LeRoy lowers to one knee and reaches for my neck. He's moving in slow motion. If I had my wits, I could give him a soft kick, and he'd tumble over.

Unfortunately, my wits have abandoned me. So has Willie. He's left the room—not that he could do much to protect me in this situation.

"LeRoy!" comes a familiar voice. "What are you doing?"

LeRoy is distracted long enough for me to crawl back on my elbows.

"What is happening?" Brian helps LeRoy to his feet. Willie is beside him.

"She attacked me," LeRoy points a bent forefinger right at me.

If I weren't so physically drained, I might laugh.

"He killed me!" Willie is screaming in Brian's ear. "He killed me!"

Brian helps LeRoy into a chair, and a nurse runs in and stumbles back when she sees me lying on the ground, surrounded by soil.

"Should I call the police?" she asks Brian.

He looks at the plant, then at his uncle, then at me, then at the plant again.

"LeRoy killed me, you idiot. Pay attention!" Willie is now in Brian's face. "I know you've got a brain in there. Use it!"

I roll to my side and rest on my elbow, still struggling to remain awake. "LeRoy accidentally killed Willie. He slipped him the wrong medicine. I bet if you check his property or his car, you'll find that broken key," I say.

Brian looks at LeRoy. "Is this true?"

LeRoy rests his hands on his knees, face pointed to the floor.

"Is it true?" Brian asks again.

LeRoy closes his eyes, clutches his chest, and falls back.

"Oh, get up, you big faker!" Willie nudges LeRoy with the tip of his shoe. "LeRoy?"

Oh, geez.

CHAPTER TWENTY-SEVEN

Dr. Girt, the same emergency room doctor who diagnosed me with an iron deficiency and prescribed me antipsychotic meds, is standing at my bedside with his iPad. "You have a minor concussion, three stitches, and you're still anemic."

"Wanna know something?" I signal Dr. Girt to come closer and cup my hand around my mouth. "I see dead people."

Dr. Girt types this information into his iPad.

"You're high," Willie says. "I want to know what they put in your IV, because I want some."

"Mmmhmmm. High as a ..." I raise my hand, searching for the right word. "As a ... as a ... My friend here invented the space ship," I tell Dr. Girt.

"A part of the fuel system," Willie corrects.

"I'm sorry." I grab the sleeve of Dr. Girt's white jacket. "He invited the fuel."

"It's *invented* not invited and ... never mind," Willie grunts.

Dr. Girt yanks his arm free. "I called your parents, and they should be here soon. Hang tight."

I salute the doctor as he pulls the curtain around my bed.

"I don't think he likes me so much," I tell Willie.

"I know he doesn't like you so much. He rock-paper-scissored with the another resident to see who had to take you when you were brought in."

"I still think calling an ambulance was over-dramatatacized."

"It's MelBorne. There are two ambulances waiting in the parking lot at all times."

"Oh. Mmmmkkaay. I'm sorry about, you know ... the whole dying thing," I say. "Sucks when your best friend kills ya, huh?" My brain filter was busted in the Pot versus Zoe battle, because I have no control over the words falling out of my mouth. "And it looks like your wife had an affair with a much younger man who is hotter than you. That *really* sucks." My empathy must have also been busted in the battle.

"Nah. It's fine. I had a good life with a lot of women. And LeRoy didn't mean to do it."

"You forgive him? Just like that?"

"I'm dead. What am I supposed to do?"

"It's always about a girl, isn't it?" I say, my voice unnecessarily loud and slurred. "Also, I don't think you were a good person when you were alive." I slap my hand over my mouth. "I didn't mean to say that."

Willie heaves a sigh. "Don't be. I'm beginning to think you're right."

I open my mouth and pause. "Oh, no. My parents are here." I can feel my mother coming.

The curtain swings open, and there she is, wearing the same tight skirt as earlier. Dad is holding her by the elbow.

"Zoe!" Mom practically throws herself onto the bed. "Your face." She touches the bandage above my right eyebrow. "Old Man LeRoy really has it out for you. I don't understand it."

"He killed Willie MacIntosh." Sheriff Vance saunters into the room, belly first. "We found the key in his backseat of his car. Then he confessed before ..."

"Before what?" Willie and I ask.

"Before he passed."

Willie and I gasp in unison.

"He *did* die," I say in almost a whisper.

"They were able to revive him enough to talk and get him here, but he ended up passing a few minutes ago," Sheriff answers, giving me a peculiar glare that—even in my drugged state—causes my insides to shrivel.

"I told you it wasn't Daniel MacIntosh," Mom is saying to the sheriff. "And that old man tried to kill my daughter not once but twice. This is unbelievable. What are you going to do about it?"

Dad taps Mom's arms. "Sweetie, Old Man LeRoy died."

Mom acts like this is the first she's hearing this information. "Oh, my. Well ... okay."

The news sinks in, and I fight with the drugs in order to truly comprehend what has happened. LeRoy is dead. I check the room. And he's not here.

Thank goodness.

But Sheriff Vance is. He's still standing at the foot of my bed, rubbing his belly.

"Do you need a statement from Zoe, Vance?" my mom asks.

"Not right now. I only came to see how she was doing and to give her the sad news." His voice has an edge. "She cracked the case. Not sure how, but she did it."

"She's always had a flare for true crime," my dad says, and I suck in my bottom lip, afraid I might blurt out the truth.

"You take care of yourself," the sheriff says to me and gives me one last glance before he leaves.

It could be the drugs, but I swear Sheriff Vance doesn't trust me.

CHAPTER TWENTY-EIGHT

The next few days fly by in a post-concussion blur. Betty is vindicated. The press is all over the story, but there is no mention of me—about which I'm equal parts relieved and peeved. Relieved no more attention has been brought to my gifts. Peeved because no one has acknowledged my help. I don't need a full-page spread in *The Gazette* or anything crazy like that, but a "Hey, thanks for solving a murder," would be nice.

Mom is as frantic as ever—is it illegal to toss a Xanax into someone's mouth while they're talking or is it just frowned upon? She drugged me. I think it's only fair I get to drug her.

No word from Brian—not even *a sorry my uncle tried to kill you. Hope you're well* note, or a phone call, or a fruit basket.

Which is fine.

I don't have time to worry about feelings and internships (assuming I still have one), because as soon as Betty was vindicated Daniel contested the will.

Which was a shock to no one.

"I still don't think we should be here," I say to Willie. There's a Bluetooth in my ear—a present from Dad. It doesn't actually connect to my phone, but it does prevent people from thinking I'm crazy.

"Daniel is not taking my money, and it's your job to make that happen. Suck it up."

"You don't have to be so grumpy," I say as I climb the courthouse steps. "If you had used a lawyer to alter your will, none of this would be happening."

"If you learned how to dress, we wouldn't be running late!"

"*Gah*! You're impossible today." I stop to rummage through my briefcase, in search of loose change for the homeless man lying across three steps. It's the same transient guy in a Davy Crockett hat with a long beard I saw walking along the frontage road near Willie's house the day I had the meltdown.

"What are you doing, person!" Willie pulls at his tie. "We're going to be late!"

"Slow your roll," I mumble and drop twenty-seven cents into the man's hand.

"Bless you," he says in a gruff voice and flashes me a toothless grin. "God bless you."

I smile back and dash up the remaining steps to the courthouse entrance before Willie has another fit. I pass through the metal detector and am deemed safe to proceed. "Are you sure you want Betty to have the money?" I ask once I'm reunited with my Bluetooth.

"Yes. Stop asking me that question."

The courtroom is busier than I anticipated. The gallery is filled with news reporters covering the case. At the front is the judge—a woman with a stiff blonde bob and purple-rimmed glasses. Betty is sitting with Jackson at one table, and Daniel is sitting beside the man with the light bulb-shaped head at another.

The judge bangs her gavel, and everyone stands.

Wait ... what? I check the time. We're fifteen minutes late. There's no way it's over.

Willie clenches his fists. "I told you to hurry up!"

"We could have left earlier if you weren't so picky about what I wear." I had on my sensible blue pantsuit, and Willie threw a toddler-like tantrum until I slipped into jeans and a pink shirt. I added the floral cardigan to tie the outfit together.

"I still think you should burn that sweater," he says.

"Noted."

A reporter gives me a sideways glance, and I point to my ear. "Bluetooth," I mouth.

Dad really is a genius.

I snake through the crowd to Betty. Jackson rolls his eyes. "What are you doing here?"

"I'm sorry," I say, feigning ignorance. "I forget. Was it *you* who vindicated your client, or was it me?" I tap my chin, pretending to be deep in thought.

Willie laughs.

So does Betty.

Jackson leaves.

"I'm glad you came." Betty leans over the divide and gives me a hug. She looks beautifully shattered. Her hair is pulled back into a low ponytail, her makeup is under-exaggerated, and *she's* wearing a sensible dark blue pantsuit with pinstripes. Although hers is tighter, and she's wearing six-inch heels.

"I'm sorry we're late," I say. "What did we miss?"

Betty heaves a telling sigh. "It doesn't look good, Zoe. Jackson said ninety-nine percent of wills sail through probate court, but this is the one percent. Daniel is arguing that I tricked Willie into giving me everything when he'd agreed all along to leave his inheritance to Daniel. And since Willie crafted the will himself and had it witnessed by two men who are dead ..." Her voice trails off, and she shifts her eyes to Daniel, who is smiling triumphantly and shaking his lawyer's hand. "I really think the judge is going to throw out the will."

"Crap!" Willie kicks at the floor and continues to push profanity through his teeth.

"What happens if the judge does that?" I ask Betty.

She looks over her shoulder then nods her head toward the exit. "It's better if we don't talk about this here."

I follow her out a side door into a small courtyard, away from reporters. "Did Willie have a will stating Daniel would get everything?" Betty asks. "Daniel said there was one, but Jackson and I have looked through all of Willie's documents and torn apart his room, but we haven't been able to locate it."

"She tore apart my room?" Willie asks. "Tell her to put it back like she found it."

"What does it matter if you're dead?" I mutter.

"Because you leave a man's room alone—dead or alive. It's common courtesy."

I roll my eyes.

"Does he know where it is?" Betty asks.

Willie kicks at the ground and whistles a jolly tune.

"Willie?" I say. "Where is it?"

He shrugs and keeps whistling.

"Willie, where is the will?"

He pretends to zip his lips and saunters off to inspect a tree.

Gah! He's back to his infuriating self.

"What happens if you can't find the original will?" I ask Betty.

"I don't know for sure. Jackson uses a lot of big words when he talks about it, but it seems like if the judge throws out the will, it would be as if there isn't one." She twists her fingers, like she isn't sure of herself. "I'd still get everything since Willie didn't have any children."

"Okay, that's good news," I say loud enough for Willie to hear.

"Except Jackson thinks Daniel will fight it."

"That's not great news," I say more at a whisper.

"I'm just tired of all this, Zoe. Would Willie be mad at me if I split the inheritance with Daniel?"

"Yes!" Willie bellows into my ear, and I stumble backwards. "I'll never forgive her."

Geez.

"Obviously Daniel didn't kill Willie. So it's not like he's this horrible person," Betty continues. "And he does have a family, and, like, he is Willie's nephew." I can tell she's trying hard to rationalize this decision.

Willie steps between Betty and me and claps his hands together, looking straight at me. "Repeat this," he says. "Tell her that I didn't marry her because she was the great love of my life or even because I wanted a wife. At first, I wanted to razz my friends. I'll admit that. And it worked, obviously, since I'm now dead. When I asked her to marry me, I never intended to actually marry her. It was after she moved in and I got to know her that I realized what a genuine person she is. I married her because I didn't want Daniel to be my legacy. I didn't want my hard work to go to a man who would buy boats, and pools, and use my money to have fun and gamble it away. Betty will use it for good. She'll donate it to all her charities, and help her friends, and the animal shelters, and all that crap. I want her to get married, have kids, and send them off to college, and have the life she always wanted. That's why I want her to have the money."

And it all makes sense.

Finally!

The sincerity of his words touches my heart, and I have a hard time repeating this to Betty without getting chocked up.

"And I don't give a damn about Ron," he adds.

"He doesn't care about you and Ron," I say to her.

Betty steps backwards, looking alarmed. "W-what about Ron?"

"We know you and Ron were together at the bed and breakfast in Trucker the night before Willie was killed."

Betty looks completely shell-shocked. "I was *not* with Ron! You take that back." Now I'm the one shell-shocked. Betty has never raised her voice before. "Why would you say that in front of Willie?"

"Where you not at Newsgate House on Monday morning? I saw the bag on your floor."

"Are you talking about the laundry bag?"

"Yes."

She shakes her head. "I offered to do his laundry because he and his wife are going through a divorce."

"Told ya!" Willie says with a triumphant smile. "No affair. You were wrong. I was right."

"Nothing happened between you and Ron?" I ask, trying to gauge her expression.

Betty lifts her eyes. "No."

I'm confused by this response; I should probably ask more precise questions. "I heard you say I love you to someone on the phone the night I slept at your house. Who were you talking to?"

"Ron," she says, her voice small.

Willie stops mid-celebration.

"We were close, but nothing *actually* happened until after Willie died," she says in a panic. "I swear, all I did was grab his laundry for him. Please don't be mad. I didn't mean for this to happen. I swear! Is Willie mad?"

Willie explodes. "The man has a horrible swing! Really? MacDonald? He plays like he's blind."

Betty's staring at me anxiously. "What does he say?"

"Um ... I think he's okay with it," I say.

"He better not touch my cars, or my clubs, or take my parking spot at the club."

I give Willie a *you're dead, why does it matter?* look.

"Tell her."

Fine. "Willie asks that Ron not touch his cars, or his clubs, and that he not take his parking spot," I say.

Betty's entire face lights up. "Willie was always very particular about his things," she says.

"Yeah, I've noticed."

CHAPTER TWENTY-NINE

According to *Reaching the Other Side*, the reason we are visited by spirits is because they have unfinished earthly business to tend to.

Willie's killer has been caught.

We know the motive.

It appears Betty will inherit Willie's fortune just as he wanted.

No one will touch his cars or his parking spot.

It seems his earthly business is finished.

Yet, here he is. Standing beside me, sulking. "I hate book festivals."

"When was the last time you went to one?"

"Never, because I *hate* them."

I ignore Willie because even though this is my first book festival, I already know that I love them. I've never seen Earl Park look better. Colorful balloons tied to every surface, triangle banners hung around the gazebo, couples strolling hand in hand eating ice cream, and popcorn, and baked goods from Butter Bakery or one of the many other vendors present. In front of the gazebo are tables dedicated to the authors who have turned out for the event.

I reach into my briefcase and pull out the Sizzling Postmen series Rosa gave to me years ago. She told me I was the only one who checked them out and she needed the shelf space. Who was I to turn down free books?

Don't fangirl, I remind myself. Keep it together and act cool, calm, and collected.

Crap, I'm almost certain I'm going to get weird. But how often does a famous author like TR Kuss come to little ol' Fernn Valley? There isn't an author picture on the back of her books, but I imagine she's in her twenties, with choppy hair and at least three tattoos. I bet she has a nose piercing and pink highlights. Her bedroom scenes are so detailed that I'm sure she's had a lot of boyfriends. Maybe she can give me a few pointers because as of yet, I've kissed exactly zero men, let alone visited anyone's bedroom, or bathroom, or locker room, or fire station, or elevator ...

"You're drooling again," Willie says.

Oops. Right.

Don't fangirl, Zoe.

Keep it cool.

I search for the TR Kuss sign and spot it beside a children's book author. I blow out a breath and step up to the table with my books clutched in my hands and ...

Willie folds over in a laughing fit.

No. No. No. No. Just ... no. Sitting behind the TR Kuss booth, with a name tag that reads TR Kuss, is a little old woman with a helmet of gray hair, a pink blazer, hooped earrings, and glasses. I *know* her! It's Jenny Clark. Mrs. Clark. Who owns the beauty parlor. The Mrs. Clark who does my mom's hair. The Mrs. Clark who does my hair. The Mrs. Clark who has, like, ten grandchildren.

"Hi, Zoe." Mrs. Clark smiles and clasps her hands.

Ok, I have nothing against the elderly. Nothing at all. But it's going to be difficult for me *not* to picture Mrs. Clark sitting behind her computer writing about burning loins and chiseled abs and creating the hot heroes of my fantasies.

"I ... I ... I didn't know you wrote ... *these* books," I say.

"I didn't know you read them." She winks. "Guess we all have our little secrets. Would you like me to sign those?" She points to the books clutched to my chest.

"Er ... sure."

Mrs. Clark, aka TR Kuss, scrawls her signature on the inside jacket of each book. "Have you checked out the Hot Billionaire series yet? This time the heroine is the billionaire." She hands me the first book in the series, and I read the back cover.

Willie peers over my shoulder. "Seductively domineering, huh? Sounds interesting."

It does.

So I buy the entire series.

Sure, I was supposed to use the money for clothes (a gift from my dad), but I'd rather spend my time reading.

"Can we go now?" Willie asks.

"We can," I say. "Do you want to walk? Or should I have my dad pick us up?"

"I don't want to walk."

I call my dad. We agree to meet in the parking lot of *The Gazette*. I buy a donut and stroll down the sidewalk, swinging my bag of books at my side. "It's a nice day, isn't it?"

"Your boyfriend is coming," Willie says.

"Huh? Where?" I spin around and come face-to-face with Brian. He's wearing jeans, a baseball cap, and sunglasses. I've never seen him so casual.

"There's donut on your lip," Willie says.

I run my tongue over my mouth. "Hi," I say with a smile, checking my reflection in Brian's glasses to be sure there's nothing stuck in my teeth.

"I'm glad I caught you," he says. "I've been meaning to stop by."

"Don't worry. It's been a hard couple of weeks. I'm sorry about LeRoy."

"Considering all that's happened, I don't think you have anything to be sorry about."

I dump my donut into the trashcan. "Don't blame yourself, Brian. It wasn't your fault."

"How did you *know*, though? When I spoke to you earlier that day, you were sure it was Ron. Who or what tipped you off? How'd you figure out it was LeRoy?"

Those are good questions. "Um ... the picture you ran in *The Gazette*. His car was facing the wrong way, and, um, what can I say? I just figured it out." I tap my temple.

"How'd you like to put this"—he taps my temple, and his finger lingers—"to work at *The Gazette*?"

"The internship?"

"Not an internship. A mind like yours needs to be a reporter. We can shake things up." He lowers his sunglasses and winks. My insides do a somersault. I'd *really* like to shake him up.

Willie waves a hand in front of my face. "Stop staring, person. You're getting weird."

I can't help it.

"Then I'll see you tomorrow?" Brian asks.

I force my mouth to move. "Sures."

"What the hell does that mean?" Willie snorts.

"I meant to say yes, but it turned into sure, and ... um ... okay." Willie tells me to stop talking. "I'll be there."

We say good-bye, and I watch Brian walk away. He stops at the Butter Bakery cart and buys a croissant.

"He would have kissed you if you were wearing different shoes," Willie says.

"Would you lay off the freaking shoes already?"

Mr. and Mrs. Batch stop and give me a look. I point to the Bluetooth in my ear. "On a call," I say.

They exchange a look then lift their bags of popcorn as if to say "cheers."

I lift my bag of books, and they continue on their way.

Phew.

Willie and I head over to the parking lot to wait for my dad. I take a seat on the curb and open the first book in the Hot Billionaire series.

"Turn the page," Willie says, reading over my shoulder.

"Wait, I'm not done."

"You're a slow reader. Hurry up."

I read the last paragraph then turn the page.

A shadow appears, blocking my reading light. I gaze up, using my hand as a visor. It's Rosa. She's hugging a clipboard with a pencil stuck behind her ear.

"I see you met TR Kuss," she says. "What did you think?"

"You never said TR Kuss was Mrs. Clark." I use a leaf to mark my page and close the book.

"Hey! I was still reading," Willie says.

"She kept her writing a secret for years," Rosa says. "I'm not sure what suddenly changed her mind, but she told me she no longer wanted to keep her talents hidden. And here she is."

"And here she is ..." I stand and dust off the back of my pants. "The day turned out wonderfully. What a fun idea."

"I'm surprised how many people came out for the event." Rosa places a hand on my shoulder and frowns. "How are you doing? You've been through quite the wringer these past few weeks."

There's an understatement.

"I'm doing better, thank you."

"Glad to hear it. Oh, excuse me." Rosa waves to the MelBorne Assisted Living van pulling into the parking lot. There's a picture on the side of an older man and woman playing cards with mega-watt smiles on their faces.

False advertisement, if you ask me.

The van parks in the handicapped spot. The door opens, and a wheelchair lift appears with a little old woman with jet black hair, a small face, and no eyebrows. Rosa gives the old woman a kiss on the cheek and speaks to her in Spanish.

"Is this your mother?" I ask.

"This is my mama." Rosa wheels her mother down the ramp. "Mama, this is Zoe," she says directly into her mother's ear then talks to her in Spanish. "Zoe, this is Mama Isabel, she doesn't speak any English, not since the stroke."

I drop my books.

Okay, there's got to be a thousand women the same age as Willie named Isabel, but the coincidence is enough to suck the air out of my lungs.

"Are you okay, dear?" Rosa asks.

My tongue has turned to mush. I bend down to gather my books off the ground. "W-w-where—how—um—did your mother grow up in Mexico?"

"Yes," Rosa answers slowly. "But she has papers."

I try not to get too excited. I mean, what are the odds? "Where did she grow up?"

"In a small town north of Mexico City ... are you okay? You look a little pale."

I turn to Willie, who looks like a statue. It *is* Isabel! The Isabel. The great love of Willie's life! The one who got away. The one whose father didn't approve. The infamous Isabel had been living in Fernn Valley, one city away for ... for ... "How long have you lived here?"

Rosa pushes her mother into the shade and down the sidewalk toward the park. "I brought Mama over from Mexico five years ago. She used to talk about moving to Fernn Valley all the time. I'm not even sure how she knew about this place. But she made it sound wonderful—it's the reason I moved here."

My thoughts are free falling, and I can't seem to put a coherent sentence together.

Willie studies Isabel's face as we walk alongside them. "That's her!" He's now in my ear. "Say I'm here! Say I'm here! Say I'm here! Say it!"

Um, sure.

But ...

Uno problemo.

Uno problemo is the only phrase I know in Spanish.

I jump in front of Rosa, and she off-roads her mother into the grass. "Sorry, but I need to talk to your mom."

"She only speaks Spanish," Rosa says.

"That's fine. You can translate for me." I lower to one knee and grab Isabel by the hand. Her hands are leathery with bulging veins and are warm to the touch. She doesn't pull away, instead she touches my cheek, her eyes glossed over. "Tell her Willie is here," I say to Rosa.

Rosa hesitates then mumbles this in Spanish.

Isabel nods along and responds.

"She says she knows," Rosa says. "But who is Willie, and where is he?"

"Tell her Willie only left to join the service so he could earn the respect of her father," I say. "When he came back, he discovered she had moved on ..." I pause to regroup. It's hard not to get emotional. I live for a good romance.

"Who is Willie?" Rosa asks, exasperated. "You're not making any sense."

"Just tell her, please?" I ask.

Rosa relents with a sigh and translates. Isabel responds in Spanish.

"Mama says that she didn't know he'd come back for her. She wished he'd said something because ... because ... Mama?" Rosa backs Isabel's wheelchair up and drops to her knee. She takes her mother by the hands and speaks to her in Spanish. I have no idea what she's saying but based on the fluctuation and tone of her voice, she's not happy.

"What is she saying?" Willie demands. "What is she saying?"

"I don't speak Spanish," I mutter out the side of my mouth.

Rosa and Isabel are going back and forth in Spanish for a while.

A long while.

Rosa throws her hands up in the air. "Mama says that ..." She massages her temples. "She says that she found out about the baby after Willie had left, and my abuelo forced her to marry to hide the family shame."

"Um ... huh?"

Rosa shakes her head. "According to Mama, this Willie person is my biological father."

I drop my books.

"I knew my biological father was a soldier, but she never spoke his name until now. Goodness me." Rosa smooths back her hair. "And this man is here? How'd you know about him?"

Willie has gone sheet white, and I realize *this* is why Willie is still here.

Not because of LeRoy.

Not because of Daniel.

Not because of his money or his murder or his parking space or his cars.

Rosa is why he's here.

After all these years, all those women, and a vasectomy.

Willie MacIntosh has a daughter, and grandchildren, and a legacy.

Holy crap.

"Rosa." I touch her shoulder. "I think you should sit down for a minute and, please, have an open mind."

CHAPTER THIRTY

And just like that, Rosa is a multimillionaire.

Of course I didn't tell her the truth. I told her I was a friend of Betty's, and we had suspected that Willie had a love child. I may have implied I was more of a PI than a medium, but whatever. I have a sinking suspicion that she knows the truth anyway.

The judge deemed the will invalid, and the fate of Willie's fortune came down to good ol' California law. Being that Betty and Willie didn't have any common property, everything was essentially split between her and Rosa—his daughter.

A ruling neither women had a problem with.

Daniel is a different story.

As soon as the judge bangs her gavel, Daniel huffs and puffs and storms out of the courtroom like he's about to blow someone's house down. I'm not sure how he'll pay for his renovations now, but as Rosa says, *agua queen no has de beber, dejala correr.*

No idea what that means, but I feel the wisdom in those words.

Also, I want to take a Spanish class.

Betty, Rosa, Willie, Jackson, and I leave the courthouse in a chatter of excitement.

"I can't believe it," Rosa says, for at least the nine hundredth time since the DNA results came back. "I just can't believe it."

"You better believe it." Betty gives her a side hug. "What does Willie think about the ruling?" she asks me.

"Um ... not sure what he thinks, since he's dead." I give her the signal. A sign we came up with the day I asked her to stop telling everyone I was a medium. I touch the tip of my nose when Willie is around. Then I wink if he's happy and suck in my bottom lip when he's not.

Right now, I'm winking.

Which isn't exactly accurate.

After he found out about Rosa, he wanted her to have everything. But I was able to convince him this was the path of least resistance and Rosa would be fine with one hundred and fifty million dollars.

But he appears to be taking the news better than I thought. Too well. He's been unusually quiet all day.

All of Rosa's children and grandchildren are waiting outside the courthouse and engulf her in a flurry of hugs and kisses on her cheeks. I watch from a short distance, giving her the space to celebrate with her family.

"I'm happy Willie knows about his daughter," Betty says.

"Me too."

Jackson looks heavenward.

"We'll make a believer out of you." Betty nudges him with her elbow. "Just you wait."

"I need a drink," he says. "We'll speak later." He gives Betty a kiss on each cheek and shakes my hand good-bye.

"Willie says you still need to work on your pitch shot," I holler after him.

Jackson thunks the heel of his hand to his forehead and continues walking.

Betty laughs and interlocks her arm in mine. "He knows you're legit, but he's just afraid to admit it."

I'm not sure about that. "So what are you going to do with your money?" I ask.

"I know exactly what I'm doing with it. But first, there's a little business to take care of." She reaches into her purse and pulls out an urn.

"Please tell me that's not me?" Willie asks, horrified.

"It's Willie." Betty flashes a smile. "I picked him up yesterday."

Willie runs his hands down his face. "I don't want to be kept in a jar. Why'd you let her pick that urn? I hate it. It's ugly."

"Why'd you bring him ... um ... here?" I ask Betty.

"Because he doesn't belong to me anymore." She steps over to Rosa and thrusts the urn into her hands. "It's Willie."

Rosa glances down at her dead father. "Oh ... thank you."

"He wants to be scattered in the lake, but that was before he knew about his daughter."

"No, I want to be in the lake!" Willie is in my ear. "In the lake!"

"He wants to be in the lake," I blurt out. "I mean. That's what his final wishes were. So, um, you should scatter him in the lake."

Rosa's son steps forward. He's a middle-aged man with a cul-de-sac of hair and three chins. "He wants to float around with a bunch of fish crap? And who knows how many dead bodies are there?"

Willie cocks a thumb. "The kid makes a point. Keep me in the urn."

"Why don't you decide," I say to Rosa. "But I need to get going."

Rosa gives me a tight hug. "Thank you for everything."

"My pleasure. I'll still see you at the library? You're not going to quit now that you could buy the place yourself, right?"

"Of course not."

I give Betty a hug good-bye and trot down the steps, stopping to give a dollar to the same Davy Crockett hat-wearing man from last week.

Brian wants a full account of how the hearing went. I place my Bluetooth in my ear and pull out my notepad. "We need to figure out how to ... Willie?" I turn around. "Willie?

I backtrack toward the courthouse and find him standing beside Rosa and laughing as her family ... *his* family ... talks.

My heart is full.

This medium gig is pretty special.

I wave to get his attention, and he appears.

"You ready?" I ask.

"I am, person. It's been a pleasure." He tips his hat.

"What are you talking about?"

"It's time to go."

"Go? No, no." I start to panic. "I don't want you to go. We have so much to do."

"Like what?"

"Like ... I don't know. Who is going to pester me about my hair or clothes? Who is going to make snarky comments when my mom goes on one of her rampages? Who is going to keep me company? Don't you want to know how the Hot Billionaire series ends?"

Willie is shaking his head before I even finish speaking. "You don't need me anymore. You're good. I'm good. They're good." He jerks his head towards Rosa. "Just remember. You are a capable and smart *person*." He winks. "You have way too much to offer this world to be hiding out. Get your own place. Your own car. Dress your age. Live a little. Hell, live a lot. I'll catch you on the other side, *Zoe* Lane."

I'm trembling all over. Tears clog the back of my throat. I'm not ready to say good-bye. "Please," I choke out, but it's too late.

Willie is gone.

CHAPTER THIRTY-ONE

Four months later.

"Attention! Attention!" Tam Woo, the mayor of Trucker, taps the microphone, and the crowd hushes. "Can I have everyone's attention please?" He pauses to smile for the camera then continues. "It is with great pleasure that I hereby dedicate the pediatric cancer wing as the Willie MacIntosh Center." Tam hands Betty the giant scissors, and she cuts the ribbon.

I shove the notepad under my arm and clap along with the crowd. Instinctually, I check around to see if Willie's here, even if I know he's not. Rosa is, though, and she's beaming with pride.

Willie was right, Betty would maintain his legacy. She donated one hundred million dollars to the pediatric cancer center at Trucker Hospital in his name. She also graduated last month and plans to use the rest of Willie's money to open a counseling center for the youth.

Betty catches my gaze, and I wink. Our sign. Even if I can't see Willie anymore, I *know* he's happy.

I move with the crowd toward the reception area, where a long table is adorned with baskets of baked breakfast goods and an assortment of jams. I grab a blueberry scone and a napkin.

Rosa comes up from behind and helps herself to a chocolate muffin. "Isn't this lovely?" she asks. "What an honor for Willie."

"It is. How are you doing?"

"I'm fine," she says, playing it off. I can tell she isn't *fine*. I'm honing in on my ability to feel others' feelings.

"It was a beautiful funeral," I say.

She tears off a piece of her muffin and gives a feeble nod of her head. "It sure was."

Isabel died the day after Willie left. There is no doubt in my mind that the two are reunited. I can't wait to see them together. Well, I mean, I *can* wait. I don't feel like dying anytime soon. But it will be a nice reunion.

"There you two are!" Betty throws her arms around our shoulders and gives us a squeeze. "Isn't this great!" She looks up, and we follow her gaze to Willie's name proudly displayed above the hospital entrance. "Anyway, I'm glad I caught you both at the same time." She tucks a strand of hair behind her ear. "Ron and I are moving to Oregon."

"What? No," I say. Betty is the first alive friend I've had, and I don't want her to go anywhere.

"There're too many whispers," she says. "Whenever Ron and I go out in public, people stare at us. If I want to make a difference, I need to go somewhere else."

"I completely understand," says Rosa. "You need a fresh start."

"We all do," says Betty. "I'm thinking that I'll sell the house and stay out of Trucker forever."

There's a business card in my briefcase with a handwritten note from my mother. Mom had said to give it to Betty the moment she talked about selling. "It's the best way to get business in Trucker," she had said. Can't argue with that.

Guess this is the right moment.

I hand the card to Betty. "Thank you," she says and tucks it in her purse. "Can I borrow you? Just for a moment."

"Sure." I give Rosa a hug good-bye and follow Betty to her car.

"The craziest thing happened to me." Betty presses a button on her key fob, and the trunk of her Escalade opens. "I had a dream last night. It was so vivid, and I talked it over with Aleena, and she said it was Willie sending me a message." She grabs a shoebox and opens it. "He said you need these." She pulls out a pair of slip-on checkered Vans. "These aren't exactly what he said in my dream, but he mentioned something youthful without arch support. I hope you like them."

All I can do is laugh. "Thank you."

"He also wants you to have this." She holds out a manila envelope.

I set the shoes down and unwind the red string that's holding the envelope closed. Out slides a pink slip and the fancy BMW i8 key fob.

"I-I-I can't take this," I say.

"But you told me you got your driver's license."

She's right. I'd completed the test last month and drive around in my parents' van—sometimes. They still mostly drove, but that's only because we have one vehicle.

I turn the key fob over in my hand, unable to conjure up the ability to move my mouth.

"Willie was quite specific in my dream about this one," Betty says. "He wanted you to have *this* car. He had so many, what am I supposed to do with them?"

"What about Rosa?"

"She knows, and she thinks it's a great idea." She grabs me by the shoulders and manually turns me around. The car is parked on the other side of the parking lot. "Take it and enjoy!"

"I don't even know what to say."

"Don't say anything. Just *live*," Betty *boops* my nose. "I'll be in touch once we're settled."

We say good-bye, and I stand there in the parking lot, staring at my fancy space car.

Mom is going to freak out.

Speaking of Mom, my cell buzzes. I flip the phone open and press it to my ear. "I don't need a ride to *The Gazette* anymore," I answer in lieu of a hello. "I'm covered."

I make it to *The Gazette* in fewer than thirty minutes. This car is much more fun to drive when I know how to drive it. I park in the space farthest from the door, under a tree. Then I move it, not wanting to risk a bird or a leaf tarnishing the shiny exterior.

It's early, and people are still slowly trickling into work. Brian isn't exactly firm on the nine o'clock start time.

Leon from accounting whistles. "Is that your car?"

"It sure is." I sling my jacket over my shoulder and lock the car without looking, feeling very James Bond.

Beth from Sports holds open the door for me. "Dang, girl. Are you having an affair with a billionaire I don't know about?"

"Not exactly."

We walk to our desks. She sits across from me, and I place my briefcase in the bottom drawer.

"Did you cover the dedication at the hospital this morning?" she asks.

"I did. Is Brian here yet? I want to go over the notes with him." I peek over at his office, but the door is closed.

"Not sure. Go check."

I think I will.

Over the last four months, Brian and I have worked on several articles together: the new stoplight off Valley Road, the

Flower Carnival, and the town hall meeting. I haven't actually written anything on my own, but it's fine. Everyone has to start somewhere, and I'll start anywhere Brian is. Sure we haven't moved our relationship past the boss/employee stage. He did tell me that I looked nice yesterday, and last week we even had a non-work related conversation about cake: he likes carrot with cream cheese frosting. I know that's not exactly a toe-curling exchange, but I can *feel* a shift in our relationship. His feelings may not be as strong as mine are, but they're there. I know it. We're just going to be one of those couples who baby-step their way to love. Which is fine by me. I can wait. Plus it's a lot easier now that I don't have a spirit following me around, vying for my attention.

I pop a mint into my mouth and smooth out my hair. I'm wearing jeans, a pink blouse, and my new Vans from Willie. I don't want to deviate from my personal style, but now that I've entered the workforce, I can see how my closet could use a little updating.

Apparently shoulder pads aren't in.

Who knew?

I knock on Brian's door and don't wait for an answer before I let myself in and …

Ahhh!

I screw my fists into my eye sockets, trying to erase the image.

Brian is kissing a tall brunette with choppy hair. Her right butt cheek is propped up on the desk, and her right leg is wrapped around Brian's waist. It's like a car accident. I can't look away, but the visual makes me want to barf. No. No. No. No. No!

I slam the door shut and retreat back to my desk, feeling a shiver down my spine. My breath huffs out in a cloud, and my fingertips go numb. I sink into my chair and look up.

Behind Beth is a girl about my age with a gaping abdomen wound. She looks around the room in a panic. We lock eyes, and she flickers in and out. "What happened?" she asks in horror. "Where am I? What happened?"

Oh, geez.

Here we go again.

THE MEDIUM PLACE BOOK #2 PREVIEW

CHAPTER ONE

Don't panic, Zoe. You can do this. No sudden movements. No staring. No talking. But really, most importantly, don't panic!

Okay, I'm feeling a little panicky.

My stomach is doing that roller coaster-lurchy thing, and my fingertips are numb. Standing in front of me is a young woman in black yoga pants, a gray tank top, with an abdomen wound.

Also, she's dead.

Last time a spirit appeared at *The Gazette*, he was a fit, thirty-something-year-old man in a dapper suit and shiny shoes. This woman looks like she walked straight off the set of a horror movie: her dark hair teased with twigs and leaves sticking out, a cut under her right eye, and mud smeared on her forehead.

Frankly, she's freaking me out.

"I heard Ira brought donuts," Beth says without taking her eyes off the computer. She's putting the finishing touches on her latest article—a recap of Fernn Valley's softball game last night against Trucker. "Do you want one?" She clicks *save* and smiles up at me, completely unaware of what's happening directly behind her.

"I'll take a glazed if there's any left," I manage to say. "Thank you."

"Not a problem. I'll be right back." Beth takes off her glasses and places them on the desk. I watch as she stands and adjusts her pants, tucks in the back of her shirt, runs a hand through her short hair, scratches her nose, and ... *holy crap. You're going to the break room not going to meet the Queen. Hurry up!*

I drum my fingers on my desk, waiting with a patient smile plastered across my face. Finally (hallelujah!) Beth deems herself break-room ready, pushes her chair in, turns around, and walks right past the spirit.

Okay. Play it cool, Zoe.

I retrieve my cell phone from my briefcase. Word of donuts in the break room travels fast, and the newsroom is empty—thank goodness. I flip open my phone and place it to my ear, giving the illusion that I'm taking a call and not talking to myself —one of the many tricks of the trade. "I'm Zoe," I say as I approach the woman slowly. "What's your name?"

She frantically surveys the room with quivering hands. "It's ... Penelope. Wh-wh-what happened?" She looks down at her stomach. "I'm hurt!"

"You're going to be just fine," I say as convincingly as I can. Truth is, I have no idea what's happening.

"I don't remember anything." Her breath quickens. "Why am I at *The Fernn Valley Gazette*? How'd I get here? *Why* am I here?"

"Penelope, I know it's hard. But try to keep calm." I inch closer, the phone still at my ear.

Beth returns. "Bad news. Mike took the last glazed. I brought you an old-fashioned." She walks *through* Penelope and slides a paper plate with my donut across the desk. "Did you hear about the Chief's visitor?" She licks frosting off her fingertips. "Everyone in the break room says she came down for the three-day weekend to—oh, shoot." She covers her mouth. "I didn't realize you were on the phone. Sorry."

"It's fine." I snap my cell shut and smile, which is really hard to do because Penelope has faded to a pale, translucent state. I'm new to this whole medium gig, and my experience is limited, but I've never seen a sprit do *that* before.

The lights around the room flicker on and off several times. Everyone lets out a collective "ah, man!" as they come in from the break room to find black computer screens.

"That was weird." Mike walks over with a paper plate stacked with not one but *three* glazed donuts.

Thanks, Mike.

"Must have been an outage, I guess," says Irwin from the corner. "Good thing I saved my story."

Oh, geez, now everyone is back at their desks, rebooting their computers. I need them all to leave again so I can get Penelope out of here. If only there were more donuts. In my four months of employment, I've come to learn that nothing clears the workroom faster than food. It doesn't even matter what kind. Chris from accounting brought in apricots from his tree last week, and it was like the freaking *Hunger Games* around here.

Speaking of death, Penelope is putting two and two together. "Am I dead?" She spins around in a complete circle and holds up her hands, studying them as if she's never seen them before. "I-I can't be dead. Is this a dream? It's a dream, right? Yeah, this is *totally* a dream."

I wish.

"So, Zoe." Mike leans against my desk, still holding his donut tower on a small paper plate. "You missed an epic game last night. We were down by two in the seventh inning when Ira *crushed* the ball into center field. Dude brought in three runs."

"Cool," I say, not quite paying attention. Mike has barely uttered more than one word to me since I started working here. I'm not sure why he chooses now of all times to be friendly. Maybe he feels guilty for being a donut hog.

"Is that Meathead Mike?" Penelope presses her nose up to his face. "It is! He works here?"

If Meathead Mike is Mike Handhoff, then yes, he does.

Here's what I know about Mike: I'm not positive what his job title is, but he always looks busy; he's in his early to mid twenties; he has a dark-coiffed mane and broad shoulders; he mostly wears white shirts; and he uses "dude" as a noun, verb, and adjective.

Also, he's still talking. "So what do you think?"

"Um ... *huh?*"

"About the game. Epic right? Dude, we celebrated *so* hard afterwards I could barely get out of bed this morning."

"The game?" I try to keep my face stoic, which is hard to do considering there's a spirit circling him.

"Now I know I'm dreaming, because Mike is looking good," Penelope says, nodding her head in appreciation.

"Zoe? You okay?" Mike asks with his mouth full.

Nope.

"I think ... um ... I think that I need to use the restroom." I jerk my head, hoping Penelope will follow me.

No such luck. She disappears and reappears in the parking lot. I watch her panicking outside the window. Good grief.

"I, um ... okay, now I need to make a private phone call." I slap my phone to my ear and hurry outside, around to the back of the building, where Penelope is holding her stomach.

"This is the worst dream I've ever had!"

"Penelope, this isn't a dream ..." I search for a way to tactfully tell her she has died. "The thing is ... well, you're dead."

Okay, so maybe that wasn't tactful.

Penelope's face blanches. It almost looks like she's going to pass out. Then, as if making some sort of inner resolution, she peers up and narrows her eyes. "If I'm dead then *why* am I bleeding, huh?"

"I don't know. But I have a feeling if you calm down you'll get better." A total guess, but it makes sense.

"Calm *down*. You want me to calm down? You're telling me I'm freaking dead!" She runs her hands down her face. "I go to church. I pray every night!" She paces the length of the walkway, hands wringing. "I've dedicated my life to religion, and when I die I'm sent to *The Gazette*! Oh, no." She covers her mouth. "Is this hell?"

"What? No!" Geez. The paper isn't *that* bad. "You're not in heaven, and you're not in hell. You're here because there is business you need to tend to before you can transition to the next phase. I'm going to help you."

"I-I'm only twenty-one years old. Of course I have a lot of business left to do on earth! Like ... living!"

"Well, first things first. Let's get out of here because um ..." I turn around. Everyone inside is gawking at me through the window.

Great.

"Wait right here," I say, my cell still at my ear. "I'll be back."

I clap my phone shut and rush inside, feeling a bit unsettled. There's a hushed silence as soon as I enter the workroom, and everyone puts their heads down, pretending to be engrossed in their work.

Well, everyone but Ira, who follows me to my desk. "Who were you talking to?"

"There's um ... an emergency at home." I grab my briefcase and go to turn off my computer then remember that I never turned it on. "My dad is ... sick."

"Really?" Beth rolls her chair over. "I just spoke to him. We have an offer on my house. I'm meeting your parents after work to sign the papers."

Well, shoot. "Um, it's recent ... food poisoning. Yeah, it's food poisoning. Came on suddenly, and he's *super* sick."

Beth's dark eyes grow in diameter. "When I spoke to him he was at Butter Bakery. He must have gotten food poisoning from there."

"Butter!" echoes several voices.

"Where'd you get the donuts, Ira?" someone else asks.

"I bought them from Butter this morning," squeaks Ira, a young guy with birdlike features and curly hair. He's over obituaries and "The Squirrel of the Week" article. When you live in a town of fewer than 800 people, you have to get creative with the news.

Side note: it used to be squirrel of the *month*, but I suggested it be weekly—because I'm innovative like that.

Beth inspects her donut. "I thought they were day-old."

"Dude, my stomach feels weird." Mike dumps his plate into the trash.

"I feel fine." Beth tears off a chunk of deep-fried dough and pops it into her mouth.

Everyone else quickly discards donuts into the trash.

"We should run a story about this," says someone.

"I think I'm going to be sick," says someone else.

"Should we call the health department?"

"I'm going to vomit!"

"I swear the donuts are fresh," Ira says in a panic. "I-I bought them this morning."

Oh, for heaven sakes.

This is precisely why you don't lie.

The Chief's door opens and out walks a slender woman with a brown choppy haircut and legs for days. Everyone watches as she glides across the floor and out into the lobby.

Beth leans over and whispers, "I heard that's his girlfriend. She lives in Portland. According to Mike, their relationship was getting rocky, and she came to win him back."

"Yeah, I think it worked." Right before Penelope arrived, I'd walked in on Brian—the editor-in-chief, and the slender, choppy-haired girl making out. Which wouldn't have been a big deal if I weren't totally and completely head-over-heels-I-want-to-have-your-babies in love with Brian Windsor.

Not that he's completely aware of my feelings.

Brian steps out of his office and adjusts the bottom of his shirt. He's a little older than I am, has black-rimmed glasses, gray eyes, dark hair, freckles across his nose, and he smiles without showing his teeth. Also, he's gorgeous. "Can I speak with you?" he asks me.

Penelope is still outside the window, holding her stomach, and she appears to be counting.

"Err, I don't have time. I need to go home."

"Me too," says Mike, stifling a burp. "Food poisoning. Don't eat the donuts in the break room." He rushes to the bathroom.

Geez. The power of suggestion is ... *well*, powerful.

"I'm not feeling so good either, Chief," Beth says. "I should probably go home." She grabs her purse and winks at me as she passes by.

Gah! I need to call Dad and tell him he has food poisoning.

"Are you sick, too?" Brian asks me.

Um ... "Yes. I. Am. Very. Sick. Gotta. Go."

Penelope appears in front of Brian, and the lights flicker again. "I can't wait anymore!"

"Zoe? Are you okay?" Brian steps forward with his arm extended. "You look like you've seen a ghost."

He has no idea.

"Zoe?" Brian tries again. "Zoe?" He waves his hand in front of my face.

THE MEDIUM PLACE BOOK #2 PREVIEW

I look from Penelope to Brian and back again.

"Is this about Vanessa?" he asks, his brow wrinkled with concern.

Vanessa?

His girlfriend's name is *Va-ness-a*?

Really?

In most every romance novel I've ever read (and I've read a lot), the other woman's name is always Vanessa. Granted, in this case, Vanessa is not technically the *other* woman since she's the girlfriend. I guess I'm the other woman, except we've had almost zero physical contact.

Bottom line: there are no grounds for me to be upset.

Except, I am.

"I have to go," I say and beeline for the door.

"Don't leave, Zoe!" Brian calls after me.

When your boss tells you not to leave, especially when you've been at work less than an hour on the Friday before a three-day weekend, you should probably stay put. But if Brian knew there was a spirit following me around, I'm sure he'd be fine with me taking a personal day.

I slap my phone to my ear. "Come with me, Penelope." I power walk to the parking lot, my briefcase swinging at my side. "Get in my car and we'll go someplace to talk privately."

Penelope's mouth falls open when we reach my copper-colored BMW i8—a hundred-thousand-dollar car with *Back to the Future* style doors. "*The Gazette* pays really well!"

"No, it doesn't. This was a present from the last spirit I helped." I slide into the driver's seat and unlock the passenger door out of habit when Penelope appears beside me. She reaches for the seat belt several times until she realizes she can't grab anything.

"Do I have to pay you? Cause I don't have any money, and I don't have a BMW!"

"Shhhh, calm down. You don't need to give me anything." I press the start button located on the center console, but nothing happens. "Shoot." I slam my foot on the brake and try again. No such luck.

"Um, no offense, but do you even know how to drive this thing?"

"Yes. *Sort of.* I've only had it about"—I check my watch—"two hours." I push a few more buttons, and the dashboard lights up. I put the car in reverse and ease out of my parking space. "Let's go someplace where no one is watching us."

"Like Irky Ira?" She points to Ira who is standing beside the dumpster holding the pink box of donuts and giving me a peculiar look.

"Yes, exactly. And why is he irky?"

"It's a nickname ... wait a second. Is your last name Lane? As in John and Mary Lane, the real estate agents?"

"I'm their daughter."

"I know you! I mean, I don't *know* you, know you. Obviously. But we call you Looney Lane."

"Yeah, well, you're dead, and I'm the only one who can see you. So perhaps we don't call me Looney Lane anymore." Like ever. Also, "Who is *we?*"

"Me and my friends. I heard you talk to yourself."

"I'm talking to dead people. Hence the reason you're here." I drive across the street to Earl Park. We appear to be the only ones here, which is perfect. I don't need an audience. But before I can deal with Penelope, I need to call my dad.

"Hid-eee-ho there, pumpkin," he answers on the first ring. My dad looks like Tom Selleck and talks like Mr. Rogers.

"Dad, I need you to do me a solid and be sick."

"But I have a meeting with Beth later today, and we're at an open house right now."

"I've um ... had a *visitor*, and it's a long story. But I need you to be sick."

"Is that Zoe?" I hear mom say in the background. Mom doesn't know about my gift. Dad does. It's better that way. Mom doesn't do paranormal.

"It is," I hear Dad say to Mom. "But"—he coughs—"I don't feel good."

"No, Dad. You need to have food poisoning."

He sighs. "Okay. I got it."

"Thank you."

We hang up, and I reach into my briefcase and grab a Bluetooth. My phone is old and has zero ability to connect to anything, but the Bluetooth is a great prop. "Okay. Back to you," I say to Penelope.

"Why do you see me if I'm dead?"

"I'm a medium. It's a gift. You're not the first spirit I've seen, and you're not the last, I'm sure. But, oddly enough, you look different than the others."

"Really?" She perks up. "Like better?"

"Honestly? Worse."

She frowns.

"Typically, spirits are restored to their prime and aren't so translucent." I extend a finger, and she leans away.

"Am I, like, a sick ghost then?"

"I don't know what's going on. Let's start with the basics." I grab a notepad from my briefcase and click my pen, which is silver and engraved with *Lane*, a present my dad gave me on my first day of work. "What's your last name?"

"Muffin."

I scribble this on the top of the paper. "Any relation to Mr. and Mrs. Muffin?"

"My dad is Arnold Muffin and Michelle is my *step*-mother." She says step as if it's a bad word.

Here's what I know about Mr. And Mrs. Muffin: they're in their mid-fifties, both are round with rosy cheeks, she is the president of the crochet club, he wears straw hats, they own Butter Bakery. When your last name is Muffin, you kind of have to, right?

I'm not much older than Penelope, but we've never met before. I've only just entered the "real world." My parents sheltered me my entire life thinking I was a schizophrenic. Turns out I'm not—I just speak to the dead.

"Do you ever work at Butter?" I ask.

"Only in the summer and on holiday breaks. I go to Trucker Community College." Trucker is one county over, about a forty-minute drive north, and twice the size of Fernn Valley.

"Can I ask about your outfit?" Penelope says. "I don't understand what's ... *happening*." She moves her hands around helplessly.

"There is nothing wrong with my clothes." I pick off a strand of cat hair from my shirt, which is a pink chiffon blouse that I bought last week. The sales lady said it looked good with my light brown hair, dark eyes, and tiny frame. I have on jeans and a pair of checkered Vans. And just *once* I'd like to connect with a spirit who will easily transition to the next phase without having an opinion on my wardrobe.

"I didn't say there was anything *wrong* with your clothes ..." Penelope holds up her palms, and I notice the paint smudged on her fingertips. "My grandma has that shirt, and I thought maybe you were old ... but, like, came back young ... I-I-I-I ... I can't be dead! You can't let me be dead!"

"Bringing people back to life isn't one of my gifts, unfortunately." Actually, no. *Fortunately*. That would be a little *too* creepy.

"You have to help me!" Her voice reaches an ear-piercing octave. "I *know* I'm not dead!"

"I'm trying to help you. We'll figure out what happened so you can transition peacefully."

"What if I don't want to transition anywhere?"

"I know this must be shocking—"

"We can't figure anything out by sitting in the car! How many ghosts have you helped?"

"*Spirits,* and really just one, but—"

"That's it? You've helped one! I need a professional. Someone who knows what they're doing. I'm in trouble. I *need* help! Don't you see? I'm not dead!"

"I'm trying to help you, Penelope. Please try to stay calm. I know this is difficult to take in—"

"Stop telling me to stay calm—" And *poof,* she's gone.

Um ...

"Penelope?" I stumble out of my car and survey the park. "Penelope?" I call out. "Hello?" I check the duck pond, behind the bushes, the trees, and the gazebo. "Hello?" I close my eyes and concentrate, hoping to feel Penelope's spirit. I don't feel anything but the wind on my face and a gnat, which has landed on my nose.

I shoo the tiny insect away and walk back to my car, feeling utterly baffled. Penelope's words roll around in my mind: *I'm in trouble. I need help!* She sounded so bone-chillingly desperate that just the memory brings goose bumps to my arms. Then there's her appearance. Her translucent like state, the abdomen wound, the twigs in her hair, and the cut under her eye. Clearly, she didn't go down without a fight. No wonder she's so frantic.

From everything I've experienced and read, a person will be restored to his or her prime after death. For example, the last spirit who visited me was in his nineties but looked thirty. Sure, Penelope is only twenty-one, which most would argue *is* your prime. So it's not like she would appear to look any different than she did when she was alive. But *why* would she still have the abdomen wound and the cut under her eye?

I take out my key fob and unlock my car. The driver's side door slowly lifts just as a horrid thought enters my mind. When the previous owner of this car showed up and declared he'd been murdered, I didn't believe him. He was old, and early reports stated he'd died of natural causes. I thought it was my job to help him accept this news. In the end, he turned out to be right. He *had been* murdered. He had known all along there was nothing natural about his death, despite my insistence, and I made a promise to never question a spirit's instinct again.

Which is problematic because Penelope did say, "*I know I'm not dead!*" She was rather adamant about it too. Why would she appear to me if she weren't dead? Can a person's spirit leave a living body ...? Oh, crap.

I bend over and put my head between my knees, feeling light-headed. I'd read about this once in a book. When a spirit made contact right before their death. It's rare, but it *has* happened. If I'm right, that means Penelope isn't entirely dead. She's not entirely alive either, which makes this situation *entirely* dire.

Find out what happens next in book two.
The Medium Place
erinhuss.com

ABOUT THE AUTHOR

Erin Huss is a blogger and the #1 Kindle bestselling author of the award-winning Cambria Clyne Mystery series. Erin shares hilarious property management horror stories at The Apartment Manager's Blog and her own daily horror stories at erinhuss.com. She currently resides in Southern California with her husband and five children, where she complains daily about the cost of living but will never do anything about it.

A NOTE FROM ERIN HUSS

Hello!

I want to personally thank you. Yes, YOU, the one with the book/phone/Kindle/tablet in your hand. I appreciate you taking the time out of your busy life to read *Making a Medium*.

If you enjoyed the book, it would make my day if you left a review on Amazon. The more reviews I get, the more books I can sell, the more sales I have, the more See's Candy I can buy, the more See's I eat, the more energy I have to write. And don't you want to know what happens next?

I'd also like to invite you to join my mailing list to stay up to date on my latest news and special sales, and get a free ebook of *Can't Pay My Rent*! You can sign up here: http://bit.ly/erinhussnews

My sincerest thanks,
  Erin

ALSO BY ERIN HUSS

Cambria Clyne Mystery Series

French Vanilla & Felonies

Rocky Road & Revenge

Double Fudge & Danger

Strawberry Swirl & Suspicion in the Pushing Up Daisies Anthology

Mint Chip & Murder (coming soon)

Find information on all of Erin's books at:

erinhuss.com

Made in the USA
Las Vegas, NV
13 March 2023